W9-ASQ-037

The Foreign Legion

Also by Clarice Lispector
from Carcanet

Family Ties
The Hour of the Star

CLARICE LISPECTOR

The Foreign Legion

Stories and Chronicles

Translated with an afterword
by Giovanni Pontiero

CARCANET

First published in Great Britain 1986 by
Carcanet Press Limited
208–212 Corn Exchange Buildings
Manchester M4 3BQ

Clarice Lispector, A Legião Estrangeira, Rio de Janeiro: Editôra do Autor, 1964
Translation and afterword copyright © Giovanni Pontiero 1986
All rights reserved

The publisher acknowledges financial assistance from
the Arts Council of Great Britain

British Library Cataloguing in Publication Data

Lispector, Clarice
    The Foreign Legion.
    I. Title   II. A Legião Estrangeira.
    English
    689.8'408   PQ9697.L5/

    ISBN 0-85635-627-1
        85635-681-6

Typesetting by Paragon Photoset, Aylesbury
Printed in England by SRP Ltd, Exeter

FOR

Eudinyr Fraga
Patricia Doreen Bins
Paul Berman

Giovanni Pontiero

Contents

Stories

The Misfortunes of Sofia

Whatever his previous occupation had been, he had abandoned it, changed his profession and drifted uneasily into teaching at a primary school: that was all we knew about him.

The teacher was burly, enormous and silent, with rounded shoulders. He wore a jacket that was far too short and rimless spectacles, with a thin band of gold bridging his great Roman nose. And I was attracted to him. Not in love with him, but drawn by his silence and by his controlled impatience as he tried to teach us, something which I observed with a sense of outrage. I started to misbehave in class. I talked in a loud voice, pestered my classmates, and interrupted the lesson with silly jokes until the teacher, turning red in the face, would say:

— Be quiet or I will send you out of the room.

Wounded but triumphant, I would answer back defiantly: Send me out then! But he didn't send me out for that would have made him seem to be obeying me. I exasperated him so much that it pained me to be an object of hatred for that man whom, in a certain way, I loved. I did not love him like the woman I would be one day; I loved him like a child who awkwardly tries to protect an adult, with the anger of someone who has not yet become a coward and sees a strong man with such round shoulders. He irritated me. At night, before I went to sleep, he irritated me. I was scarcely nine years old, a difficult age like the unbroken stem of a begonia. I taunted him and when I finally succeeded in provoking him, I could taste, in glorious martyrdom, the unbearable acidity of the begonia when it is crushed between teeth; and I bit my nails in triumph. In the morning, as I walked through the school gates, feeling pure, nourished on coffee and milk, and with my face washed, it was a shock to meet in the flesh the man who had clouded my thoughts for one abysmal moment before falling asleep. On the surface of time it was only a moment, but in the depths of time they were bygone centuries of the darkest sweetness. In the morning — as if I had not counted on the real existence of the man who had unchained my black dreams of love — in the morning, confronted by that enormous man with his short jacket, I was suddenly overcome by shame, bewilderment, and a terrifying hope. Hope was my greatest sin.

Each day I resumed the farcical struggle which I had initiated in order to save that man. I wanted what was good for him, and in return, he hated me. Bruised, I became his demon and tormentor, the symbol of the hell it must have been for him to teach that grinning, inattentive class. To torment him had already become a vindictive pleasure. The game, as always, fascinated me. Without knowing that I was observing time-honoured traditions, yet with that insight which the wicked are born with — those evil people who bite their nails in amazement — without knowing that I was complying with one of the most common situations in the world, I was playing the whore and he the saint. No, perhaps it was not that. Words anticipate and outstrip me, they seduce and transform me, and if I am not careful it will be too late: things will be said before I have even uttered them. Or, at least, it was not only that. My puzzlement stems from the fact that a rug is woven from so many threads that I cannot resign myself to pursuing one only; my confusion stems from the fact that a story is made up of many stories. And I cannot narrate all of them — resounding echoes of a truer word might topple my lofty glaciers from the precipice. Therefore I will speak no more of the maelstrom that raged within me as I daydreamed before falling asleep. Otherwise, even I will begin to think that it was only that subdued whirlpool that drew me towards him, forgetting my desperate sacrifice. I became his temptress, a duty which no one had imposed on me. It was sad that the task of saving him by means of temptation should have fallen into my clumsy hands, because of all the adults and children of that time, there was probably no one less capable. 'This flower isn't for smelling,' as our maid used to say. But it was as if finding myself alone with a mountaineer paralysed by his terror of the precipice, I could not but try to help him descend, however useless I might feel. The teacher had suffered the misfortune of finding himself alone in his wilderness with the most fool-hardy of his pupils. However risky it might be, I felt obliged to pull him over to my side because his was fatal. That was what I did, like a tiresome child tugging at the tails of a grown-up's jacket. He did not look back nor ask what I wanted, and shook me off with a slap. I went on tugging at his jacket, for insistence was my only weapon.

And of all this, he only noticed that I was tearing his pockets. It is true that I myself was not entirely sure what I was doing, my life with the teacher was invisible. Yet I sensed that my role was wicked and dangerous: it drove me to a craving for a real existence that was slow in coming. Worse than incapable, I even enjoyed tearing his pockets. Only God could forgive what I was, because He alone knew of what matter He had made me and for what purpose. So I allowed myself to be His matter. Being God's matter was my only virtue. And the source of a nascent mysticism. Not mysticism for Him, but for His matter, for a crude life filled with pleasure. I worshipped. I accepted the vastness of things beyond my understanding and confided therein the secrets of the confessional. Was it towards the dark depths of ignorance that I was luring the teacher with the zeal of a cloistered nun? A happy and monstrous nun, alas! Not even of this could I boast: in the classroom we were all equally monstrous and sweet, the avid matter of God.

But if the teacher's heavy round shoulders and his tight jacket affected me, my outbursts of laughter only made him all the more determined to pretend that he had forgotten me, and all that self-control made him look even more hunched. The hatred this man felt for me was so strong that I began to hate myself. To the point where my laughter finally supplanted my impossible weakness.

As for learning, I did not learn anything during those lessons. The game of making him unhappy had taken much too great a hold over me. Enduring with undisguised resentment my lanky legs and my always shabby shoes, mortified at not being a flower, and, above all, tortured by an enormous childhood that I feared would never end — I was determined to make him even more unhappy and I flaunted my only wealth: the flowing hair which I planned to have beautifully permed one day and in anticipation of the future I tossed my hair at every opportunity. As for studying, I did not study. I trusted in my idleness which had never let me down and which the teacher accepted as one more provocation from a horrid little girl. In that he was mistaken. The truth is that I had no time to study. Happiness kept me occupied, remaining attentive took up days and days of my time: there were the history books which I read passionately, biting my nails to the quick. In my first ecstasies of sadness, a refinement which I had recently discovered: there were boys whom I had chosen but they had not chosen me. I spent hours suffering because they were unattainable, and yet more hours suffering by warmly accepting them, for man was my King of Creation; there was the promising peril of sin, and I occupied myself with anxious waiting; not to mention that I was permanently occupied with wanting or not wanting to be what I was. I could not decide which part of me I wanted, but I could not accept all of me; having been born was to be full of errors that needed correcting. No, it was not to irritate the teacher that I did not study; I only had time to grow. Which I did on all fronts, with a gracelessness that suggested some miscalculation; my legs did not go with my eyes and my mouth was expressive while my grubby hands dangled at my sides — in my haste I grew without any sense of direction.

A photograph from that time reveals a healthy girl, savage and sweet, with thoughtful eyes under a heavy fringe, and this real image does not belie me, yet it portrays a ghostly stranger whom I would not understand even if I were her mother. Only much later, after I had finally accepted my physical presence and felt basically more self-assured, could I bring myself to study a little; before that, however, I could not risk learning, I did not wish to unsettle myself — I took intuitive care with what I was, since I did not know what I was, and I proudly cultivated the integrity of ignorance. It was a pity that the teacher was never to see the person I unexpectedly became four years later: at thirteen, with clean hands, freshly bathed, composed and pretty, he would have seen me looking like a Christmas poster displayed on the veranda of a large house. But, instead of the teacher, a former chum of mine walked by and called out my name, without realizing that I was no longer a tomboy but a dignified young lady whose name could not be called out along the city pavements. 'What is it?' I asked the intruder coldly. I then received the news aloud that the teacher had died that morning. Pale, and with wide eyes, I looked at the street whirling under my feet. My composure shattered like a broken doll.

Going back four years. It was perhaps because of everything I have just narrated, mixed up and jumbled together, that I wrote the composition the teacher had assigned, the dénouement of this story and the nucleus of others. Or perhaps it was only because I wanted to finish my work as quickly as possible and play in the park.

— I am going to tell a story, he said, and you will write a composition. But use your own words. When you have finished, you may go out to play without waiting for the bell.

This was the story: a very poor man dreamed that he had discovered treasure and had become very rich; on awakening, he packed his bundle and went in search of the treasure; he had travelled the wide world and still hadn't found the treasure; weary, he returned to his modest house and since he had nothing to eat, he started to plant seeds in his poor little yard; he planted so much, reaped so much, and began to sell so much that he ended up by becoming very rich.

I listened with disdain, blatantly playing with my pencil, as if I wanted to make it quite clear that his stories did not fool me and that I knew perfectly well who he was. He told the story without looking even once in my direction. Clumsy in my efforts to love him, I took pleasure in persecuting him, I pursued him with my gaze: to everything he said I answered with a simple direct glance, which nobody in all conscience could have condemned. The look I affected was quite angelic and pure, completely open, like innocence confronting crime. And it always achieved the same result: perturbed, he avoided my eyes, and began to stutter. And this filled me with a sense of power that condemned me. And with pity. Which, in its turn, irritated me. It irritated me that he should force a little brat like me to understand a man.

It was almost ten in the morning and the recreation bell was about to ring. My school was a rented building in one of the city parks and had the biggest playground I have ever seen. It afforded me as much pleasure as it might have given a squirrel or a horse. It had trees scattered here and there, extended undulations and broad expanses of lawn. It seemed never-ending. Everything there was extensive and wide, made for the long legs of a little girl, with space for piles of bricks and wood of unknown origin, for thickets of sour begonias which we ate, for sunlight and shadows where bees made honey. There was room there for an abundance of fresh air. And we lived life to the full; we rolled down every slope, whispered earnestly behind every pile of bricks, ate the different varieties of flowers, and into all the tree trunks we carved with our penknives dates, sweet obscenities and hearts pierced with arrows: girls and boys made their honey there.

I was finishing my composition and the scent of the hidden shadows was already beckoning me. I hurried. Since I only knew how 'to use my own words', writing was simple. What also made me hurry was the desire to be the first to walk across the room — the teacher had ended up banishing me to the back of the classroom — and to hand in my composition arrogantly, thus showing him how quick I was, a quality which struck me as being essential in order to live and which, I felt sure, the teacher could not fail to admire.

I handed him my notebook and he took it without even looking at me. Offended that he should not have praised my quickness, I skipped out into the big park.

The story which I had transcribed into my own words was exactly the same as the one he had narrated. Only at that time, I was beginning to 'extract the moral of the story', which made me feel virtuous but later threatened to smother me in austerity. Anxious to impress him, I made several additions to his closing sentences. Sentences which hours later I read and re-read to see what there was in them that had finally succeeded in provoking the man when I myself had so far failed. Probably what the teacher had wanted to leave implicit in his sad tale was that hard work is the only way to make a fortune. Facetiously, I drew the opposite moral: something about the hidden treasure, which exists where one least expects to find it, which is only waiting to be discovered. I think I talked about squalid backyards with hidden treasure. I cannot recall, I do not know if those were my precise words. I cannot imagine with what childish phrases I expressed a simple idea which somehow turned into something complicated. I suppose that by wilfully contradicting the real meaning of the story, I had somehow in writing promised myself that idleness rather than work would yield me many gratuitous rewards, the only rewards to which I aspired. It is also possible that even then the theme of my existence was irrational hope, and that my perverse stubbornness was already manifest. I would give everything I possessed for nothing, but I wanted everything in return for nothing. Unlike the labourer in the story, in my composition I shrugged off all responsibilities and came away free and poor, carrying treasure in my hands.

I went out to play, only to find myself alone with the useless reward of having been the first, scratching at the earth, waiting impatiently for my classmates who, one by one, emerged from the classroom.

In the midst of our rowdy games, I decided to look for something in my satchel, I do not remember what, to show to the park-warden, my friend and protector. Dripping with perspiration, I flushed with an irrepressible happiness which at home would have earned me a few slaps — I fled in the direction of the classroom, crossed it at a run, so flustered that I did not see the teaching leafing through the notebooks piled on his desk. The object I had gone to fetch was already in my hand and I was just about to run out again — when my glance fell awkwardly on the man. Standing alone by his desk, he looked at me.

It was the first time we had come face to face on our own. He was looking at me. My steps faltered almost to a standstill.

For the first time I found myself alone with him, without the whispered support of my classmates, without the admiration that my insolence aroused. I tried to smile, feeling the blood rushing to my cheeks. A bead of sweat ran down my forehead. He was looking at me. His look was like a soft, heavy paw resting on me. But if that paw was soft, it froze me like a cat's paw as it quickly catches a mouse by the tail. The bead of sweat ran down over my nose and on to my mouth, cutting my smile in half. Just that: his face drained of any expression, he was staring at me. I began to skirt the wall with lowered eyes, taking refuge in my smile, the only feature left in a face which had lost every contour. I had never noticed before just how long the classroom was; only now, to the slow pace of fear, could I judge its real dimensions. Lack of time had not allowed me to perceive until that moment just how bare and high those walls were; and solid, I could feel the solid wall against the palm of my hand. In a nightmare, in which smiling played some part, I scarcely believed that I could reach the doorway — from where I would run, oh, how I would run! and hide among the other children. As well as concentrating on my smile, I was most careful not to make any noise with my feet, and thus I adhered to the intimate nature of a danger about which I knew nothing more. With a shudder, I caught a sudden glimpse of myself as if in a mirror: a perspiring thing pressed against the wall, advancing slowly on tiptoe, with an ever more intense smile. My smile had crystallized the room into silence and even the sounds that came from the park reverberated on the outer shell of silence. I finally reached the door, and my unruly heart began to beat so loudly that it threatened to awaken the immense world from its sleep.

That was when I heard my name.

Suddenly, nailed to the spot, my mouth dry, I stood there with my back to him, too scared to turn round. The breeze which came from the open door had dried the perspiration from my body. I turned round slowly, controlling within my clenched fists the impulse to run.

At the sound of my name the room had become dehypnotized.

And very slowly I began to see the teacher in his entirety.

Very slowly I saw that the teacher was huge and ugly, and that he was the man of my life. A new and greater fear. Small, somnambulant, alone, I confronted what my fatal freedom had finally brought me to. My smile, which was all that remained of my face, had also been obliterated. I was a pair of numbed feet too paralysed to move, and a heart so parched that it might die of thirst. There I stood, out of the man's reach. My heart was dying of thirst, yes. My heart was dying of thirst.

As calm as if he were about to commit a murder in cold blood, he said:

— Come closer . . .

How did the man intend to avenge himself?

Was I about to receive, smack in the face, the ball of the

world which I myself had thrown to him and which none the less I did not understand?

Was I about to retrieve a reality which would not have existed if I had not rashly perceived it and thus given it life? To what extent was that man, a mountain of compact unhappiness, also a mountain of fury? But my past was too remote now. A stoic repentance kept my head erect. For the first time ignorance, which until then had been my faithful guide, abandoned me. My father was at work, my mother had been dead for several months. I was the only one.

— Take your notebook, he added.

I looked at him suddenly in surprise. Was that all, then? The unexpected relief was almost more alarming than my former fear. I took a step forward, and hesitantly held out my hand.

But the teacher remained still and made no attempt to hand over my notebook.

To my sudden distress, without averting his gaze, the teacher slowly began to remove his spectacles. He looked at me with naked eyes protected by thick eyelashes. I had never seen his eyes, which, with those thick eyelashes, looked like two sweet cockroaches. He stared at me. And I did not know how to exist in the presence of a man. Evasively I gazed at the ceiling, the floor, the walls, and kept my hand outstretched because I did not know how to withdraw it. He looked at me gently, inquisitively, with his eyes uncombed as if he had just woken up. Would he crush me with an unexpected hand? Or demand that I kneel and beg forgiveness? My thread of hope was that he might not know what I had done to him, just as I myself no longer knew, and, indeed, had never known.

— How did you get the idea of the hidden treasure?

— What treasure? I murmured sheepishly.

We stood there looking at each other in silence.

— Oh, the treasure! I blurted out, not really understanding, anxious to admit some fault, imploring him that my punishment should be simply to feel forever guilty, that eternal torture should be my punishment, anything but this unknown life.

— The treasure which is hidden where you least expect to find it. That is only waiting to be discovered. Who told you that?

The man has taken leave of his senses, I thought to myself, for what has all this got to do with the treasure? Stunned, unable to understand and passing from one surprise to another, I sensed, nevertheless, that I was on less dangerous ground. In our school races I had learned to carry on running after a fall, however serious, and I regained my composure at once: 'It was the composition about the treasure! So that was my mistake!' Feeling weak, and still treading carefully on this new and slippery reassurance, I had recovered sufficiently from my fall to be able to toss, in imitation of my former arrogance, my permanent waved hair of the future.

— Gosh, nobody . . ., I replied haltingly. I made it up myself, I said nervously, but already beginning to sparkle once more.

If I felt some relief at having something concrete to battle with at last, I was also aware of something much worse. The teacher's sudden lack of anger. Puzzled, I looked at him askance. And little by little, with the utmost suspicion. His lack of anger began to frighten me, it implied new threats which I could not fathom. His staring eyes refused to leave me — eyes void of anger . . . I was perturbed, and for no good reason, I was losing my enemy and my support. I looked at him in surprise. What did he want from me? He made me feel uneasy. And those eyes without anger began to irk me more than the brutality which I had feared. A gentle fear, cold and moist, gripped me by degrees. Slowly, lest he should notice, I backed away until my shoulders touched the wall, and then drew back my head until it could go no further. From the wall where I had embedded my entire body, I looked at him furtively.

And my stomach filled with the waters of nausea. I cannot describe it.

I was a very inquisitive child and, despite my paleness, I could see. Agitated, and ready to be sick, although to this day, I cannot say for certain what I saw. But I certainly saw. As if looking deep into someone's mouth, I suddenly saw the chasm of the world. What I saw was as anonymous as a belly split open for an intestinal operation. I saw his expression change — a hardened disquiet surfaced awkwardly on his skin. I saw his grimace falter before breaking through the crust — but that thing which was being uprooted in mute destruction, that thing showed no more resemblance to a smile than if a human liver or foot should try to smile, so help me. What I saw, I saw so closely that I do not know what I saw. It was as if my inquisitive eye had become glued to the keyhole and unexpectedly met another glued eye staring at me from the other side. I saw the inside of an eye. Something as incomprehensible as an eye. An open eye with its quivering gelatine. With its organic tears. An eye weeping by itself, laughing by itself. Until the man's concentrated effort began to peter out and in childish triumph he revealed — a pearl snatched from an open belly — that he was smiling. I saw a man with entrails, smiling. I saw his grim determination to avoid making any mistakes, his earnest application like some backward student, his clumsy movements as if he had suddenly become left-handed. Unable to understand, I knew that I was being asked to accept him and his open belly; to receive his manly weight. My shoulders pressed desperately against the wall, I drew back — it was much too soon for me to see so much. It was much too soon for me to see how life is born. Life being born was much more bloody than dying. Dying is uninterrupted. But to see inert matter slowly trying to raise itself like a great living corpse — to see hope, filled me with fear, to see life filled me with nausea. Too much was being asked of my courage just because I was courageous, too much was being asked of my strength just because I was strong. 'But what about me?' I screamed ten years later because of a lost love, 'who will witness my weakness!' I looked at him in surprise, and forever I did not know what I saw, what I had seen was capable of blinding the inquisitive.

Then, making use of the smile he had just acquired for the first time, he said:

— Your composition about the treasure is most appealing. The treasure that is only waiting to be discovered. You . . . — he paused for a moment. He scrutinized me, gently, indiscreetly, as intimately as if he were my heart. — You are a funny child, he said at length.

For the first time in my life, I felt deeply mortified. I lowered my eyes, unable to bear the defenceless gaze of the man whom I had deceived.

Yes, my impression was that, in spite of his anger, he somehow trusted me, and that I had deceived him with all that nonsense about the treasure. At that time, I believed that everything that one invented was a lie, and that only my conscience tormented by sin could redeem me from evil. I lowered my eyes in shame. I preferred his former rage, which had helped me in my struggle with myself, because it crowned my strategies with failure and one day might even reform me. What I did not want was gratitude, which was not only the worst punishment, because undeserved, but also because it encouraged my perverse existence which I so greatly feared. Living perversely appealed to me. I wished to make it clear to him that treasure is not discovered at will. But looking at him, I lost heart: I could not find the courage to disappoint him. I had already become accustomed to protecting the happiness of others, that of my father, for example, who was even more vulnerable than I. But how difficult it was for me to remain silent about happiness which I had so irresponsibly provoked. He was like a beggar showing his gratitude for a plate of food, oblivious to the fact that the meat was rancid. The blood rushed to my face, which felt so hot that I thought my eyes must be bloodshot, while he, probably under some new delusion, must have thought that I was blushing with pleasure at his words of praise. That same night all this would be transformed into an irrepressible fit of vomiting that would keep all the lights on in my house.

— You — he then repeated slowly, as if under some spell he was gradually uttering words which had accidentally formed on his lips — you are a funny child. You are a foolish little girl . . . he said, once more adopting the smile of a little boy who takes his new shoes to bed with him. The teacher had no idea how ugly he looked when he smiled. Trusting, he allowed me to see his ugliness, which was his most innocent feature.

I had to swallow as best I could the outrage he inflicted on me by believing in me, I had to swallow my compassion for him and my own shame. 'You fool!' I felt like shouting at him, 'that story about the hidden treasure was all made up, it's downright childish!' I was very conscious of being a child, which helped to explain all my serious faults, and I put such faith in growing up one day — and that big man had allowed himself to be fooled by a wretched little girl. He was the first person to destroy my faith in adults: a grown man, he also believed like me in the great untruths . . .

Suddenly my heart was pounding with disillusionment. I could not bear it a minute longer — without taking the notebook, I ran out to the park, one hand over my mouth as if someone had broken my teeth. With my hand over my mouth, horror-stricken, I ran and ran as if never to stop, a deep prayer asks for nothing, the deepest prayer asks no more — terrified, I ran and ran.

Contaminated, I was relying on grown-ups for my redemption. The need to believe in my future goodness led me to venerate grown-ups whom I had made to my image, but an image of me cleansed at last by the penance of growing, delivered at last from the impure soul of a little girl. And now the teacher was destroying all this, he was destroying my love for him and for me. There could be no salvation for me: for that man was also me. My bitter idol who had ingenuously fallen into the snares of a confused and wilful child, and who had meekly allowed himself to be guided by my diabolical innocence . . . Pressing my hand to my mouth, I ran through the dust of the park.

When it finally dawned on me that I was well beyond the teacher's orbit, I came to an exhausted halt; close to collapsing, I leaned my full weight against a tree trunk, panting furiously. I stood there, gasping for breath with my eyes closed, swallowing the bitter dust from the tree trunk, my fingers mechanically stroking the rough grooves . . . forming a heart and arrow. Suddenly, closing my eyes tightly, I moaned, understanding a little more clearly: was he trying to say that . . . that I was a hidden treasure? That treasure hidden where one least expects to find it . . . Oh, no, no, poor thing, poor King of Creation, so much in need . . . of what? What was he in need of . . . that made him transform even me into a treasure?

I had enough strength to run even further, forced my dry throat to recover its breath, and angrily pushing the tree trunk, I set off once more in the direction of the world's end.

But the shadowed edges of the park were still invisible and my steps were growing slower and slower from sheer exhaustion. I could go no further. Perhaps because I was so tired,

I finally gave up. My steps became slower and slower and the foliage of the trees swayed slowly. My steps became confused. Hesitantly, I came to a halt, the trees circled overhead. The strangest sweetness left my heart weary. I paused in fear. I was alone on the lawn, unsteady on my feet, and without any support. My hand was over my weary breast like some virgin in an annunciation scene. Weary, lowering to that first sweetness a head that was submissive at last, and that from a distance might even suggest the head of a woman. The crest of the trees swayed to and fro. 'You are a very funny child, you are a foolish little girl,' he had said. It was almost like being in love.

No, I was not funny. Unconsciously, I was most serious. No, I was not a foolish little girl, reality was my destiny, and it was that part of me which offended others. And, by God, I was not a treasure. But if I had already discovered in myself all the vicious poison with which human beings are born and use to destroy life — only at that moment of honey and flowers did I discover how I would cure whoever loved me, whoever suffered on my account. I was dark ignorance with its hunger and laughter, with small deaths nourishing my inevitable life — what was I to do? I already knew that I was inevitable. But if I was worthless, I was all that man possessed just then. For once at least, he was being obliged to love, and without loving anyone — to love through someone. And I alone was there. Even if this were his sole advantage: having only me, and being forced to start by loving the wicked, he had started with something few achieve. It would be much too easy to desire the pure; the ugly was beyond love's reach; to love the impure was man's deepest longing. Through me, someone difficult to love, he had charitably received the substance of which we are made. Did I understand all this? No. Nor do I know what I understood at the time. But just as for one brief moment I had seen with horrified fascination the world in my teacher — and to this day I do not know what I saw, only that forever and in one brief moment I saw — so I understood us, even though I shall never know whom I understood. I shall never know what I understand. Whatever I understood in the park was, with a shock of extreme sweetness, understood by my ignorance. An ignorance which stood there — in the same numbed solitude as the surrounding trees — an ignorance which I fully recovered with its incomprehensible truth. There I stood, the girl who was too knowing by far, and behold how all that was unworthy in me served both God and man. All that was unworthy about me, was also my treasure.

Yes, just like a virgin in an annunciation scene. In allowing me to make him smile at last, the teacher had brought about this annunciation. He had just transformed me into something more than the King of Creation: he had made me the wife of the King of Creation. For suddenly it fell to me, armed with claws and dreams as I was, to pluck the barbed arrow from his heart. Suddenly it became clear why I had been born intransigent, why I had been born resistant to pain. For what purpose those long nails? To claw you to death and pluck out the fatal thorns, the wolf-man replies. For what purpose that cruel, hungry mouth? To bite you, then blow on the wound so that it will no longer hurt you, my love, for I must hurt you. I am the inevitable wolf and for this reason I was given life. For what purpose those burning grasping claws? So that we may grasp others, for our need is so great, so great, so great — the wolves howled, looking nervously at their own claws before snuggling up to one another to make love and sleep.

. . . Thus it came about that in the large park surrounding my school, I slowly began to learn how to be loved, while enduring the sacrifice of not being worthy, if only to lessen the pain of one who does not love. No, that was only one of the reasons. The others make up different stories. In some, other claws, swollen with cruel love, have plucked the barbed arrow from my heart, indifferent to my screams of pain.

The Sharing of Bread

It was Saturday and we had been invited to lunch out of a sense of obligation. But we were all much too fond of Saturday to go wasting it in the company of people whom we did not care for. Each of us had experienced happiness at some time or other and had been left with the mark of desire. As for me, I desired everything. And there we were, trapped, as if our train had been derailed and we had been forced to settle down among perfect strangers. No one there cared for me and I did not care for them. As for my Saturday — it swayed outside my windows in acacias and shadows. Rather than spend it badly, I preferred to hold it in my clenched fist, where it could be crumpled like a handkerchief. Waiting for lunch to be served, we half-heartedly drank a toast to the health of resentment: tomorrow it would be Sunday. I have no desire to be with you, our gaze was saying without any warmth, as we slowly blew smoke from our dry cigarettes. The avarice of refusing to share our Saturday eroded little by little and advanced like rust, until any happiness would have been an insult to a greater happiness.

Only the mistress of the household did not appear to save her Saturday in order to exploit it on a Thursday evening. But how could this woman, whose heart had experienced other Saturdays, have forgotten that people crave more and more? She did not even betray impatience with this heterogeneous gathering in her home, daydreaming and resigned, as if waiting for the next train to leave, any train — rather than remain in that deserted railway station, rather than have to restrain the horse from bolting furiously to join more and more horses.

We finally moved into the dining room for a lunch without the blessing of hunger. When taken by surprise, we came face to face with the table. This could not be for us . . .

It was a table prepared for men of good will. Who could the expected guest be who had simply failed to turn up? But it was we ourselves. So that woman served the best no matter the guest? And she was content to wash the feet of the first stranger. We watched, feeling uneasy.

The table had been covered with solemn abundance. Sheaves of wheat were piled up on the white table-cloth. And rosy apples, enormous yellow carrots, round tomatoes with their skins ready to burst, green marrows with translucent skins, pineapples of a malign savageness, oranges golden and tranquil, gherkins bristling like porcupines, cucumbers stretched tight over watery flesh, red, hollow peppers that caused our eyes to smart — were all entangled in moist whiskers of maize, as auburn as if bordering human lips. And the berries of the grape. The purplest of the grapes that could barely wait to be pressed. Nor did they mind who pressed them. The tomatoes were circular for no one: for the atmosphere, for the circular atmosphere. Saturday belonged to anyone who cared to turn up. The oranges would sweeten the tongue of the first person to arrive. Beside the plate of each unwanted guest, the woman who washed the feet of strangers had placed — even without choosing or loving us — a sheaf of wheat, a bunch of fiery radishes, or a crimson slice of water-melon with its merry seeds. All dissected by the Spanish acidity visible in the green lemons. In the earthenware jugs there was milk, as if it had crossed a rocky desert with the goats. Wine that was almost black after being thoroughly trampled shuddered in the clay vessels. Everything was set before us. Everything cleansed of perverse human desire. Everything as it really is, and not as we would wish it to be. Simply existing and intact. Just as a field exists. Just as the mountains exist. Just as man and woman exist, but not those of us who are consumed by greed. Just as Saturday exists. Simply existing. It exists.

On behalf of nothing, it was time to eat. On behalf of no one, it was good. Without any dream. And on a par with day, we gradually became anonymous, growing, rising, to the height of possible existence. Then, like the landed aristocracy, we accepted the table.

There was no holocaust: everything there was anxious to be eaten just as we were anxious to eat it. Saving nothing for the following day, there and then I offered my feelings to that which aroused those feelings. It was a feast for which I had not paid in advance with the suffering of waiting, the hunger that comes as we bring the food to our lips. For now we felt hungry, an all-consuming hunger which embraced the entire spread down to the crumbs. Those who drank wine kept a watchful eye on the milk. Those who slowly sipped milk could taste the wine that the others were drinking. Just outside, God among the acacias. Acacias which existed. We ate. Like someone giving water to a horse. The carved meat was shared out. The friendly exchanges were homely and rustic. No one spoke ill of anyone because no one spoke well of anyone. It was a harvest reunion and a truce was declared. We ate. Like a horde of living creatures, we slowly covered the earth. As busy as someone who cultivates existence, and plants, and reaps, and kills, and lives, and dies, and eats. I ate with the honesty of the man who does not belie what he is eating; I ate the food and not its name. God was never so possessed by what He is. The food was saying, brusque, happy, austere: eat, eat and share. Everything there was mine, it was my father's table. I ate without affection, I ate without the passion of mercy. Without offering myself to hope. I ate without any longing whatsoever. And I was wholly deserving of that food. For I cannot always be my brother's keeper, just as I can no longer be my own keeper, for I have ceased to love myself. Nor do I wish to form life because existence already exists. It exists like some territory where we all advance. Without a single word of love. Without a word. But your pleasure comprehends mine. We are strong and we eat. For bread is love among strangers.

The Message

At first, when the girl said she felt *anguish*, the boy was so surprised that he blushed and quickly changed the subject, to conceal his quickening heartbeat.

For many years now — ever since childhood — he had courageously overcome the childish tendency to speak of events as 'a coincidence'.

Or rather — *progressing* fast and no longer believing in such a thing — he regarded the expression 'a coincidence' as some novel word-game and a renewed mockery.

So, having suppressed the involuntary happiness which this alarming coincidence provoked — that she, too, should be feeling anguish — he found himself conversing with her in his own anguish, and with a girl at that! he who from a woman's heart had received no more than a maternal kiss.

He found himself conversing with her, while really disguising his amazement at being able to speak at last about things that really mattered: and with a girl at that! They also discussed books, barely able to conceal how anxious they were to catch up on all the things they had never discussed. Even so, they never exchanged certain words. This time it was not because their expression might be one more snare which the *others* exploited to deceive the young. But because he felt embarrassed. Because he could never summon the courage to say everything, even though she, as someone who felt anguish, was a person of trust. Nor would he ever speak of a *mission*, although that very word, which he, in a manner of speaking, had created, burned on his lips, longing to be expressed.

Naturally, the fact that she was also suffering simplified the problem of how to treat a girl, by giving her a virile quality. He began treating her as a comrade.

She also began to manifest her own anguish with haloed modesty as if it were a new sex. Hybrids — who so far had not chosen a personal life-style, who so far had not acquired any distinctive handwriting and took notes in class with a different lettering each day — hybrids, they searched out each other, scarcely able to conceal their earnestness. From time to time, he still felt that incredible acceptance of coincidence: that someone as odd as him should have met a girl who spoke his language! Little by little, they made a pact. It was sufficient for her to say as if she were giving a password 'yesterday I spent a miserable evening' and he knew with austerity that she was suffering what he was suffering. They shared sorrow, pride and courage.

Until even the word anguish began to jar, showing how spoken language can be deceptive. (They hoped to write one day.) The word anguish started to take on that tone which *others* used, and provoked mild hostility between them. When he was suffering, he found it indiscreet of her to speak of anguish. 'I have already *outgrown* that word', he always *outgrew* everything before she did, and it was only later that the girl caught up with him. Gradually she grew tired of being the only anguished female in his eyes. Although this conferred intellectual status, she, too, was cautious about this kind of error. For they both desired, above all, to be *authentic*. She, for example, wanted no misunderstandings even in her favour, she wanted the *truth* however bad it might be. Besides, sometimes it was much better than it should be, 'however bad it might be'. Most of all, the girl now resented being treated as a male whenever she showed the least sign . . . of being a person. If flattered and somehow offended her at the same time: it was as if he was surprised to find her capable, precisely because he judged her incapable. Although, if they were not careful, the fact that she was female might suddenly surface. They were careful.

But, naturally, there was confusion, the absence of any possible explanation, and time was passing. Even months.

Although the hostility between them was gradually increasing, like hands drawing close without ever touching, they could not prevent themselves from seeking out each other. Because — if on the lips of *others* the word 'young' sounded offensive — between themselves 'to be young' was a mutual secret, and the same irremediable disaster. They could not help themselves from seeking out each other because, although hostile — with the repudiation which human beings of the

opposite sex reveal when they feel no desire for each other —
although hostile, they believed in their sincerity *versus* the
great lie spread by others. Their outraged hearts could not
forgive the lie told by others. They were sincere. And because
they were not small-minded, they ignored the fact that they
themselves were extremely adept at telling lies — as if all that
really mattered was the sincerity of their imagination. So they
continued to seek out each other, vaguely proud of being
different from the *others*, different to the extent of not even
being in love. Those *others* who did nothing except exist.
Vaguely conscious that there was something false about their
relationship. As if they were homosexuals of the opposite sex
and unable to unify their separate misfortunes. They only
agreed on the one point that united them: the error that existed
in the world and the tacit certainty that if they did not save the
world, they would be traitors. As for love, they obviously did
not love each other. She had even spoken to him of her recent
infatuation with one of her teachers. He even got round to
telling her — since she was just like another chap for him — he
even got round to telling her, with a coolness which unexpectedly exploded into a thumping heartbeat, that a chap is
forced to tackle 'certain problems', if he wants to be able to
think clearly. He was sixteen and she was seventeen. Not even
his own father knew that from time to time he tackled certain
problems with severity.

Once they had found the secret part of their inner self, there
came the temptation and the hope that one day they might
reach the maximum. What maximum?

What did they want in the end? They themselves did not
know, and they used each other like someone clinging to the
smaller rocks until they are able to scale the largest and most
difficult rock of all, unaided; they used each other in order to
prepare themselves for initiation; they used each other impatiently, teaching each other to flap their wings so that finally
— alone and free — they might embark on the great solitary
flight which would also mean separation. Was that it? They
needed each other for a time, irked by each other's clumsiness,
the one criticizing the other's lack of experience. They failed
with every encounter, like two people who disappoint each
other in bed. What did they want in the end? They wanted to

learn. To learn what? They were both disastrous. Oh, they could not say that they were uhappy without feeling ashamed for they knew that some went hungry; they ate with hunger and shame. Unhappy? How? When for no apparent reason they were actually touching the extreme edge of happiness as if the world had shaken and a thousand fruits had fallen from that enormous tree. Unhappy? if they were bodies with blood like flowers in the sun. How? if they were standing forever on their own weak legs, puzzled, free, miraculously on their feet, her legs hairless, his uncertain, yet ending up in a size 44 shoe. How could creatures such as them be unhappy?

They were most unhappy. They sought out each other, weary, expectant, forcing a continuation of that initial and casual understanding which had never been renewed — and without even loving each other. Their ideal suffocated them, time was passing in vain, urgency summoned them — they did not know where they were heading, but the path beckoned them. They asked a great deal of each other, but they both had the same needs, and they would never seek out an older couple to teach them, for they were not fools to surrender themselves so readily to the adult world.

One possible way of still achieving salvation might be what they never referred to as *poetry*. What could poetry be? What did that compelling word really mean?

Could it be that they would meet when, by coincidence, a sudden shower of rain fell over the city? Or perhaps, while sitting in a café, they would both look simultaneously at the face of a woman passing on the street? Or that they might even meet each other, by coincidence, in an ancient night of moon and wind? But both were born with the word poetry already printed in bold letters in the supplements of the Sunday newspapers. Poetry was a word used by grown-ups. And their distrust was enormous, like that of animals. Whose instinct warns them that one day they will be hunted down. They had already been deceived far too often to be able to believe now. They would need to be hunted down with the utmost caution, a powerful scent, much cunning and an even more cautious affection — an affection that would not offend them — so that taking them unawares, they might be caught in the net. And, with even more caution, so as not to awaken them, to carry them by stealth to the world of the corrupted, to the world already created; for such was the role of grown-ups and spies. After being deceived for so long, they were proud of their own bitterness, and felt a loathing for words, especially when a word — like poetry — was so ingenious that it came close to expressing something — for that was precisely when it became clear just how little it expressed. In truth, they both despised the majority of words, words which scarcely helped them to communicate, for they still had not succeeded in inventing any better words. Stubborn rivals, they constantly misunderstood each other. Poetry? Oh, how they loathed it. As if it were sex. They were also convinced that *the others* wanted to hunt them down not for sex, but for their *normality*. They were frightened, scientific, exhausted by experience. Yes, they discussed the word experience without embarrassment and without explanation: the word tended to vary in meaning. Sometimes, experience even became confused with *message*. They used both words without really probing their meaning.

Besides, they probed nothing, as if there was no time, as if there were far too many things waiting to be discussed. Oblivious to the fact that they never discussed anything.

Well, it was not only that, or quite so simple. It was not only that: meanwhile, time was passing, confused, vast, interrupted, and the heart of time was fear, and there was that hostility towards the world which no one was to tell them was desperate love and compassion. They possessed the sceptical wisdom of the ancient Chinese, a wisdom that could suddenly shatter revealing two disconcerted faces because they did not know how to sit naturally in a café eating ice-cream: then everything exploded, suddenly denouncing two imposters. Time was passing, they discussed nothing, and nevermore would they understand each other as perfectly as on that first occasion when she said that she was feeling *anguish* and, miraculously, he replied that he felt exactly the same, and their horrible pact was sealed. And nevermore was anything to happen that would finally dispel the blindness with which they stretched out their hands, preparing themselves for the destiny which impatiently awaited them in order to finally separate them forever.

Perhaps they were ready to free themselves from each other

like a drop of water on the point of falling, and they were only waiting for something to symbolize the plenitude of *anguish* so that they could separate. Perhaps, mature as a drop of water, they had provoked the event which I am about to relate.

The vague event around the old house only occurred because they were both prepared for it. It was simply an old abandoned house. But their existence was impoverished and eager as if they were never to grow old, as if nothing would ever happen to them — and then the house was transformed into an event. They had come away after the last day of term. They had caught the bus, got off, and started walking. As usual, they rushed headlong along the road or unexpectedly slowed down, without ever striking quite the right pace, uncomfortable in each other's company. It was a *bad* day for both of them, the beginning of the summer holidays. The final lesson had left them without a future and free of obligations, both of them contemptuous of the future their respective families guaranteed them in terms of love and misunderstanding. Without tomorrows and obligations, they were worse off than before, speechless and wide-eyed.

That afternoon, the girl clenched her teeth as she looked at everything with resentment or passion, as if she were searching in the wind, in the dust, in the extreme poverty of her own soul for some further cause for anger.

The boy — in that road whose name they did not even know — in that unfamiliar road the boy showed little resemblance to the man of Creation. The day was pale, and the boy paler still, involuntarily young, exposed to the wind and obliged to exist. However, he looked gentle and uncertain, as if suffering only made him look even younger, unlike the girl who behaved aggressively. In their formless state, they found everything possible, and sometimes they even exchanged certain qualities . . . she became virile, and he acquired the almost ignoble sweetness of a young girl. On several occasions, he came close to saying goodbye, but vague and empty as he felt, he would be at a loss for something to do on returning home, as if the end of term had severed the final link. So he walked on silently behind her, following her with the meekness of someone who had been abandoned. Only some seventh sense barely attuned the world, sustained him, linking him to tomorrow with some dark promise. No, the two of them were not exactly neurotic and — despite their vindictive thoughts about each other in moments of ill-suppressed hostility — it did not appear that psychoanalysis would entirely solve the problem. Or perhaps it would.

It was one of those roads that end up at the St John the Baptist Cemetery, polluted with dust, gravel on the street and black youths loitering in the doorways of the bars.

They walked along the cracked pavement which was so narrow that there was scarcely room for both of them. She made a sudden gesture — he thought that she was about to cross the road and he made to follow her — she turned round, not knowing which side he was on — he hesitated trying to locate her. In that split second in which they anxiously searched for each other, they simultaneously turned their backs on the bus — and found themselves facing the house, the look of someone still searching on their faces.

Perhaps everything stemmed from that look of searching on their faces. Or perhaps because the house was set right on the pavement and so very 'close'. They had barely any room to stand back in order to look at it, crowded as they were on that narrow pavement, between the dangerous rumbling of the bus and the utter stillness of the house. No, no it had not been bombarded; it was only a broken-down house, as a child might say. It was large, broad, and tall like the two-storeyed houses in the old quarters of Rio. A large house with deep foundations.

Caught up in a search which was much more significant than the question written on their faces, they had both turned inadvertently at the same time, and the house seemed as close to them as if, looming from nowhere, a wall had suddenly been erected before their very eyes. Behind them stood the bus, before them stood the house — there was no means of escaping from that spot. Were they to move back, they would collide with the bus, were they to move forward they would crash into the monstrous house. They were trapped.

The house was tall, and close. They could not look at it without having to gaze up like little children, a gesture which suddenly made them look tiny and transformed the house into a huge mansion. It was as if nothing had ever stood so close to them. The house must have been painted once. But whatever the original colour of the windows, they were now merely old and solid. Dwarfed, they opened their eyes in amazement: the house was *anguished*.

The house was anguished and tranquil. As no word had ever been. It was a building that weighed in the hearts of a boy and a girl. A two-storeyed house reminiscent of someone lifting a hand to their throat. Who? Who had built it, erecting that monstrosity, stone by stone, that cathedral of petrified horror? Or was it time that had stuck to those bare walls giving them that air of strangulation, that silence of someone who has been hanged and was now at peace? The house was compact like a boxer with no neck. And a head attached directly on to shoulders was anguish. They looked at the house like tiny children standing at the bottom of a flight of stairs.

At last, they had unexpectedly reached their goal and found themselves before the sphinx. Dumbfounded, in an extreme union of fear and respect and paleness, in the presence of truth. Naked anguish had taken a leap and landed before them — not even as familiar as the word that they had become accustomed to using. Simply an enormous house, rustic, with no neck, only that ancient might.

I am that very thing you have been searching for all this time, the large house said.

And most ironic of all, I hold no secrets, the large house said.

The girl stared, as if in a daze. As for the boy, his seventh sense had fastened on to the innermost part of the building and he could perceive on the end of a thread the faintest trembling of a reply. He dared not move for fear of startling his own attentiveness. The girl had anchored herself to fear, afraid to emerge only to confront the terror of some discovery. They dared not speak lest the house should come tumbling down. Their silence left the two-storeyed house intact. But just as they had been forced to look at it before, even if they were to be assured that they could now escape, they would remain there, transfixed by fascination and horror. Transfixed before that monster which had been built long before they were born, that relic of another age, now drained of all meaning. But what of the future? Oh God, grant us our future! The house without eyes, with the power of a blind man. And if it had eyes, they were the round, vacant eyes of a statue. Oh God, do not make us the children of that empty past, deliver us to the future. They wanted to be someone's children. But not the children of that fatal, brittle carcass, for they did not understand the past: oh deliver us from the past, let us carry out our arduous duty. For it was not freedom that the boy and girl desired, what they desired most of all was to be persuaded, to be won over and guided — but it would have to be by something more powerful than the great power that was beating in their breasts.

The girl suddenly turned away her face. I am so unhappy, more unhappy than I have ever been, classes have come to an end, everything has come to an end! — for in her eagerness she showed no gratitude for a childhood that had probably been happy. The girl suddenly turned away her head with a groan.

As for the boy, he quickly foundered in a haze of uncertainty as if left without any thoughts. That, too, might have been due to the evening light: it was a harsh light without any sense of time. The boy's face was greenish and calm, and he no longer received any guidance from the words of the *others*: the very thing he had courageously set out to achieve one day. Except that he had not counted on the misery that ensues when someone is unable to express himself.

Green and filled with nausea, they were unable to express themselves. The house symbolized something that they would never comprehend, even were they to spend the rest of their lives searching for words to express it. Searching for words to express it, even though it might require a lifetime, would be a pastime in itself, bitter and disquieting, but nonetheless a pastime, and it would serve as a diversion and gradually lead them away from dangerous truth — and ensure their salvation. One day soon — having already invented their own future with desperate cunning in their will to survive — they would both become writers with such determined effort as if by expressing the soul it might finally be suppressed. And should it not be suppressed, it would be a means of knowing only that we tell lies in the solitude of our own hearts.

Just as they would no longer be able to play with the house of the past. Now, dwarfed by the house, it seemed to them that they had merely played at being young and sorrowful, and at delivering the *message*. Now, in terror, they finally possessed what they had dangerously and imprudently asked for: they were two young people who had truly lost their way. As grown-ups might say: 'They have got their just deserts'. And they were as guilty as guilty children, as guilty as criminals are innocent. Oh, if only they could still pacify the world they had offended, by saying reassuringly: 'We were only playing! we are a couple of imposters!' But it was too late. 'Surrender unconditionally, and make yourselves a part of me for I am the past' — future life was saying to them. And how could anyone, dear God, expect them to believe that the future would be theirs? Who? but who was prepared to clear up the mystery, without telling lies? — was there someone functioning in this sense? This time, they were lost for words and it did not even occur to them to reproach society.

Suddenly, the girl turned her face away with a groan, something akin to weeping or coughing.

'Just like a girl to cry at a time like this', he thought from the depths of his perdition, without quite knowing what he meant by 'at a time like this'. But this was the first sign of stability that he had discovered for himself. Holding on to this first life-line, he could come struggling back to the surface, and, as always, before the girl. He turned round before she did, and saw a house standing with a placard announcing 'To rent'. He heard the bus behind him, saw an empty house, and at his side the girl with a sickly face, which she tried to hide from the man who had already been awakened: for some reason, she tried to hide her face.

Still hesitant, he waited politely until she regained her composure. Yes, he waited hesitantly, but a man. Thin, and irremediably young certainly, but a man. A man's body provided the stability that would always help him to recover. Now and then, when his need was greatest, he became a man. Then, with an unsteady hand, he would awkwardly light a cigarette, as if he were the *others*, taking advantage of the gestures which the freemasonry of men provided for his support and guidance. And she?

The girl emerged from all this painted with lipstick, her rouge half smudged, a blue necklace adorning her neck. Plumes which a moment sooner had been part of a situation and of a future, but now she looked as if she had not washed her face before going to bed and had woken up with the shameless traces of the previous night's orgy. For, now and then, she was a woman.

With consoling cynicism, the boy watched inquisitively. And saw that she was a mere girl.

— I'm staying here, he told her, arrogantly dismissing her, he who no longer had any set time for returning home and who could feel the front door key in his pocket.

They said goodbye, and they who never shook hands because it would be too conventional, shook hands. For she — in her confusion at finding herself with breasts and a necklace at such an unfortunate moment — she had clumsily stretched out her hand. The contact of those two moist hands touching without love, embarrassed the boy as if it were some shaming operation, and he blushed. And she, with lipstick and rouge, tried to conceal her own adorned nakedness. She was a nonentity, and withdrew as if she were being pursued by a thousand eyes, evasive in her humiliation upon finding herself with a condition.

Watching her leave, the boy studied her in disbelief and amusement: 'Is it possible that women are capable of truly understanding what anguish means?' This uncertainty gave him a feeling of great strength. 'No, women were good for something else, that no one could deny.' And what he needed was a comrade. Yes, a loyal friend. He now felt pure and frank, with nothing to hide, loyal as a man. From any tremor of the earth, he emerged with a brisk forward movement, with the same proud inconsequence that causes a horse to neigh. While she withdrew, skirting the wall like an intruder, close to being the mother of the children she would bear one day, her body foretelling her submission, that sacred and impure body with which she was burdened. The youth watched her, astonished that he should have been fooled by the girl for so long, and he almost smiled, he almost flapped the wings he had just grown. I am a man, his sex told him in dark victory. From every struggle or truce, he emerged ever more a man; to be a man nourished itself on that wind that even now was blowing dust through the streets near the St John the Baptist Cemetery. The same dusty wind which caused that other creature, the female, to cower wounded, as if no clothing could ever protect her nakedness, that wind blowing through the streets.

The boy saw her leave, accompanying her with pornographic and inquisitive eyes that did not miss the smallest detail about the girl. The girl who suddenly began to run in desperation for fear of missing the bus . . .

Startled, fascinated, the boy watched her run like someone demented for fear of missing the bus. Intrigued, he saw her board the bus like a monkey wearing a short skirt. The false cigarette dropped from his fingers . . .

Something alien unbalanced him. What was it? He was momentarily seized by utter disquiet. But what was it? Urgently, anxiously: what was it? He watched her run swiftly even though he could perceive that the girl's heart was pale. And he watched her, full of impotent love for humanity, boarding the bus like a monkey — and afterwards he saw her sitting, quiet and composed, re-arranging her blouse as she waited for the bus to leave . . . Was that it? But what was causing him to feel uneasy and vigilant? Perhaps the fact that she had run in such desperation, for the bus was still not ready to leave, so there was still time . . . There was no need for her to run . . . But what was there about all this that was making him prick up his ears, anguished and attentive, with the deafness of someone who will never hear the explanation?

He had just been born a man. But no sooner had he accepted his birth, than he found himself carrying that burden in his heart: no sooner had he accepted his glory when an unfathomable experience gave him his first wrinkle of the future. Oblivious and uneasy, he had barely accepted his masculinity, when a new avid hunger was born, an unhappy thing like a man who never weeps.

Was he experiencing the first fear that something might be impossible? The girl was a nonentity in that stationary bus, and meanwhile, man as he now was, the boy suddenly needed to turn to that nonentity, to that girl. Not even to turn to her as equal to equal, or to turn to her in order to concede . . . But, imprisoned in his kingdom of man, he needed her. For what reason? To remind himself of some law? So that she or some other woman might not allow him to stray too far and lose himself? So that he might sense with apprehension, as he was sensing even now, that there was the possibility of error? He hungered after her in order never to forget that they were made of the same flesh, that poor flesh out of which, as she boarded the bus like a monkey, she appeared to have carved a fatal itinerary. What is it? What is finally happening to me? he asked himself in fear.

Nothing. Nothing. Let us not exaggerate, it was only a moment of weakness and uncertainty, nothing more, there was no danger.

Only a moment of weakness and uncertainty. Yet within that system of harsh and final judgement, which forbids even a moment of disbelief lest the ideal should collapse, he looked at the long road in a daze — everything was now in ruins and arid as if his mouth were full of dust. Now, alone at last, he was defenceless and at the mercy of the hasty lie with which the *others* tried to teach him to be a man. But what about the message? The message reduced to dust which the wind was blowing towards the grating over the sewer. Mummy, he said.

Monkeys

The first time we had a monkey in the house was about the New Year. We were without water and without a maid, people were queueing for meat, and there was a sudden spell of hot weather — when, speechless and perplexed, I saw the monkey enter the house, eating a banana, already inspecting everything rapidly, and swishing its long tail. It looked more like a chimpanzee and, although still quite small, its latent powers were tremendous. It climbed over the washing hanging on the clothes-line, from where it cursed like a sailor, and threw banana skins in every direction. I felt exhausted. Sometimes forgetting, I entered the kitchen, lost in thought, then the sudden shock: to find that happy creature there. My younger son knew before I did, that I would get rid of the monkey: 'And if I should promise that the monkey will become ill and die one day, would you let him stay? and suppose he were somehow to fall out of the window one day and die down there on the pavement?' My feelings avoided his eyes. The happy and foul unconsciousness of the little monkey made me responsible for his destiny, since he himself did not accept any blame. A woman friend understood the bitterness of my acceptance, the crimes which encouraged my vague expression, and she abruptly came to the rescue: some urchins had appeared in merry uproar, they carried off the grinning monkey, and that unnerving New Year, at least I acquired a house without a monkey.

A year later, I had just had a happy experience when there in Copacabana I saw a crowd gather. A man was selling tiny monkeys. I thought of the children, of the joys they gave me gratis, which bore no relation to the worries they also gave me gratis, and I visualized a chain of happiness: 'Whoever receives this, should pass it on to another', and another to another, like a quivering trail of smoke. And there and then, I bought the little monkey whom we christened Lisette.

She almost fitted into my hand. She wore a tiny skirt,

earrings, a necklace, and a bracelet from Bahia. She looked like an immigrant, who disembarks wearing the national costume of her native country. No less peculiar to the immigrant were those big round eyes.

As for the little monkey, she was a woman in miniature. She remained with us for three days. Her bones were so incredibly delicate. And she was very sweet. Her expression was even rounder than her eyes. At the slightest movement, her earrings jingled; the skirt always looked neat, the necklace a brilliant red. The little monkey slept a great deal, but when it came to eating she was slow and listless. Her rare displays of affection consisted of a gentle bite that left no mark.

On the third day we were in the kitchen, admiring Lisette and the way in which she belonged to us. 'A little too gentle,' I thought, longing for my ape. And unexpectedly my heart replied with utter cruelty: 'That is not sweetness. It is death.' The lack of communication pacified me. Then I said to the children: 'Lisette is dying.' Watching her, I perceived just how far our love had gone. I wrapped Lisette in a napkin and went with the children to the nearest dispensary, where the vet could not attend to us because he was carrying out an emergency operation on a dog. Another taxi — Lisette imagines that she is being taken for a drive, mummy — another dispensary. There they gave her oxygen.

With the breath of life, a Lisette was suddenly revealed to us whom we did not recognize. Her eyes were much less round, more secretive, more laughing, and on that protruding, unremarkable face there was a certain ironic hauteur: a little more oxygen, and she felt an urge to say outright that she hated being a monkey; but she was, and she had much to relate. Shortly, however, she succumbed once more, exhausted. More oxygen, and this time a serum injection. As the needle went in, she reacted with an angry swipe, her bracelet tinkling. The vet's assistant smiled: 'Lisette, my pet, keep still!'

The diagnosis: she would not live without a ready supply of oxygen, and even then, her survival seemed unlikely. 'People should not buy monkeys on the street,' the vet rebuked me, shaking his head, 'they are often sold in poor condition.' No, people should have some guarantee before buying a monkey, know something of its origin, be assured of at least five years of domestication, know what it will do or not do, just as if choosing a partner for marriage. I consulted the children briefly. And I said to the vet's assistant: 'You have taken a liking to Lisette. So why not allow her to stay here for a few days where oxygen is at hand, and, if she recovers, she is yours?' He was thinking. 'Lisette is so pretty,' I pleaded. 'She is delightful,' he agreed pensively. Then he sighed and said: 'If I can cure Lisette, she's yours.' We departed with an empty napkin.

The following day they telephoned from the dispensary and I informed the children that Lisette had died. The little one asked me: 'Do you think she died wearing her earrings?' I answered yes. One week later, the older boy said to me: 'You look just like Lisette!' 'I am fond of you, too,' I replied.

The Egg and the Chicken

In the morning I see the egg on the kitchen table.

I take in the egg at a single glance. I immediately perceive that I cannot be seeing an egg. To see an egg never remains in the present. No sooner do I see an egg than I have seen an egg for the last three thousand years. The very instant an egg is seen, it is the memory of an egg — the only person to see the egg is someone who has already seen it. — Upon seeing the egg, it is already too late: an egg seen is an egg lost. — To see the egg is the promise of being able to see the egg one day. — A brief glance which cannot be divided; if there is any thought; there is no thought; there is the egg. Looking is the necessary instrument which, once used, I shall put aside. I shall remain with the egg. — The egg has no *itself*. Individually, it does not exist.

To see the egg is impossible: just as there are supersonic sounds, the egg is supervisible. No one is capable of seeing the egg. Does the dog see the egg? Only machines see the egg. The hoist sees the egg. — When I was ancient, an egg rested on my shoulder. — Love for the egg cannot be felt. Love for the egg is supersensitive. Mankind is unaware of loving the egg. — When I was ancient, I was the depositary of the egg and I walked softly to avoid disturbing the egg's silence. When I died, they carefully removed the egg from inside me. It was still alive. — Only someone who has seen the world can see the egg. Like the world, the egg is obvious.

The egg no longer exists. Like the light of an extinguished star, the egg, strictly speaking, no longer exists.

— Egg, you are perfect. You are white. — To you, I dedicate the beginning of time. To you, I dedicate the first moment.

To the egg, I dedicate the Chinese nation.

The egg is a suspended thing. It never settles. When it comes to rest, it is not the egg that has come to rest. It is something that remains beneath the egg. — I look at the egg in the kitchen

inattentively in order not to break it. I take the greatest care not
to understand it. Since it is beyond understanding, I know that
if I should understand it, it is because I am mistaken. To
understand is the proof of my mistake. To understand it, is not
the way to see it. — Never to think about the egg is one way to
have seen it. — Is it possible that I know about the egg? It is
almost certain that I know. Thus: I exist, and immediately I
know. — What I do not know about the egg is what really
matters. What I do not know about the egg gives me the egg,
strictly speaking. — The moon is inhabited by eggs.

The egg is an exteriorization. To have a shell is to give
oneself. — The egg denudes the kitchen. It transforms the
table into a slanting plane. The egg lays bare. — Anyone who
fathoms the egg, anyone who penetrates the egg's surface,
desires something else: that person is hungry.

The egg is the soul of the chicken. The awkward chicken.
The reliable egg. The terrified chicken. The reliable egg. Like a
stationary missile. For the egg is an egg in space. The egg
above the blue. — Egg, I love you. I love you like a thing that
does not even know that it loves another thing. — I do not
touch it. It is the aura of my fingers that sees the egg. I do not
touch it. — But to dedicate myself to the vision of the egg
would be to renounce my worldly existence, and I need both
the yolk and the white. — The egg sees me. Does the egg
idealize me? Does the egg contemplate me? No, the egg only
sees me. It is immune to harmful understanding. — The egg
has never struggled. It is a gift. — The egg is invisible to the
naked eye. — From egg to egg, one arrives at God, Who is
invisible to the naked eye. Perhaps the egg was once a triangle
which rolled so far into space that it gradually became oval. —
Is the egg essentially a vessel? Perhaps the first vessel modelled
by the Etruscans? No. The egg originated from Macedonia.
There it was calculated, the fruit of the most painstaking
spontaneity. On the sands of Macedonia, a man with a rod
in his hand, designed it. And then erased it with his bare
foot.

An egg is something that requires care. That explains why
the chicken is the egg's disguise. The chicken exists so that the
egg may traverse the ages. That is what it means to be a
mother. The egg is persecuted because it is always ahead of its

time. — The egg for the present is always revolutionary. — It lives inside the chicken so that no one may call it white. The egg is truly white. But it must not be called white. Not because this would do the egg any harm, but those people who call the egg white — renounce life. To define what is white as white, might easily destroy humanity. A man was once accused of being what he was, and he was referred to as That Man. They were not lying: He was. But to this day, generation after generation, we still have not recovered. The universal law so that we may go on living decrees: one may say 'a pretty face', but anyone who says 'the face' dies; having exhausted the topic.

With the passage of time, the egg has become the egg of a chicken. It is not. But once having adopted it, the egg uses the surname. — We have to say 'the egg of a chicken'. If we simply refer to 'egg', the topic is exhausted, and the world remains naked. — In relation to the egg, there is the danger that we might discover what could be called beauty, that is to say, its veracity. The egg's veracity has no semblance of truth. Should this be discovered, it might be forced to become rectangular. The egg is in no danger, for it would not become rectangular. (Our guarantee is that it cannot: that is the egg's great strength: its supremacy comes from the greatness of not being able to, which radiates like unwillingness.) But anyone struggling to make it rectangular would be in danger of losing his own life. Therefore, the egg exposes us to danger. Our advantage is that the egg is invisible. And as for the initiated, the initiated disguise the egg.

As for the chicken's body, the chicken's body is the clearest proof that the egg does not exist. It is enough to look at the chicken to see that the egg cannot possibly exist. And the chicken? The egg is the chicken's great sacrifice. The egg is the cross that the chicken carries through life. The egg is the chicken's unattainable dream. The chicken loves the egg. She does not know that the egg exists. Were she to know that she has an egg inside her, would she be saved? Were she to know that she has the egg inside her, would she lose her condition as a chicken? To be a chicken is the chicken's survival. To survive is salvation. For it appears that to live does not exist. To live leads to death. Therefore, what the chicken does is permanently to survive. To survive means sustaining the struggle against life which is mortal. That is what it means to be a chicken. The chicken looks ill at ease.

It is essential that the chicken should not know she has an egg. Otherwise she might possibly be saved as a chicken, but would lose the egg. Therefore, she does not know. The chicken exists so that the egg may use her. She was only there to fulfil herself, but came to enjoy it. The chicken's downfall stems from this: enjoyment was no part of being born. It hurts to enjoy being alive. — As for what came first, it was the egg that discovered the chicken. The chicken was not even summoned. The chicken is chosen spontaneously. — The chicken lives as in a dream. She has no sense of reality. The chicken's timid nature is the result of always having her daydreams interrupted. The chicken is one great slumber. — The chicken suffers from some unknown malaise. The chicken's unknown malaise is the egg. — She cannot explain it: 'I know that the error is somewhere inside me', she refers to her life as an error. 'I no longer know what I feel', etc.

'Etc. etc. etc.' is what the chicken clucks the whole day long. The chicken possesses a great deal of inner life. To tell the truth, inner life is all she possesses. Our vision of her inner life is what we call 'chicken'. The chicken's inner life consists in behaving as if she understood. The slightest threat and she makes an uproar as if she were demented. All this to ensure that the egg does not break inside her. The egg that breaks inside the chicken is like blood.

The chicken looks towards the horizon. As if she were watching an egg slowly advance from the line on the horizon. Apart from being a means of transport for the egg, the chicken is stupid, idle and shortsighted. How can the chicken understand herself if she is the contradiction of an egg? The egg is still the same egg which originated in Macedonia. The chicken is ever the most modern of tragedies. She is ever uselessly up to date. And she is continuously being designed anew. The most appropriate form for a chicken has still to be discovered. While my neighbour answers the telephone, he absentmindedly designs the chicken anew with his pencil. But there is no way out for the chicken: it is inherent in her condition to be of no use to herself. Since her destiny is more important than the chicken herself and her destiny is the egg, her personal life does not interest us.

The chicken does not recognize the egg inside her nor does she recognize it once it is outside her. When the chicken sees the egg, she thinks that she is struggling with something impossible. And with her heart beating, with her heart beating furiously, she fails to recognize the egg.

Suddenly, I look at the egg in the kitchen and all I see there is something to eat. I fail to recognize it and my heart is beating. A transformation is taking place inside me. My perception of the egg becomes less clear. Excepting each particular egg, excepting each egg one eats, the egg does not exist. I can no longer bring myself to believe in an egg. I find it increasingly difficult to believe in it, for I am weak and dying, farewell. I have looked at an egg for far too long and it has lulled me to sleep.

The chicken who did not wish to sacrifice her life. The one who opted for being 'happy'. The one who failed to perceive that if she spent her life designing the egg inside her as in an illuminated manuscript, she would be serving some purpose. The chicken who did not know how to bring about her own ruin. The one who thought that she was covered in feathers to protect her precious skin, unable to comprehend that the feathers were only intended to lighten her burden while she carried the egg, because intense suffering could harm the egg. The one who thought that pleasure was a gift, unable to perceive that it was intended to keep her wholly distracted while the egg was being formed. The one who did not know that 'I' is only one of the words people form with their lips when answering the telephone, a mere attempt to find some more apt expression. The one who thought that 'I' means to possess a 'selfness'. The chickens who are likely to harm the egg are those who show themselves to be a relentless 'I'. With them, the 'I' is so constant that they can no longer pronounce the word 'egg'. But who can tell, perhaps this is exactly what the egg needs. Because if they were not so distracted, if they were to pay closer attention to the great life that is forming inside them, they could upset the egg.

I began by speaking about the chicken, and for some considerable time I have said nothing about the chicken. I am still speaking about the egg.

And lo and behold, I do not understand the egg. I only understand a broken egg: I break it into the frying pan. So indirectly I pledge myself to the egg's existence: my sacrifice is to reduce myself to my inner self. From my joys and sorrows I have shaped my hidden destiny. And to possess only one's own life represents a sacrifice for anyone who has seen the egg. Like those in a convent, who sweep the floors and wash the linen, serving without the glory of any higher office, my task is to live my joys and sorrows. It is essential that I should possess the modesty of living.

In the kitchen I take one more egg and break its shell and form. And from that precise moment the egg no longer exists. It is absolutely necessary that I should be kept occupied and distracted. I am essentially one of those who renege. I belong to the freemasonry of those who have seen the egg once and then deny it as a means of ensuring its protection. We are those who refrain from destroying, only to be destroyed ourselves. Agents in disguise, assigned to less conspicuous duties, occasionally we recognize each other. A certain manner of looking, a certain way of shaking hands, helps us to recognize each other, and we call this love. And then concealment is no longer necessary: though no one speaks, no one tells lies either, although no one speaks the truth, there is no need to go on pretending any longer. Love exists when one is allowed to participate a little more. Few desire love, because love is the greatest disillusionment of all. And few can bear to sacrifice all their other illusions. There are some who volunteer for love, believing that love will enrich their personal life. It is quite the contrary: love is poverty in the end. Love is to possess nothing. Love is also the disillusionment of that which was believed to be love. Since it is not a prize, it does not encourage conceit; love is not a prize, it is a state conceded exclusively to those who would otherwise taint the egg with their personal sorrow. This does not make an honourable exception of love: it is conceded precisely to unworthy agents, to those who would upset everything unless they were permitted to have vague intuitions.

Many advantages are given to all the agents so that the egg may take form. It is not a question of being jealous, because even some of the conditions, worse than those imposed on the others, are simply the ideal conditions for the egg. As for the pleasure of the agents, they receive that, too, without conceit. They experience all the pleasures with austerity: it is, moreover, our sacrifice so that the egg may take form. A nature has already been imposed on us which is wholly apt for endless pleasure. This makes things much easier. And at least it makes pleasure less painful.

There are instances of agents who commit suicide: they find the few instructions they have been given are insufficient, and feel a lack of support. There was the case of the agent who publicly revealed his identity because he could no longer tolerate not being understood, just as he could no longer tolerate not being respected by others; he died after being run over as he was leaving a restaurant. There was another agent who did not even need to be eliminated: he slowly consumed himself in rebellion, a rebellion which gripped him when he discovered that the handful of instructions he had received included no explanation. There was yet another who was also eliminated, because he thought that 'the truth must be spoken courageously', and he began initially to look for truth: it was said of him that he died in the name of truth, but the fact is that he was simply obstructing the truth with his innocence; his apparent courage was folly, and his desire for loyalty ingenuous; he had failed to understand that to be loyal is not something pure, to be loyal is to be disloyal to all the rest. These extreme cases of death are not provoked by cruelty. There is a task to be accomplished which might be termed cosmic, and, sadly, individual cases cannot be taken into consideration. For those who succumb and become individuals, there exist institutions, charity, an understanding which does not discriminate between motives: our human life in short.

The eggs spurt in the frying pan, and lost in a dream, I prepare breakfast. Without any sense of reality, I call out to the children who spring from various beds, draw up their chairs and start eating, and the work of the day which has just dawned begins, shouting, laughing, eating, the white and the yolk, happiness mingled with quarrelling, the day is our salt, and we are the salt of the day, living is quite tolerable, living occupies and distracts, living excites laughter.

It makes me smile in my mystery. My mystery consists of my being simply a means, and not an end, and this has given me the most dangerous of freedoms. I am not stupid, and take full advantage of my freedom. I even do harm to others, believe me . . .

I convert the false credentials they have given me by way of concealment into my real occupation; I even take advantage of the money they pay me on a daily basis to make life easier so that the egg may take form, by using that money for other purposes, a misappropriation of funds. Recently I have bought shares in a brewery, and I am a rich woman. I still refer to all this as the essential modesty of living. There is also the time they have given me, and which they give us so that the egg may take its form in honest idleness, because I have used this time for forbidden pleasures and forbidden sorrows, completely forgetting about the egg. This is my simplicity.

Or is that exactly what they want to happen to me, so that the egg may fulfil itself? Is this freedom or am I being compelled? For it is now becoming clear that every error on my part has been exploited. My grievance is that in their eyes I count for nothing, I am merely precious: they look after me second by second with the most complete absence of love; I am merely precious. With the money they give me, I have recently taken to drinking. Am I abusing your confidence? It is simply that no one knows how the person feels whose occupation consists in pretending to be a traitor and who ends up believing in his own betrayal. Whose occupation consists in forgetting each day. The person of whom apparent dishonour is exacted. My mirror no longer reflects a face which can be called mine. Either I am an agent or this is truly betrayal.

But I sleep the sleep of the just, knowing that my futile existence does not hinder the march of infinite time. On the contrary: it would appear that I am required to be extremely futile, that I am required to sleep like the just. They want me occupied and distracted, by whatever means. For with my wandering thoughts and my solemn folly, I might obstruct that which is being made through me. The fact is that I myself, I myself strictly speaking, have only served to obstruct. The idea that my destiny transcends me suggests that I might be an agent: they should have allowed me to foresee at least this, for I am one of those people who do a job badly unless they are allowed to have some intuition; they made me forget what they had allowed me to foresee, but I have vaguely remained with the notion that my destiny transcends me, and that I am the instrument of their work. At all events, I could only be the instrument, for the work could never be mine. I have already tried to establish myself in my own right without success; this hand of mine has trembled to this day. Had I been a little more insistent, I should have lost my health forever. Ever since then, ever since that abortive experience, I try to reason in the following manner: I have already received a great deal, and they have already made every possible concession; and other agents, vastly superior to me, have also worked only for what they did not know. And with the same meagre instruments. I have already received a great deal; this, for example: now and then, with my heart beating at the privilege, at least I know that I am not acknowledging anything! with my heart beating with emotion, at least, I do not understand! with my heart beating with confidence, at least, I do not know. But what about the egg? This is one of their pretexts: while I was talking about the egg, I had forgotten about the egg. 'Speak, speak', they instructed me. And the egg remains completely protected by so many words. 'Go on speaking' is one of their instructions. I am so tired.

Out of devotion to the egg, I forgot about it. My necessary forgetfulness. My calculating forgetfulness. For the egg is an evasion. Confronted by my possessive adoration, the egg can withdraw never to return. But suppose the egg were to be forgotten. Suppose I were to make the sacrifice of only living my life and forgetting about the egg. Suppose the egg were to be impossible. Then — free, delicate, without any message for me — perhaps once more the egg might move through space right up to this window which I have always kept open. And, as day breaks, it might descend into our apartment. Serenely move into the kitchen. Illuminating it with my pallor.

Temptation

She was sobbing. And as if the bright glare of the afternoon were not enough, she had red hair.

In the empty street, the stones vibrated with heat — the little girl's head was aflame. Seated on the steps in front of the house, she was bearing up. The street was deserted except for a solitary figure waiting in vain at the tram stop. As if her submissive and patient gaze were not enough, her sobs kept interrupting her and caused her chin to tremble as it rested dejectedly on one hand. What was to be done with a sobbing child with red hair? We looked at each other in silence, dismay confronting dismay. In the deserted street there was no sign of the tram. In a land of brunettes, to have red hair was an involuntary act of rebellion. What did it matter if one day this characteristic would cause her to raise a woman's head with an air of defiance? For the present, she was seated on a sparkling doorstep, at two o'clock in the afternoon. What saved her was a woman's discarded handbag, with a broken strap. She held it as if experienced in conjugal love, clutching it to her knees.

At that moment she was approached by her other half in this world, a soul-mate in Grajaú. The possibility of communication emerged on a street-corner in a haze of sweltering heat; accompanying a woman and embodied in the form of a dog. It was a beautiful and pitiful basset-hound, sweet beneath its destiny. It was a red-haired basset.

There he came trotting, ahead of his owner, dragging his long body. Off-guard, accustomed, a dog.

The little girl opened her eyes in astonishment. Gently warned, the dog halted before her. His tongue quivered. They eyed each other.

Among so many creatures who are ready to become the owners of another creature, there was the little girl who had come into this world to possess that dog. He trembled gently, without barking. She looked at him from under her hair, fascinated and solemn. How much time had passed? A great discordant sob shook her whole body. The basset did not even tremble. She, too, overcame her sob and continued to stare at him.

Both of them had short, red hair.

What did they say to each other? No one knows. We only know that they communicated rapidly with each other, for there was no time to lose. We also know that, without speaking, they invoked each other. They invoked each other with urgency, embarrassment and surprise.

In the midst of so much vague impossibility and so much sun, there was the solution for the red-haired girl. And in the midst of so many streets to be trotted, of so many bigger dogs, of so many dry sewers — there was a little girl as if she were the flesh of his own red flesh. They stared at each other, absorbed, forgetful of Grajaú. Another second and the hovering dream would shatter, yielding perhaps to the solemnity with which they invoked each other.

But they were both pledged. She to her impossible childhood, the centre of that innocence which could only open out when she became a woman. He, to his imprisoned nature.

The dog's owner waited impatiently beneath her parasol. The red-haired basset finally detached himself from the little girl and trotted off as if in a dream. She remained terrified, holding the event in her hands with a muteness which neither a father nor a mother could understand. She accompanied the basset with black eyes, watching him in disbelief, slumped over the handbag pressed against her knees, until she saw him disappear round the next corner.

But he was stronger than she was. He did not look back even once.

Journey to Petrópolis

She was a tiny, shrivelled-up old woman who, sweet and obstinate, did not seem to understand that she was all alone in the world. Her eyes were always watering, her hands resting on her black, opaque dress, the fading document of her life. In the fabric which had become hard there were small crumbs of bread stuck together by the spittle which appeared once more as she recalled her childhood. There was a yellowish smudge, the remains of an egg she had eaten two weeks earlier. And tell-tale signs of the places where she had slept. She always found somewhere to doss down, someone's house here or there. When they asked her name, she would reply in a voice refined by failing strength and many years of good breeding:

— Missy.

People smiled. Pleased at the interest she had aroused, she would explain:

— Name, my real name is Marguerite.

Her body was tiny and sallow, even though she had once been tall and fair. She once had a father, and a mother, a husband and two children. They had all died one by one. She alone has remained with her rheumy, expectant eyes, which were almost entirely covered by a white, velvety membrane. Whenever anyone gave her alms, they gave her very little, for she was so minute and really did not need much food. When they gave her a bed to sleep on, it was invariably narrow and hard, for Marguerite had physically shrunk over the years. She herself was sparing in her thanks. She would smile and nod her head.

She was now sleeping, no one knew for what reason, in a room at the back of a large house in a tree-lined street in Botafogo. The family found Missy quaint but ignored her existence most of the time. For they were also dealing with a mysterious old girl. She got up early each morning, made her bed fit for a dwarf, and darted out hastily, as if the house were on fire. No one knew where she was heading. One day, one of the daughters in the house asked her where she was going. She replied with an amiable smile:

— I'm going for a stroll.

They found it amusing that an old woman living on charity should go for a stroll. But it was true. Missy was born in Maranhão, where she had always lived. She had only recently arrived in Rio accompanied by a kind-hearted woman who planned to intern Missy in a hospice, but this turned out to be impossible: the woman had travelled on to Minas and given Missy some money to get herself settled in Rio. And the old woman strolled the streets to get to know the city. It was sufficient, however, for someone to sit down on a bench in any square in order to see Rio de Janeiro at a glance.

Missy's life ran smoothly until one day it dawned on the family in the house in Botafogo just how long she had been there, and they decided it was time she moved on. To some extent, they were right. Everyone in that household was kept extremely busy; from time to time, there were weddings, parties, engagements, social visits. And when they encountered the old woman, as they rushed backwards and forwards, they were startled as if they had been stopped in their tracks, and accosted with a tap on the shoulder and a sudden: 'Hey there!' One of the girls in particular felt irritated and uneasy, the old woman got on her nerves for some reason. Especially that permanent smile, even though the girl realized that it was a harmless rictus. Perhaps because there was never any time, no one discussed the matter. But the moment someone suggested sending her to live in Petrópolis, at the house of their German sister-in-law, the consensus was more lively than any old woman could have expected to provoke.

So when the son of the household, accompanied by his girl friend and his two sisters, went to spend a weekend in Petrópolis, they took the old woman with them in the car.

What had kept Missy awake the previous night? Just to think of a journey caused her parched, diseased heart to shed its rust inside that brittle body as if she had swallowed a large pill without any water. At times, she even found it difficult to breathe. She spent the night talking to herself, sometimes aloud. The excitement of the promised excursion and a different life suddenly clarified certain ideas. She remembered things that some days before she would have sworn had never existed. Beginning with the son who had been run over and died beneath a tram in Maranhão — if he had lived amidst the traffic of Rio de Janeiro, he would have been run over and died right here. She remembered her son's hair, his clothes. She remembered the coffee cup that Maria Rosa had broken, and how she had screamed at her. If only she had known that her daughter would die giving birth, she would never have screamed at her. And she remembered her husband. She could only remember her husband in his shirt-sleeves. But that was difficult to understand for she was certain that he always went to the office dressed formally as befitted a clerk; he always went to functions wearing a jacket and obviously he would never have attended the funerals of his own children in his shirt-sleeves.

Trying to remember her husband's jacket only made the old woman feel even more exhausted, as she tossed and turned in her bed. Suddenly she discovered that the bed was hard.

— What a hard bed, she said in a very loud voice in the middle of the night.

Her whole body had become sensitive. Parts of her body which she had ignored for some considerable time now reclaimed her attention. And suddenly — she felt a terrible hunger! Delirious, she got up, untied her tiny bundle, and took out a stale chunk of buttered bread, which she had furtively kept for two days. She devoured the bread like a rat, causing her gums to bleed. As she ate, she became more and more animated. She succeeded, however fleetingly, in visualizing her husband saying goodbye as he left for work. Only after the image had passed did she realize that she had forgotten to observe if he was in his shirt-sleeves. She lay down once more, scratching her feverish body which was itching all over. She spent the rest of the night playing this obsessive game of seeing something for an instant only to lose sight of it. Hours later, she fell asleep.

And, for the very first time, it was necessary to rouse her. The house was still in darkness when one of the girls came to call her with a kerchief tied round her head and a suitcase in one hand. Unexpectedly, Missy begged a few minutes to comb her hair. Her trembling hands clutched the broken comb. She had never been the sort of woman who went for a stroll without first combing her hair properly.

When she finally approached the car, the young man and the girls were surprised at her cheerful expression and her brisk steps. 'She's fitter than I am,' the young man quipped. He reminded his girlfriend: 'And to think I almost felt sorry for her.'

Missy sat on the back seat of the car near the window, somewhat cramped by the two girls who shared the same seat. She remained silent, smiling. But when the car gave the first jolt, throwing her backwards, she felt a stab of pain in her breast. It was not simply happiness, it was affliction. The young man turned round:

— I hope you won't be sick, granny!

The girls laughed, especially the one who sat at the front, who from time to time rested her head on the young man's shoulder. Out of politeness, the old woman wanted to reply, but could find no words. She wanted to smile, but no smile came. She looked at all of them, her eyes watering, which they no longer mistook for weeping. Something in Missy's expression numbed any sense of happiness and gave her an air of stubbornness.

The journey was most agreeable.

The girls were jovial, Missy was now smiling again. And although her heart was still beating furiously, she felt much better. They passed a cemetery, a grocer's shop, a tree, two women, a soldier, a cat! hoardings — all swallowed up by the speed at which they were travelling.

When Missy woke up, she did not know where she was. The road had become visible in the morning light: it was narrow and dangerous. The old woman's mouth was burning, but her hands and feet were so cold that they had become detached from the rest of her body. The girls were conversing, the one in front resting her head on the young man's shoulder. Parcels kept toppling over.

Then Missy's brain started functioning. Her husband appeared to her wearing his jacket — I've found it, I've found it! My jacket was hanging in the wardrobe all the time. She remembered the name of Maria Rosa's friend, the girl who lived opposite: Elvira, and Elvira's mother who was lame.

These memories almost made her call out. Then she slowly moved her lips and muttered some words in a whisper.

The girls were chatting:

— Thank you, I want no such present!

That was when Missy finally began not to understand. What was she doing in this car? How had she met her husband and where? How did the mother of Maria Rosa and Rafael, their own mother, come to be in the car with these people? A moment later she calmed down again and accepted the situation.

The young man said to his sisters:

— I think it's better if we don't stop in front of the house, to avoid any scenes. The old girl will get out, we'll show her where the house is, and she will go there alone and explain that she's come for good.

One of the girls felt apprehensive. She feared that her brother, with that lack of tact which was so typical of men, might say too much in front of his girlfriend. They no longer visited their brother in Petrópolis, much less their sister-in-law.

— That's right, she interrupted him before he could say any more. Listen Missy, you go down that side-street and you won't go wrong: at the red-brick house ask for Arnaldo, my brother, do you understand? Arnaldo. Tell him that you cannot stay with us any longer, tell Arnaldo that he's got room for you and that you might even keep an eye on their child, is that clear . . .

Missy got out of the car, and stood there for some time, hesitant and dazed as she hovered over the wheels. The fresh breeze flapped her long skirt between her legs.

Arnaldo was not at home. Missy entered the small sitting-room, where the mistress of the house, a duster covering her head, was drinking coffee. A fair-haired little boy — clearly the child Missy was supposed to look after — was seated before a plate of onions and tomatoes which he ate almost dozing, while his white, freckled legs dangled under the table. The German woman filled the child's plate with gruel and pushed some buttered toast within his reach. The flies droned. Missy felt weak. If she were to drink a little coffee, perhaps she would get some warmth into her body.

The German woman stared at her from time to time in silence. She did not believe the tale about her sister-in-law's recommendation, although one could expect anything from 'that lot'. Perhaps the old woman had got their address from someone else, perhaps even from a stranger on a tram, because such things happened, one only had to open a newspaper to see what could happen. But there was something fishy about her story, the old woman had a shifty look, and she made no attempt to disguise that knowing smile. It would be wise not to leave her alone in the sitting-room with the display cabinet full of valuable china.

— I must finish my coffee first. Then when my husband arrives, we'll see what's to be done.

Missy did not understand her very well, for she spoke like a foreigner. But she understood that she was to remain seated. The smell of coffee gave her the most unbearable thirst and a vertigo which cast the whole room into darkness. Her parched lips were burning and her heart was beating furiously of its own accord. Coffee, coffee, she looked on smiling, her eyes watering. At her feet the dog was chewing its own paw and growling. The maid brought a plate of soft white cheese to the table. Tall, with a very thin neck and a big bosom, she also looked rather foreign. Without a word, the mother spread a thick layer of cheese on a slice of toast and pushed it towards the little boy. The child ate everything and, once his belly was full, he grabbed a tooth-pick and left the table.

— Mum, I need some money.

— Certainly not. What do you need money for?

— To buy sweets.

— No. Sunday is your day for pocket-money and that's tomorrow.

A glimmer of light illumined Missy: Sunday? What was she doing in that house on the eve of the Sabbath? She would never know. But she would dearly love to take that child in hand. She had always had a weakness for fair-haired children: all fair-haired children resembled the Infant Jesus. What was she doing in that house? For no good reason, they despatched her from one place to another, but she would spill the beans, she would let them see a thing or two. She smiled, feeling awkward: she would not tell them anything for all she really wanted was a cup of coffee.

The mistress of the house shouted in the direction of the kitchen, and the apathetic maid brought a soup plate, full of dark gruel. These foreigners eat such a lot in the morning, as Missy remembered from her days in Maranhão. The mistress of the house with that unfriendly expression, because foreigners in Petrópolis were as sullen as those in Maranhão, the mistress of the house took a large spoonful of white cheese, mashed it with a fork and stirred it into the gruel. Frankly, the kind of muck only a foreigner would relish. The German woman then started to eat, lost in thought, with the same bored expression Missy had seen on the faces of foreigners in Maranhão. Missy sat watching her. The dog growled at the fleas.

Arnaldo finally arrived when the sun was at its brightest, the china in the display cabinet gleaming. Arnaldo was not fair. He spoke to his wife in a low voice, and after a lengthy discussion he informed Missy with firmness and a hint of curiosity: No, it's out of the question, there is no room here.

And since the old woman made no protest and went on smiling, he spoke louder:

— There's no room here, do you hear?

Missy remained seated. Arnaldo tried gesticulating. He looked at the two women in the sitting-room and vaguely sensed the absurd contrast they provided. His wife tense and red in the face. Behind her, the old woman, wrinkled and sallow, layers of dry skin sagging everywhere. Confronted with the old woman's malicious smile, he lost his patience:

— And now, if you'll excuse me, I'm rather busy. I'll give you some money to catch the train to Rio, do you understand? Go back to my mother's house, and when you get there, you tell them: Arnaldo's house is not a refuge, have you got that? there is no room here. Just tell them what I said: Arnaldo's house is not a refuge.

Missy took the money and headed towards the door. As Arnaldo was about to sit down to eat, she reappeared:

— Thanks, may God bless you.

Back in the street, she began to think once more about Maria Rosa, Rafael and her husband. She did not feel the slightest nostalgia. But she remembered. She headed for the main road, walking further and further away from the station. She smiled, as if she were playing a trick on someone: instead of returning to Rio immediately, she would go for a little stroll. A man passed. Then something very curious and of no interest became clear: the men, when she was still a woman. She could not form a precise image of the men, but she could visualize herself with blouses in bright colours and long hair. The thirst came back, burning her throat. The sun was fierce and sparkled on every white pebble. The Petrópolis road is quite charming.

At a fountain made of lustrous black stone, set in the middle of the road, a black woman in her bare feet was filling a can with water.

Missy remained still, watching her. She saw the black woman join her hands in the form of a shell and drink.

When the road was deserted once more, Missy moved forward as if emerging from a hiding place, and stealthily approached the fountain. Threads of icy water trickled down the inside of her sleeves right up to her elbows, tiny drops of water gleamed, caught in her hair.

Her thirst sated, she continued to walk, terrified, wide-eyed, conscious of the violent gyrations the heavy water was making in her stomach, awakening tiny reflexes like flashing lights throughout her entire body.

The road climbed steeply. The road was much more charming than any road in Rio de Janeiro, and it climbed steeply. Missy sat down on a boulder beside a tree to admire the view. The sky was immense, and without a cloud. And there were lots of birds flying from the chasm towards the road. The road bleached by the sun stretched over a green chasm. Then, because she felt tired, the old woman rested her head against the tree-trunk and died.

The Solution

She was called Almira and she had grown much too fat. Alice was her best friend. At least that was what she anxiously told everyone, wishing to compensate with her own vehemence for the lack of affection she received from Alice.

Alice was pensive and smiled without listening to Almira, as she went on typing.

The more Alice's friendship waned, the more intense Almira's friendship became. Alice had an oval face with skin like velvet. Almira's nose was always shiny. Almira's face betrayed an eagerness which it had never occurred to her to conceal: the same eagerness she showed for food, her most direct contact with the world.

Why Alice tolerated Almira, no one could understand. They were both typists and workmates, but that did not explain anything. They took their coffee breaks together, but even that did not explain anything. They left the office together at the same time and waited for a bus in the same queue. Almira always dancing attendance upon Alice. The latter, aloof and dreamy, allowing herself to be adored. Alice was small and delicate. Almira had a very broad face, sallow and greasy: lipstick did not last long on her lips, for she was one of those girls who eat their lipstick unintentionally.

— I thoroughly enjoyed the programme sponsored by the Ministry of Education, Almira said, trying to ingratiate herself somehow. But Alice received everything as if it were her due, including the cultural programme sponsored by the Ministry of Education.

Only Almira's nature was delicate. With that huge body of hers, she was capable of losing a whole night's sleep because of some word that would have been best left unsaid. And a piece of chocolate could suddenly taste bitter in her mouth at the thought that she might have been unjust. She was never without a piece of chocolate in her handbag, always apprehensive that she might have given offence. It was not a question of goodness. Probably a case of weak nerves in a weak body.

On the morning of the day the incident occurred, Almira went rushing out to work, still chewing a piece of bread. When she arrived at the office, she looked at Alice's desk only to discover that she was not there. An hour later, Alice appeared, her eyes red from weeping. She refused to offer any explanations and made no reply to Almira's anxious questions. Almira almost wept into her typewriter.

At last it was time for lunch, and Almira pleaded with Alice to join her and offered to pay. It was precisely during this lunch that the incident occurred.

Almira continued to question Alice why she had arrived late for work and why her eyes were red. Broken-hearted, Alice could scarcely bring herself to speak. Almira ate avidly and went on insisting, her eyes filled with tears.

— You fat bitch! Alice turned on her, white with rage. Can't you leave me in peace?

Almira choked on her food, tried to speak and began stuttering. From Alice's soft lips had come words which refused to go down, just like the food which was stuck in the throat of Almira G. de Almeida.

— You're a bloody nuisance and always poking your nose into other people's affairs, Alice exploded once more. You want to know what happened, don't you?

Well, I'll tell you, Miss Nosey Parker. Zequinha has gone off to Porto Alegre and she isn't coming back! Are you satisfied, fatty?

In truth, Almira appeared to have grown even fatter during the last few minutes, with the food still stuck in her throat.

And then she suddenly came to life. With surprising agility for one so fat, she grabbed a fork and embedded it in Alice's neck. Everybody in the restaurant, as the newspapers subsequently reported, rose to their feet at the same time. But fat Almira, even after the assault, remained seated gazing at the floor, oblivious to the fact that Alice was losing blood.

Alice was rushed to hospital, from where she emerged with her neck all bandaged, her eyes still staring in horror. Almira was arrested on the spot.

Some people insinuated that there was something odd about their relationship. While others, friends of the family, related that Almira's grandmother, Dona Altamiranda, had been a very eccentric old woman. No one remembered that elephants, according to the experts on the subject, are extremely sensitive creatures, right down to their great feet.

Committed to prison, Almira proved to be docile and contented, a little melancholy perhaps, but truly contented. She was unfailingly kind to the other inmates. At last she had friends. She was put in charge of the laundry and got on extremely well with the prison warders, who from time to time would slip her a bar of chocolate. Just as if she were a circus elephant.

The Evolution of Myopia

She did not know if he was intelligent. To be or not to be intelligent depended upon the instability of the others. At times, the things he said suddenly provoked a satisfied and sly look in the adults. Satisfied, because they concealed the fact that they found him intelligent and did not pamper him: sly, because they gained more than he himself did from the things he said. And so when he was considered intelligent, he had at the same time the uneasy sensation of unconsciousness; something had escaped him. For at times, in trying to imitate himself, he said things that were certain to provoke anew the rapid movement on the chessboard, for this was the impression of automatic mechanism which he associated with the members of his family: the moment he said something intelligent, the adults would rapidly exchange glances, with a smile clearly suppressed on their lips, a smile barely indicated with their eyes, 'just as we should be smiling now were we not such good educators' — and, just as in a square-dance in some western film, everybody would somehow change their partner and place. In short, the members of the family understood each other; and they understood each other at his expense. Besides understanding each other at his expense, they misunderstood each other permanently, as if it were a new form of square-dancing: even when they misunderstood each other, he felt that they were obeying the rules of a game, as if they had agreed to misunderstand each other.

At times, then, he tried to reproduce those phrases which had succeeded in provoking movement on the chessboard. Not exactly to reproduce past successes, nor exactly to provoke the silent movement from his family. But to try to gain possession of the key to his 'intelligence'. His efforts, however, to establish laws and causes met with failure. Whenever he tried to repeat one of his successful phrases, it brought no reaction whatsoever from the others. His eyes blinking with curiosity, the first symptoms of myopia, he pondered why he had once succeeded in setting his family in motion, while failing the second time. Was his intelligence judged by the lack of discipline in others?

Much later, when he substituted the instability of others with his own, he entered into a state of conscious instability. Grown to manhood, he maintained this habit of suddenly blinking at his own thoughts, and twitching his nose at the same time, which caused his spectacles to slip sideways — expressing with this nervous tic an attempt to substitute the judgement of others with his own, in his efforts to probe his own bewilderment. But he was a child with a capacity for balancing forces: he had always been capable of maintaining bewilderment as bewilderment, without it becoming transformed into some other feeling.

That he was not in possession of his own key was something which he had got used to knowing, even as a child, when his eyes would blink and his nose twitch, causing his spectacles to slip sideways. That no one held the key was something which he had gradually perceived without any disillusionment, his tranquil myopia demanding lenses that were ever more powerful.

Strange though it might seem, it was precisely because of this state of permanent uncertainty and because of this premature acceptance that no one held the key — it was because of all this that he started growing normally, and living in a state of tranquil curiosity. Patient and curious. A trifle nervous, they said, referring to the tic which caused his spectacles to slip sideways. But 'nervous' was the name which the family gave to their own unstable judgement.

Other names which these inconstant adults conferred on him were 'well-behaved' and 'docile'. Thus giving a name not to what he was, but to the varying requirements of the moment.

Now and then, in the extraordinary calm of his spectacles, there occurred inside him something brilliant and almost spasmodic, akin to inspiration.

As, for example, when they told him that in a week's time he would spend the whole day at the home of a cousin. This married cousin was childless yet she adored children. 'The whole day' included lunch, tea and dinner, before returning home almost asleep. As for his cousin, his cousin meant a surfeit of love with the unexpected advantages and an incalculable eagerness — and all this would open the way for special requests to be heeded. At his cousin's house, everything that he was would have its value guaranteed for a whole day. There love, so much more likely to be constant if merely for a day, would provide an opportunity for unstable judgements: for one whole day he would be judged the same boy.

During the week that preceded 'the whole day' he began by trying to decide if he would behave naturally or otherwise with his cousin. He tried to decide if he should say something intelligent upon arrival — which would result in his being judged intelligent for the whole day. Or if he should do something upon arrival that she would judge 'well-behaved', which would mean that for the whole day he would be the well-behaved boy. To have the possibility of choosing what it should be and for the very first time, for one whole day, caused him to adjust his spectacles every other minute.

During the preceding week, the range of possibilities had gradually widened. And, with his capacity for tolerating confusion — he was precise and calm when confronted with confusion — he ended up by discovering that he could even capriciously decide to be a clown, for example, for a whole day. Or, if he so wished, he could spend that day being utterly miserable. What consoled him was to know that his cousin, with her love of children and, above all, with her lack of experience in dealing with children, would accept the way in which he decided he wanted to be judged. It also reassured him to know that nothing he might be during that day would really change him. For prematurely — being a precocious child — he was superior to the instability of others and to his own instability. He somehow hovered over his own myopia and that of others. And this gave him considerable freedom. At times, it was simply the freedom of tranquil scepticism. Even when he grew up, and used the thickest of lenses, he never became conscious of this kind of superiority that he had over himself.

The week preceding the visit to his cousin was one of continuous anticipation. At times his stomach became cramped with anxiety: for in that house without children he would be totally at the mercy of the undiscriminating love of a woman. 'Undiscriminating love' represented a threatening stability: it would be permanent, and would almost certainly result in a unique way of judging, and that was stability. For him, stability now meant danger: if the others should err in the first stages of stability, the error would become permanent, without the advantage of instability, which is a possible means of correction.

Another thing which worried him beforehand, was what he would do for a whole day in his cousin's house apart from eating and being loved. Well, there was always the solution of being able to go to the bathroom from time to time, and that would make the time pass more quickly. But, with the experience of being loved, he was already feeling apprehensive that his cousin, who was a stranger to him, would regard his trips to the bathroom with infinite affection. Generally speaking, the mechanism of his life had become a motive for tenderness. Well, it was also true that, as for going to the bathroom, the solution might be not to go to the bathroom even once. But not only would that be impossible to achieve for a whole day, but — but he did not wish to be judged as 'a boy who does not go to the bathroom' — this, too, did not offer any advantage. His cousin, stabilized by her permanent desire to have children, would find herself, were he to go to the bathroom, with a false trail of immense love.

During the week that preceded 'the whole day', he did not suffer on account of these evasions. For he had already taken the step that so many never get round to taking: he had accepted uncertainty, and was struggling with its components as intently as someone peering through the lens of a microscope.

During that week, as ideas came to him somewhat spasmodically, they gradually changed in substance. He abandoned the problem of deciding what elements he would give to his cousin so that she in turn might give him temporarily some certainty of 'who he was'. He abandoned these meditations and tried to establish beforehand the smell of his cousin's house, the size of the small backyard where he would play, the cupboards he would open when she was not looking. And finally, he came to the question of his cousin herself. In what way should he confront his cousin's love?

Meantime, he had overlooked one detail: his cousin had a gold tooth on the left side. And it was this detail — upon finally entering his cousin's house — it was this detail which upset in a flash the entire scene he had anticipated.

The rest of the day could be described as horrible, were the boy inclined to see things in terms of being horrible or not horrible. Or it could be described as wonderful, were he one of those people who hope that things either are or are not.

There was the gold tooth, with which he had not reckoned. But, with the reassurance that he derived from the idea of a permanent unpredictability, so much so that he wore spectacles, he did not become insecure upon encountering at the outset something with which he had not reckoned.

Afterwards, the surprise of his cousin's love. His cousin's love was not obvious at once, contrary to what he had imagined. She received him in a natural manner, which he found offensive to begin with, but soon afterwards it offended him no longer. She explained at once that she must tidy up the house and that he could play in the meantime. This gave the boy, quite unexpectedly, a whole sunny day to himself.

Some hours later, wiping his spectacles, he tried, with an air of indifference, to impress her with his intelligence and made an observation about the plants in the yard. For when he made an observation aloud, he was always thought to be very observant. But his cold observation about the plants received in reply a simple 'of course', amidst rapid strokes with a broom. So he went to the bathroom, where he decided that, since everything had failed miserably, he would play at 'not being judged': for a whole day he would be nothing, he simply would not exist. And he yanked the door open in a gesture of freedom.

As the sun rose higher, the gentle pressure of his cousin's love started making itself felt. And when he became aware of it, he was someone who was loved. At lunch, the food became pure love, errant and stable: beneath his cousin's tender gaze, he adapted himself with curiosity to the strange taste of that food, perhaps due to the type of oil, he adapted himself to a woman's love, a new love which was quite unlike the love of other adults: it was a love seeking fulfilment, for his cousin was not pregnant, which is already in itself a maternal love fulfilled. But it was a love without any pregnancy beforehand. It was a love seeking conception *a posteriori*. In short, impossible love.

The whole day long, love demanded a past that might redeem the present and the future. The whole day long, without saying a word, his cousin demanded from him that he might have been born from her womb. His cousin wanted nothing from him other than that. She demanded from the boy with spectacles that she should not be a woman without children. On that day, therefore, he knew one of the rare forms of stability: the stability of an impossible desire. The stability of an unattainable desire. For the first time, he, who was a creature given to moderation, for the first time, he felt himself attracted to the immoderate: an attraction for the impossible extreme. In a word, for the impossible. And for the first time he experienced passion.

And it was as if his myopia had vanished and he could see the world clearly. The deepest and most simple glimpse he had ever had of the kind of universe in which he lived and where he would continue to live. Not a mental glimpse. It was as if he had removed his spectacles, and myopia itself was helping him to see. Perhaps it was from that moment that he formed the habit which he would have for the rest of his life: whenever he was overcome by confusion and he could barely see anything, he would remove his spectacles on the pretext of cleaning them, and, without spectacles, he would stare at the person who was addressing him with the reverberating intensity of a blind man.

The Fifth Story

This story could be called 'The Statues'. Another possible title would be 'The Killing'. Or even 'How To Kill Cockroaches'. So I shall tell at least three stories, all of them true, because none of the three will contradict the others. Although they constitute one story, they could become a thousand and one, were I to be granted a thousand and one nights.

The first story, 'How To Kill Cockroaches', begins like this: I was complaining about the cockroaches. A woman heard me complain. She gave me a recipe for killing them. I was to mix together equal quantities of sugar, flour and gypsum. The flour and sugar would attract the cockroaches, the gypsum would dry up their insides. I followed her advice. The cockroaches died.

The next story is really the first, and it is called 'The Killing'. It begins like this: I was complaining about the cockroaches. A woman heard me complain. The recipe follows. And then the killing takes place. The truth is that I had only complained in abstract terms about the cockroaches, for they were not even mine: they belonged to the ground floor and climbed up the pipes in the building into our apartment. It was only when I prepared the mixture that they also became mine. On our behalf, therefore, I began to measure and weigh ingredients with greater concentration. A vague loathing had taken possession of me, a sense of outrage. By day, the cockroaches were invisible and no one would believe in the evil secret which eroded such a tranquil household. But if the cockroaches, like evil secrets, slept by day, there I was preparing their nightly poison. Meticulous, eager, I prepared the elixir of prolonged death. An angry fear and my own evil secret guided me. Now I coldly wanted one thing only: to kill every cockroach in existence. Cockroaches climb up the pipes while weary people sleep. And now the recipe was ready, looking so white. As if I were dealing with cockroaches as cunning as myself, I carefully spread the powder until it looked like part

of the surface dust. From my bed, in the silence of the apartment, I imagined them climbing up one by one into
the kitchen where darkness slept, a solitary towel alert on the
clothes-line. I awoke hours later, startled at having overslept.
It was beginning to grow light. I walked across the kitchen.
There they lay on the floor of the scullery, huge and brittle.
During the night I had killed them. On our behalf, it was
beginning to grow light. On a nearby hill, a cockerel crowed.

The third story which now begins is called 'The Statues'. It
begins by saying that I had been complaining about the cockroaches. Then the same woman appears on the scene. And so it
goes on to the point where I awake as it is beginning to grow
light, and I awake still feeling sleepy and I walk across the
kitchen. Even more sleepy is the scullery floor with its tiled
perspective. And in the shadows of dawn, there is a purplish
hue which distances everything; at my feet, I perceive patches
of light and shade, scores of rigid statues scattered everywhere. The cockroaches that have hardened from core to shell.
Some are lying upside down. Others arrested in the midst of
some movement that will never be completed. In the mouths
of some of the cockroaches, there are traces of white powder. I
am the first to observe the dawn breaking over Pompei. I
know what this night has been, I know about the orgy in the
dark. In some, the gypsum has hardened as slowly as in some
organic process, and the cockroaches, with ever more tortuous movements, have greedily intensified the night's
pleasures, trying to escape from their insides. Until they turn
to stone, in innocent terror and with such, but such an expression of pained reproach. Others — suddenly assailed by
their own core, without even having perceived that their inner
form was turning to stone! — these are suddenly crystallized,
just like a word arrested on someone's lips: I love . . . The
cockroaches, invoking the name of love in vain, sang on a
summer's night. While the cockroach over there, the one with
the brown antennae smeared with white, must have realized
too late that it had become mummified precisely because it did
not know how to use things with the gratuitous grace of the *in
vain*: 'It is just that I looked too closely inside myself! it is just
that I looked too closely inside . . .' — from my frigid height
as a human being, I watch the destruction of a world. Dawn

breaks. Here and there, the parched antennae of dead cockroaches quiver in the breeze. The cockerel from the previous
story crows.

The fourth story opens a new era in the household. The
story begins as usual: I was complaining about the cockroaches. It goes on up to the point when I see the statues in
plaster of Paris. Inevitably dead. I look towards the pipes
where this same night an infestation will reappear, swarming
slowly upwards in Indian file. Should I renew the lethal sugar
every night? like someone who no longer sleeps without the
avidity of some rite. And should I take myself somnambulant
out to the terrace early each morning? in my craving to encounter the statues which my perspiring night has erected. I
trembled with depraved pleasure at the vision of my double
existence as a witch. I also trembled at the sight of that
hardening gypsum, the depravity of existence which would
shatter my internal form.

The grim moment of choosing between two paths, which I
thought would separate, convinced that any choice would
mean sacrificing either myself or my soul. I chose. And today I
secretly carry a plaque of virtue in my heart: 'This house has
been disinfected'.

The fifth story is called 'Leibnitz and The Transcendence of
Love in Polynesia' . . . It begins like this: I was complaining
about the cockroaches.

A Sincere Friendship

We had not been friends for very long. We had only started to know each other well during our last year at school. From that moment onwards we were never apart. For a long time, we had both needed a friend in whom we could confide. Our friendship reached the point where we could not keep a thought to ourselves: the one would telephone the other immediately, arranging to meet without a moment's delay. After talking to each other, we felt as pleased as if we just had introduced ourselves. This continuous communication reached such a pitch of exaltation that on those days when we had nothing to confide, we anxiously searched for some topic of conversation. But the topic had to be serious, because any old topic could never accommodate the vehemence of this sincerity we were experiencing for the first time.

Already at this stage, the first signs of tension between us began to appear. Sometimes one of us would telephone the other, we would meet, and then have nothing to say to each other. We were very young and we did not know how to remain silent. From the outset, when we could find no topic of conversation, we tried to discuss other people. But we were both well aware that we were debasing the nucleus of our friendship. To attempt to discuss our mutual girlfriends was also out of the question, for a fellow did not talk about his love affairs. We tried to remain silent — but became uneasy the moment we separated.

Upon returning from similar encounters, my solitude was immense and arid. I started to read books just to be able to discuss them. But a sincere friendship demanded the most pure sincerity. In my search for such sincerity, I felt nothing but emptiness. Our encounters became ever more unsatisfactory. My sincere poverty gradually became manifest. I knew that my friend had also reach an impasse.

About this time, my family moved to São Paulo. My friend was living alone for his family had settled in Piauí. So I invited him to move into our apartment, where I had been left in charge. We felt so excited! We eagerly arranged our books and records, and planned the ideal setting for friendship. When everything was ready — here we were in our home, somehow at a loss, silent, full only of friendship.

We were so anxious to save each other. Friendship is a question of salvation.

But all the problems had already been touched on, all the possibilities examined. All we possessed was this thing which we had eagerly sought from the beginning and found at last: sincere friendship. The only way we knew, and how bitterly we knew, to escape the solitude every spirit carries in its body.

But how artificial we discovered friendship to be. As if we were trying to expand a truism into a lengthy discourse which could be exhausted with one word. Our friendship was as inextricable as the sum of two numbers: it was useless to attempt to elaborate for more than a second on the fact that two and three make five.

We tried to organize some wild parties in the apartment, but it was not only the neighbours who protested, so that was no use.

If only we could at least do each other favours. But there was never the opportunity, nor did we believe in giving proof of a friendship that needed no proof. The most we could hope to do was what we were already doing: simply to know that we were friends. Yet this was not enough to fill our days, especially the long summer holidays.

The start of our real troubles dates from those long summer holidays.

The friend to whom I could offer nothing except my sincerity, turned out to be an accusation of my poverty. Moreover, our solitude at each other's side while listening to music or reading was much greater than when we found ourselves alone. Not only much greater, but also disturbing. There was no longer any peace. When we finally retired to our respective rooms, we felt so relieved that we could not bring ourselves to look at each other.

It is true that there was a pause in the course of these developments, a truce which gave us more hope than the reality of our situation justified. This occurred when my friend ran into some trouble with the Authorities. It was nothing serious, but we treated it as such in order to exploit the situation. For by that time we were already showing our readiness to do each other favours. I went eagerly from the office of one family friend to another, mustering support for my friend. And when the time came to start rubber-stamping the documents, I went all over the city — I can say in all conscience that there was not a single authorized signature which I had not been instrumental in securing.

During this crisis, we spent our evenings at home, worn out and animated: we related the day's achievements and planned our next move. We did not probe very deeply into what was happening, it was sufficient that all this activity should have the seal of friendship. I thought I could now understand why bride and groom pledge themselves to each other; why the husband insists upon providing for his bride, while she solici-tously prepares his meals, and why a mother fusses over her children. It was, moreover, during this crisis, that at some cost I gave a small gold brooch to the woman who was to become my wife. It was only much later that I came to realize that just to be there is also a form of giving.

Having settled the problem with the Authorities — let it be said in passing, with a successful outcome for us — we re-mained close friends, without finding that word which would surrender our soul. Surrender our soul? but after all, who wanted to surrender their soul? Whatever next?

But what did we want after all? Nothing. We were worn out and disillusioned.

On the pretext of spending a holiday with my family, we separated. Besides, my friend was off to Piauí. With an emotional handshake we said goodbye at the airport. We knew that we would never see each other again, unless by accident. More than this: that we did not wish to see each other again. And we also knew that we were friends. Sincere friends.

The Obedient

What follows is an ordinary situation, an episode to be related and forgotten.

But if anyone is imprudent enough to pause for a moment longer than he should, he will founder and be compromised. From the moment that we, too, put ourselves at risk, it is no longer an episode to be related, the words are suddenly missing which would not betray it. At this point, because we have foundered so badly, the episode ceases to be an episode and becomes only its widening repercussions. Which, were it to be delayed unduly, would eventually explode as on this Sunday afternoon, when there has not been rain for weeks, and when, like today, a dessicated beauty persists, although still beautiful. In the presence of which I become solemn as if standing before a tomb. At this point, where is the initial episode going? It has become transformed into this afternoon. Not knowing how to fight it, I hesitate before becoming aggressive or retreating battle-scarred. The initial episode is suspended in the sun-drenched dust of this Sunday afternoon — until I am summoned to the telephone and go leaping off to express my gratitude by licking the hand of the person who loves and frees me.

Chronologically, the episode occurred as follows: a man and a woman got married.

Simply to discover this fact caused me to founder.

I was obliged to think of something. Even were I to say nothing more and finish the story with this discovery, I should have already compromised myself with my most impenetrable thought. It would be as if I had seen a black stroke over a white background, a man and a woman. And my eyes would be fixed on this white background and find enough to observe there, for every word has its own shadow.

This man and this woman began — without any intention of going too far, and perhaps drawn by one of those urges which people have — began trying to live with greater intensity. In search of that destiny which precedes us? and to which our instinct seeks to draw us? instinct?

This attempt to live with greater intensity led them, in turn, to a constant verification, as it were, of income and expenditure, to an assessment of what was and what was not important. They did these things in their own way: with a lack of skill and experience, with modesty. They fumbled. With an addiction they were both to discover much too late in life, they each persisted in trying to distinguish between the essential and the non-essential, not that they would ever have used the word *essential*, for it had no meaning in their milieu.

But nothing came of the vague, almost self-conscious effort they were making: the plot escaped them daily. Only when they reviewed each day gone by did they get the impression of having — somehow and without any awareness or merit on their part — the impression of having lived. But by then it was already night, they were putting on their slippers and it was night.

None of this really constituted a situation for the couple. That is to say, something that each of them might recount even to themselves as they turned and tossed in bed, their eyes momentarily open before they finally fell asleep. People so badly need to be able to tell their own story. They had no story to tell. With a sigh of comfort, they closed their eyes and fell into a troubled sleep. And when they weighed up their lives, they could not even include this attempt to live with greater intensity, or deduct it, as with income tax. A weighing-up which they gradually started to engage in more frequently, even without the technical equipment or a terminology attuned to their thoughts. If this represented a situation, it was not a situation with which one could ostensibly live.

But it did not happen just like this. In truth, they were even serene because 'not to lead', 'not to invent', 'not to err', was for them much more than a habit, it was a point of honour, tacitly assumed. They would never remember to disobey.

From this noble self-awareness came the bold conviction that they were two individual human beings among thousands like them. 'To be an equal' was the role they were given to fulfil, the task with which they were entrusted. The two of them, honoured and serious, corresponded with gratitude and civility to the confidence that their equals had placed in them. They belonged to a caste. The role they fulfilled with a certain emotion and decorum was that of anonymous persons, of children of God, of members of some club.

Yet, perhaps due to the insistent passage of time, all this had started to become daily, daily, daily. Sometimes breathless. (The man as well as the woman had already reached the critical age.) They would open the windows and comment that it was extremely hot. Without exactly living a life of boredom, it was as if no one ever sent them any news. Besides, boredom formed part of a life of honest sentiments.

But since all of this was beyond their understanding, and they found so many points above their heads which, even if expressed in words, they would fail to recognize — all these factors taken together and dismissed as being over and done with, resembled irremediable life. To which they submitted with total silence and that somewhat wounded expression which is common among men of good will. It resembled that irremediable life for which God has destined us.

Life irremediable, but not concrete. In truth, it was a life of dreams. Sometimes, when they spoke of someone eccentric, they would say, with the benevolence that one class shows towards another: 'Ah, that one leads the life of a poet.' You could perhaps say, using the few words known to have been spoken by the couple, that they both led, except for its extravagance, the life of a bad poet: a life of dreams.

No, no, that is not true. It was not a life of dreams, for that would never have given them any guidance. But one of unreality. Although there were moments when suddenly, for one reason or another, they would plunge into reality. And then they had the impression of having touched depths, which no one could hope to transcend.

As, for example, when the husband came home earlier than usual to find his wife still had not returned from some shopping expedition or a visit to friends. The husband felt as if a chain had been interrupted. He sat down diligently to read the newspaper in a silence so hushed that even a corpse at his side would have broken the spell. There he sat, pretending with grave honesty to be wholly engrossed in his newspaper, but listening attentively. It was then that the husband would touch rock-bottom with startled feet. He could not remain for long like this, without the risk of drowning, for to touch rock-bottom was the same as having water above one's head. Thus were his concrete moments. Which caused him, level-headed and sensible as he was, to extricate himself at once. He extricated himself at once, although strangely with some reluctance, for his wife's absence was such a promise of dangerous pleasure that he experienced what might be termed disobedience. He extricated himself reluctantly but without any argument, responding to what they expected of him. He was not a deserter who might betray the trust of others. Moreover, if this was reality, there was no way of living in it or by it.

As for his wife, she touched on reality rather more frequently, for she had more freedom and fewer facts to contend with, such as colleagues at work, overcrowded buses, and administrative jargon. She would sit down to do some mending, and little by little she was confronted by reality. The sensation of sitting down to do some mending was intolerable while it lasted. The sudden way the dot would fall on the i, that manner of adapting completely to what existed, and everything retaining its identity so clearly — was unbearable. But when it passed, it was as if the wife had drunk from some possible future. Little by little, that woman's future became something which she carried into the present, something contemplative and secret.

It was surprising how the two were not touched, for example, by politics, by the change of government, by developments in general, although, like everyone else, they also discussed these things from time to time.

Truly, they were so reserved these two that, were anyone to suggest that they were reserved, they would have been surprised and flattered. It would never have occurred to them to think of themselves as being reserved. Perhaps they would have seen the point if someone were to say to them: 'You are the very symbol of soldierly reserve'. Some acquaintances said of them after all this took place: they were decent people. And there was nothing more to be said, for they were decent people.

There was nothing more to be said. They lacked the weight

of a serious error, which very often is what is needed casually to open a door. Sometimes they took something quite seriously. They were obedient.

Not simply out of submissiveness: as in a sonnet, it was obedience because of their love for symmetry. For them, symmetry was the feasible art.

How was it that each of them reached the conclusion that, alone, the one without the other, they would live longer? — it would be a long road of rehabilitation and of useless effort, because from several different angles they had already arrived at the same point.

The wife, under the continuous spell of fantasy, not only arrived rashly at this conclusion, but found her life transformed into something broader and more disturbing, into something richer and more superstitious. Each thing appeared to be the sign of something else, everything was symbolic, and even vaguely spiritualistic within the limits perceived by catholicism. Not only did she rashly come to this conclusion but — provoked solely by the fact that she was a woman — she came to believe that some other man would save her. Which was not altogether absurd. She knew that it was not. To be half right confused her and plunged her into meditation.

The husband, affected by the atmosphere of anguished masculinity in which he lived, and by his own masculinity, which was diffident but real, started to believe that numerous love affairs would represent life.

Dreamers, they began to tolerate dreamers; it was heroic to be tolerant. Silent about what each of them could foresee, disagreeing about the most convenient hour to dine, the one serving as a sacrifice for the other, because love is a sacrifice.

And so there came the day when the woman was finally roused from her dream: she bit into an apple and felt one of her front teeth breaking. With the apple still in her hand, she examined herself closely in the bathroom mirror — and thus losing all perspective — she saw the pale face of a middle-aged woman, a broken tooth and her own eyes . . . Touching rock-bottom, and the water already up to her throat, fifty-one years of age and without a ticket. Instead of going to the dentist, she threw herself out of the apartment window, a person for whom one could feel so grateful, a figure of soldierly reserve and the pillar of our disobedience.

As for her husband, once the river-bed was dry and without any water in which he might drown, he walked over the bottom without looking at the ground, as nimble as if he were using a cane. The river-bed was unexpectedly dry. Puzzled and without danger, he walked over the bottom with the swiftness of someone who is about to fall flat on his face at any minute.

The Foreign Legion

If I were to be asked about Ofélia and her parents, I would reply with decorous honesty: I scarcely know them. Before the same jury I should testify: I scarcely know myself — and to each member of the jury I should say with the same innocent look of someone who has hypnotised herself into obedience: I scarcely know you. But sometimes I wake from a long sleep and turn submissively towards the delicate abyss of disorder.

I am trying to speak about that family which disappeared years ago without leaving any traces in me, and of which there remains only a faded and distant image. My sudden acquiescence in knowing was provoked today when a little chick appeared in the house. It was brought by a hand which wanted to experience the pleasure of giving me some living thing. Upon releasing the chick from its box, its charm overwhelmed us. Christmas Day is tomorrow, but the moment of silence I await the whole year has come on the eve of Christ's birth. Something chirping by itself arouses the most gentle curiosity, which beside a manger is adoration. Well, whatever next, said my husband. He felt much too big and clumsy. Scruffy and with gaping mouths, the children approached. I, a little presumptuously, felt happy. As for the chick, it went on chirping. But tomorrow is Christmas, the older boy said self-consciously. We smiled, defenceless and curious.

But sentiments are like sudden water. Presently — just as the same water changes when the sun makes it extremely soft, and changes again when it becomes enervated trying to devour a stone, and changes yet again when it engulfs someone's immersed foot — presently we no longer had on our faces simply an aura and illumination. Kind and solicitous, we gathered round the chick. Kindness leaves my husband gruff and morose, something to which we have become accustomed; to some extent he crucifies himself. With the children, who are more serious, kindness is a passion. As for me, kindness frightens me. Very soon, the same water had changed, and we watched, feeling uneasy, caught up in our clumsiness at being kind. And once the water had changed, we gradually betrayed on our faces the burden of an aspiration, our heart weighed down by a love which was no longer free. The chick's fear of us also made us feel uncomfortable; there we were, and no one was worthy of appearing before a chick; with every chirp it drove us away. With each chirp, it reduced us to helplessness. The constancy of its terror accused us of a thoughtless merriment which by now was no longer merriment, but annoyance. The chick's moment had passed, and with ever greater urgency it banished us while keeping us imprisoned. We adults would already have suppressed any feeling. But in the children there was a silent indignation. They accused us of doing nothing either for the chick or for humanity. The persistent chirping had already brought us, the parents, to an uneasy resignation: things are just like this. Only we had never said so to the children, for we were ashamed; and we postponed indefinitely the moment when we should summon them in order to tell them openly that this is the way things are. Each time it became more difficult, the silence increased, and they resisted, to some extent, the eagerness with which we tried to give them love in return. If we had never discussed things, all the more reason why we should hide from them now the smile that came to our faces as we listened to the desperate squawks coming from that beak; a smile as if it was up to us to bless the fact that this is the way things are, and we had just complied by giving our blessing.

As for the chick, it was chirping. Standing on the polished table, it dared not make a move as it chirped from within. I never knew that so much terror could exist inside a creature that was made only of feathers. Feathers covering what? half a dozen fragile little bones which had been loosely put together for what reason? to chirp terror. In silence, out of respect for our inability to understand each other, out of respect for the children's revolt against us, in silence, we watched impatiently. It was impossible to give the chick those words of reassurance which would allay its fears and bring consolation to that creature which was terrified just to have been born. How could one promise it protection? A father and a mother, we knew just how brief the chick's life would be. The chick also

knew, in the way that living creatures know; through profound fear.

Meanwhile, there was the chick full of charm, an ephemeral
and yellow creature. I wanted the chick to feel the grace of life,
just as we had been expected to feel it; the chick which was the
happiness of others, and not its own. That the chick should feel
that it was gratuitous, even superfluous — one of the chicks
has to be useless — to have been born simply for the greater
glory of God made it the happiness of mankind. But was to
love our dear little chick, to wish that it should be happy
simply because we loved it? I also knew that only a mother
determines birth, and ours was the love of those who take
pleasure in loving; I rejoiced in the grace of having devoted
myself to loving; bells, bells were pealing because I know how
to adore. But the chick was trembling, a thing of terror, not of
beauty.

The younger boy could stand it no longer:

— Do you want to be its mummy?

Startled, I answered yes. I was the messenger assigned to
that creature which did not understand the only language I
knew: I was loving without being loved. My mission was
precarious and the eyes of four children waited with the in-
transigence of hope for my first gesture of effective love. I
recoiled a little, smiling and solitary; I looked at my family and
wanted them to smile. A man and four little boys stared at me,
incredulous and trusting. I was the mistress of that household,
the provider. I could not understand the impassiveness of these
five males. How many times would I fail, so that, in my hour
of fear, they might look at me. I tried to isolate myself from the
challenge of those five males, so that I, too, might expect love
from myself and remember what love is like. I opened my
mouth, I was about to tell them the truth: exactly how, I
cannot say.

But if a woman were to appear to me in the night holding a
child in her lap. And if she were to say: Take care of my child. I
would reply: How can I? She would repeat: Take care of my
child. I would reply: I cannot. She would insist: Take care of
my child. Then — then, because I do not know how to do
anything and because I cannot remember anything and
because it is night — then I would stretch out my hand and

save a child. Because it is night, because I am alone in another person's night, because this silence is much too great for me, for I have two hands in order to sacrifice the better of the two, and because I have no choice.

So I stretched out my hand and held the chick.

It was at that moment that I saw Ofélia again. And at that same moment I remembered that I had been the witness of a little girl.

Later, I remembered how my neighbour, Ofélia's mother, was as dark-skinned as an Indian. She had dark shadows round her eyes which made them very beautiful and gave her a languid appearance which caused men to take a second look. One day, when we were seated on a bench in the square, while the children were playing, she told me with that stern expression of someone scanning the desert: 'I have always wanted to take a course in confectionery.' I remembered that her husband — who was also dark-skinned, as if they had chosen each other for their colouring — wanted to prosper in life through his particular line of business: the manager or perhaps even the owner of a hotel, I was never quite sure. This made him courteous but haughty. When we were forced into more prolonged contact in the lift, he accepted an exchange of words with that arrogant tone which he had acquired in greater battles. By the time we reached the tenth floor, the humility which his cold manner forced from me had already placated him a little: perhaps he might even arrive home rather more chastened. As for Ofélia's mother, because we lived on the same floor, she feared we might become too intimate, and started avoiding me, oblivious to the fact that I was also on my guard. The only intimacy between us had been that day on the bench in the square, where, with those dark shadows round her eyes and those thin lips, she had talked about decorating cakes. I did not know what to say and I ended up by agreeing, so that she might know that I liked her, that I, too, would find a course in confectionery most interesting. That one moment of mutual intimacy divided us even more, out of fear that any mutual understanding might be taken for granted. Ofélia's mother was even rude to me in the lift: the next day I was holding one of my children by the hand, the lift was going down slowly, and feeling oppressed by the silence which gave the other woman strength — I said in an affable tone, which I, too, found repugnant as I spoke:

— We are going to visit his grandmother.

And she, to my horror, snapped in reply:

— No one asked you where you are going. I never poke my nose into my neighbours' affairs.

— Well I never, I mumbled in a low voice.

This made me think there and then, that I was being made to pay for that moment of intimacy on the bench in the square. This in turn made me think that she was afraid of having confided more than she actually had confided that day. And this in turn made me wonder if she had not told me more, in fact, than either of us had perceived. By the time the lift finally reached the ground floor, I had reconstituted that obstinate, languid air of hers on the bench in the square — and I gazed with new eyes at the proud beauty of Ofélia's mother. 'I won't tell a soul that you enjoy decorating cakes', I thought, giving her a furtive glance.

The father aggressive, the mother remaining aloof. A proud family. They treated me as if I were already living in their future hotel and as if I had offended them by not paying my bill. Above all, they treated me as if I did not believe, nor could they prove, who they were. And who were they? I sometimes asked myself that question. Why was that slap imprinted on their faces, why that exiled dynasty? Nor could they forgive that I should carry on without having been forgiven: if I met them on the street, outside the zone to which I had been confined, it terrified me to be caught out of bounds: I would draw back to let them pass, I gave them precedence — my three dark-skinned and well-dressed neighbours passed as if they were on their way to Holy Mass, a family that lived under the sign of some proud destiny or hidden martyrdom — purple as the flowers of the Passion. Theirs was an ancient family.

But contact was made through the daughter. She was a most beautiful child with her long hair in plaits, Ofélia, with the same dark shadows round her eyes as her mother, the same gums looking a little red, the same thin lips as if someone had inflicted a gash. But those lips talked. She started coming to visit me. The door-bell would ring, I would open the spy-hole

without seeing anyone, and then I would hear a resolute voice:
— It's me, Ofélia Maria dos Santos Aguiar.

Disheartened, I would open the door. Ofélia would enter. She came to visit me, for my two little boys were far too small then to be treated to her phlegmatic wisdom. I was a grown-up and busy, but she came to visit me: she arrived all intent, as if there was a time and place for everything, she would carefully lift her flounced skirt, sit down, and arrange the flowers — and only then would she look at me. In the midst of duplicating the office files, I worked and listened. Ofélia would then proceed to give me advice. She had firm opinions about everything. Everything I did was not quite right in her opinion. She would say 'in my opinion' in a resentful tone, as if I should have asked her advice, and since I had not asked for it, she was giving it. With her eight proud and well-lived years, she told me that in her opinion, I did not rear my children properly: for when you give children an inch, they take a mile. Bananas should not be mixed with milk. It can kill you. But obviously, you must do what you think is best: everyone knows their own mind. It was rather late for me to be wearing a dressing-gown: her mother dressed as soon as she got up, but everyone must live as they see fit. If I tried to explain that I still had to take my bath, Ofélia would remain silent and watch me closely. With a hint of tenderness and then patience, she added that it was rather late to be taking a bath. I was never allowed the last word. What last word could I possibly offer when she informed me: vegetable patties should not be covered. One afternoon in the baker's shop, I found myself unexpectedly confronting the useless truth: there stood a whole row of uncovered vegetable patties. 'But I told you so,' I could hear her say, as if she were there beside me. With her plaits and flounces, with her unyielding delicacy. She would descend like a visitation into my sitting-room, which was still waiting to be tidied up. Fortunately she also talked a lot of nonsense, which made me smile, however low I felt.

The worst part of this visitation was the silence. I would raise my eyes from the typewriter and wonder how long Ofélia had been watching me in silence. What could possibly attract this child to me? I even irritated myself. On one occasion, after one of her lengthy silences, she calmly said to me: you are a strange woman. And as if I had been struck on the face without any form of protection — right on the face which is the reverse of ourselves and therefore very sensitive — struck full on the face, I thought to myself in a rage: you are about to see just how strange I can be. She who was so well protected, whose mother was protected, whose father was protected.

However, I still preferred her advice and criticism. Much less tolerable was her habit of using the word *therefore*, as a way of linking sentences into a concatenation which never failed. She told me that I bought far too many vegetables at the market — therefore — they would not fit into my small fridge and — therefore — they would go bad before the next market day. A few days later I looked at the vegetables, and they had gone bad. Therefore — she was right. On another occasion, she saw fewer vegetables lying on the kitchen table, as I had secretly taken her advice. Ofélia looked and looked. She seemed prepared to say nothing. I waited, standing there aggressive and silent. Ofélia said phlegmatically:

— It won't be long before there is another market day.

The vegetables had run out towards the middle of the week. How did she know? I asked myself bewildered. Probably she would reply with 'therefore'. Why did I never, never know? Why did she know everything, why was the earth so familiar to her, and I without protection? Therefore? Therefore.

On one occasion, Ofélia actually made a mistake. Geography — she said, sitting before me with her hands clasped on her lap — is a way of studying. It was not exactly a mistake, it was a slight miscalculation — but for me it had the grace of defeat, and before the moment could pass, I said to her mentally: that's exactly how to do it! just go on like that, and one day it will be easier or more difficult for you, but that's the way, just go on making mistakes, ever so slowly.

One morning, in the midst of her conversation, she announced peremptorily: 'I'm going home to get something but I'll be right back.' I dared to suggest: 'If you've got something to do, there's no need to hurry back.' Ofélia looked at me, silent and questioning. 'There exists a very nasty little girl,' I thought very clearly so that she might see the entire sentence written on my face. She kept on looking at me. A look wherein — with surprise and sadness — I saw loyalty, patient confidence in me, and the silence of someone who never spoke. When had I thrown her a bone — that she should follow me in silence for the rest of my life? I averted my gaze. She sighed tranquilly. And said with even more decisiveness: 'I'll be right back.' What does she want? — I became nervous — why do I attract people who do not even like me?

Once when Ofélia was sitting there, the door-bell rang. I opened the door and came face to face with Ofélia's mother. She came in all solicitous and flustered:

— Is Ofélia Maria here by any chance?

— Yes, she is, I said, excusing myself as if I had abducted her.

— Don't do that again — she said to Ofélia with a tone of voice that was directed at me: then she turned to me and suddenly sounded peevish: I'm sorry if you've been troubled.

— Not at all, your little girl is so clever.

The mother looked at me in mild surprise — but suspicion flickered across her eyes. And in her expression I could read: what do you want from her?

— I have already forbidden Ofélia to come bothering you, she now said with open distrust. And firmly grabbing the little girl by the hand to lead her away, she appeared to be defending her from me. Feeling degenerate, I watched them through the half-opened spy-hole without making a sound: the two of them walked down the corridor leading to their apartment, the mother sheltering her child with murmured words of loving reproach, the daughter impassive with her trembling plaits and flounces. Upon closing the spy-hole, I noticed that I was still in my dressing-gown and that I had been seen like this by the mother who dressed the moment she got up. I thought somewhat impudently: Well, now that her mother despises me, at least there will be no more visits from the daughter.

But naturally, she came back. I was much too attractive for that child. I had enough defects to warrant her advice, I was apt terrain for the development of her severity, I had already become the domain of that slave of mine: of course, she came back, she lifted her flounces and sat down.

On this occasion, since Easter was drawing near, the market was full of chicks and I had brought one home for the children.

We played, then the chick was put in the kitchen while the children went out to play. Afterwards, Ofélia appeared for her daily visit. I was typing and from time to time I assented, my thoughts elsewhere. The girl's monotonous voice, the voice of someone reciting from memory, made me feel quite dizzy, her voice filtered between the words typed on the paper, and she talked and talked.

At that point, the impression that everything had come to a sudden standstill. The torture suspended, I looked at her hazily. Ofélia Maria's head was erect, her plaits transfixed.

— What's that? she asked.

— What's what?

— That! she said unbending.

— What?

We might have remained there forever in a vicious circle of 'that?' and 'what!', were it not for the extraordinary resolve of that child, who, without saying a word, but with an expression of intransigent authority, forced me to hear what she herself was hearing. Forced into attentive silence, I finally heard the faint chirping of the chick in the kitchen.

— It's the chick.

— The chick? she said, most suspiciously.

— I bought a chick, I replied submissively.

— A chick! she repeated, as if I had insulted her.

— A chick.

And there the matter would have rested had I not seen something which I had never noticed before.

What was it? Whatever it was, it was no longer there. A chick had flickered momentarily in her eyes only to become submerged in them, as if it had never existed. And a shadow formed. A dark shadow covering the earth. From the moment her trembling lips almost involuntarily mouthed the words: 'I want one too' — from that moment, darkness intensified in the depths of her eyes into revocable desire, which if touched, would close up like the leaf of the opium poppy. She retreated before the impossible, the impossible which had drawn near, and which, in a moment of temptation, had almost become hers; the darkness of her eyes oscillated like a gold coin. Slyness was written on her face — and had I not been there, she would slyly have stolen something. In those eyes, which blinked to feigned wisdom, in those eyes there was a marked tendency to steal. She looked at me rapidly, and it was envy: you have everything; and censure: why are we not the same person then I would have a chick; and covetousness — she wanted me for herself. Slowly I slumped into my chair, her envy denuded my poverty and left my poverty musing; had I not been there, she would have stolen my poverty as well; she wanted everything. After the tremor of covetousness had passed, the darkness of her eyes endured everything: it was not only to a face without protection that I was exposing her. I was now exposing her to the best of the world: to a chick. Without seeing me, her moist eyes stared at me with an intense abstraction, which made intimate contact with my intimacy. Something was happening which I could not understand with the naked eye. And once more, desire returned. This time her eyes were full of anguish, as if they could do nothing with the rest of her body which had become detached and independent. And those eyes grew wider, alarmed at the physical strain as her inner being began to disintegrate. Her delicate mouth was that of a child, a bruised purple. She looked at the ceiling — the dark shadows round her eyes gave her an air of supreme martyrdom. Without stirring, I watched her. I knew about the high incidence of infant mortality. The great question she raised involved me: is it worth while? I do not know, my ever greater calm replied, but it is so. There, before my silence, she surrendered to the process, and if she was asking me the great question, it had to go unanswered. She had to give herself — for nothing. It had to be. And for nothing. She held back, unwilling to surrender. But I waited. I knew that we are that thing which must happen. I could be useful to her as silence. And, dazed by misunderstanding, I could hear a heart beating inside me that was not mine. Before my fascinated eyes, like some emanation, she was being transformed into a child.

Not without sorrow. In silence, I saw the sorrow of her awkward happiness. The slow colic of a snail. She slowly ran her tongue over her thin lips. (Help me, her body said, as it painfully divided into two. I am helping, my paralysis replied.) Slow agony. Her entire body became swollen and deformed. At times, her eyes became pure eyelashes with the avidity of an egg about to be hatched. Her mouth trembling with hunger. Then I almost smiled, as if stretched out on an operating table, and insisting that I was not suffering much pain. She did not lose sight of me: there were footprints she could not distinguish, someone had already walked this way, and she perceived that I had walked a great deal. She became more and more deformed, almost identical to herself. Shall I risk it? shall I give way to feeling? she asked herself. Yes, she replied to herself, through me.

And my first yes enraptured me. Yes, my silence replied to her, yes. Just as when my first son was born, I had said to him: yes. I had summoned the courage to say yes to Ofélia, I who knew that one can also die in childhood without anyone noticing. Yes, I replied enraptured, for the greatest danger does not exist: when you go, you go together, you yourself will always be there: this, this you will carry with you whatever may become of you.

The agony of her birth. Until then I had never seen courage. The courage to be one's other self, the courage to be born of one's own parturition, and to cast off one's former body. And without any reassurance that it was worthwhile. 'I', her body tried to say, washed by the waters. Her nuptials with herself.

Cautious because of what was happening to her, Ofélia asked slowly:

— Is it a chick?

I did not look at her.

— Yes, it's a chick.

From the kitchen there came a faint chirping. We remained silent, as if Jesus had just been born. Ofélia sighed and sighed.

— A tiny little chick? she confirmed, trying to overcome her uncertainty.

— Yes, a little chick, I said, guiding her carefully towards life.

— Ah, a little chick, she said pensively.

— A little chick, I repeated, without treating her brutally.

For some minutes now, I had found myself in the presence of a child. The metamorphosis had taken place.

— It's in the kitchen.

— In the kitchen? she repeated, pretending not to understand.

— In the kitchen, I repeated, sounding authoritarian for the first time, and without adding anything further.

— Ah, in the kitchen said Ofélia, shamming and looking up at the ceiling.

But she was suffering. Feeling somewhat ashamed, I noted that I was taking my revenge at last. Ofélia was suffering, shamming, looking up at the ceiling. Her mouth, those shadows around her eyes.

— Why don't you go into the kitchen and play with the little chick?

— Me . . .? she asked slyly.

— Only if you want to.

I know that I should have ordered her to go rather than expose her to the humiliation of such intense desire. I know that I should not have given her any choice, and then she could say that she had been forced to obey. At that moment, however, it was not out of revenge that I tormented her with freedom. The truth is that that step, that step, too, she had to take alone. Alone and without delay. It was she who had to go to the mountain. Why — I wondered — why am I trying to breathe my life into her purple mouth? Why am I giving her my breath? how can I dare to breathe inside her, if I myself . . . is it only so that she may walk, that I am giving her these painful steps? Am I only breathing my life into her so that one day she may momentarily feel in her exhaustion that the mountain has come to her?

Did I have the right? But I had no choice. It was an emergency as if the girl's lips were turning more purple every second.

— Go and see the little chick only if you want to, I then repeated with the extreme harshness of someone who is saving another.

We stood there facing each other, dissimilar, body separated from body; united only by hostility. I sat quiet and motionless in my chair so that the girl might suffer inside some other being, unyielding so that she might struggle inside me; I felt increasingly strong as I witnessed Ofélia's need to hate me, her determination that I should resist the suffering of her hatred. I cannot live this for you — my coldness told her. Ofélia's struggle came ever closer and then inside me, as if that creature who had been born endowed with the most extraordinary strength, were drinking from my weakness. In using me, she bruised me with her strength: she clawed me as she tried to cling to my smooth walls. At last she muttered, in tones of suppressed rage:

— Well, I'm off to see the chick in the kitchen.

— Yes, off you go, I said slowly.

She withdrew hesitantly, conscious of her dignity, even as she turned her back on me.

She re-emerged from the kitchen immediately — she looked startled, shamelessly holding out the chick in one hand, and examining me from head to foot with questioning eyes.

— It's a little chick! she said.

She looked at the chick in her outstretched hand, then looked at me, then looked once more at her hand — and suddenly she became nervous and excited, which automatically made me feel nervous and excited.

— But it's only a little chick! I said, and this reproach flickered across her eyes at once as if I had not told her who was chirping.

I laughed. Ofélia looked at me, deeply offended. And suddenly — suddenly she laughed. Then we both laughed, somewhat stridently.

When we stopped laughing, Ofélia put the chick down on the floor to see it walking. When it ran, she went after it. She seemed to be giving the chick its freedom only in order to feel nostalgia, but if it cowered, she rushed to protect it, pitying it for being subjected to her power: 'Poor little thing, he's mine': and when she held the chick, it was with a hand deformed by delicacy. — Yes, it was love, tortuous love. He's very tiny, therefore he needs a lot of attention. One cannot fondle him for that could be really dangerous; don't let people handle him unless they know what they're doing, and do as you think best, but corn is far too big for his little open beak; for he's very fragile, poor little thing, and so tiny; therefore, you shouldn't let your children play with him; I'm the only one who knows how to look after him; he keeps slipping all over the place, therefore, the kitchen floor is obviously no place for a little chick.

For quite some time now, I had been attempting to get back

to my typing, in order to make up for lost time, while Ofélia's voice droned on. Little by little, she was only speaking to the little chick, and loving for love's sake. For the first time she had cast me aside, she was no longer I. I watched her, all golden, and the chick, all golden, and the two of them hummed like distaff and spindle. This also meant my freedom at last and without any quarrel; farewell, and I smiled with nostalgia.

Much later, I realized that Ofélia was talking to me.

— I think — I think I'll put him in the kitchen.

— Off you go then.

I did not see her leave, nor did I see her return. At a given moment, quite by chance and somewhat distracted, I realized that there had been silence for some time. I looked at her for a moment. She was sitting with her hands folded on her lap. Without quite knowing why, I looked at her a second time.

— What is it?

— I . . .?

— Do you want to go to the lavatory?

— I . . .?

I gave up and carried on with my typing. Some time later, I heard a voice:

— I must go home now.

— Of course.

— If you don't mind.

I looked at her in surprise: Now then, if you wish . . .

— Well, she said, well I'm going.

She walked away slowly and closed the door quietly behind her. I went on staring at the closed door. What a funny child you are, I thought to myself. I went back to my work.

But I was stuck at the same sentence. Well — I thought impatiently, looking at my watch — now what's the matter? I saw there, searching restlessly in my mind, searching in my mind to discover what was troubling me. Just as I was about to give up, I saw once more an extremely tranquil face: Ofélia. I was struggling with an idea, when unexpectedly, she was leaning over me in order to be able to hear what I was feeling. I slowly pushed away the typewriter. Reluctantly, I put the chairs out of the way, until I came to a halt in the doorway of the kitchen. On the floor lay the dead chick. Ofélia, I impulsively called after the girl who had fled.

From an infinite distance, I saw the floor. Ofélia. From afar, I tried to reach the heart of that silent girl, in vain. Oh, do not be so frightened! Sometimes people kill for love, but I promise you that one day you will forget everything, I promise you! People do not know how to love, do you hear me, I repeated as if I might reach her before, in refusing to serve truth, she should proudly serve nothingness. I who had not remembered to warn her that without fear there was the world. But I swear that this is breathing. I was very tired. I sat down on the kitchen stool.

Where I am now sitting, slowly beating the mixture for tomorrow's cake. Sitting, as if throughout all these years I have been patiently waiting in the kitchen. Beneath the table today's chick shudders. The yellow is the same, the beak is the same. As we are promised at Easter, He returns in December. It is Ofélia who did not return: she grew up. She went away to become the Indian princess whose tribe awaited her in the desert.

Chronicles

Author's Introduction

BOTTOM DRAWER

The second part of this book is entitled 'Bottom Drawer' at the suggestion of the never sufficiently recognized Otto Lara Resende.[1] But why should we store all the things which accumulate in every household in our bottom drawer? Read the poem by Manuel Bandeira[2] where he confides: so that death may find me with 'my house in order, the table laid, and everything in its proper place'.[3]

Why should I rescue from my bottom drawer 'The sinner burned at the stake', for example, which was written simply for my own amusement when I was expecting my first child? Why publish what is worthless? Perhaps because the worthy is also worthless. Besides, what is obviously worthless has always fascinated me. I have a real affection for things which are incomplete or badly finished, for things which awkwardly try to take flight only to fall clumsily to the ground.

[1] Otto Lara Resende (1922–) Brazilian journalist, critic, poet and writer.
[2] Manuel Bandeira (1886–1968) One of Brazil's most distinguished poets in this century and an influential figure in launching the Brazilian Modernist Movement in the 1920s.
[3] The closing lines of Manuel Bandeira's poem 'Consoada' (Vigil Feast) from the collection *Opus 10* (1952).

GASTÃO MANOEL HENRIQUE[1]

The paintings and sculptures of Gastão Manoel Henrique take us by surprise with their fearless approach to symmetry. An artist requires experience or courage in order to revalue symmetry, when it is so easy to imitate what is spuriously termed 'asymmetrical', one of art's most hackneyed claims to originality. The symmetry of Gastão Manoel Henrique take centrated and assured. But never dogmatic. It is also hesitant, as tends to happen with artists who cherish the hope that two asymmetrical forms will finally result in symmetry. Thus providing a third solution: synthesis. Perhaps this will explain the atmosphere of despoilment, the delicacy of something lived and then relived, as opposed to the blatant audacity of less experienced artists. It is not quite tranquillity that we discover there. What we are witnessing is the arduous struggle of something which, although corroded, endures, and in the densest of colours; what we see there is the lividness of something which even when contorted, remains standing. His crosses have become crooked from centuries of mortification. Altars perhaps? At least they possess the silence of altars. The silence of portals. The greenish colouring is reminiscent of something hovering between life and death, the intense colouring of twilight. There is an ancient bronze in those quiet colours, and the quality of steel; and everything is amplified by the silence of things found on the road. We sense a long, dusty road before finally arriving at the focal point in the picture; for somehow this is a resting place which receives the viewer. Even though Gastão Manoel Henrique's portals do not open. Or are those portals the church itself, and have we already arrived there? In the work of Gastão Manoel Henrique there is evidence of a struggle to avoid any transposition. And in none of his paintings do we find written the word: church. These are the walls of a Christ who is missing, but the walls are there, and everything is tangible, ultimately tangible for anyone who comes from afar. For his painting is tangible: our hands also observe it. Gastão Manoel Henrique creates his material before painting it, and the wood becomes as essential to his painting

[1] Gastão Manoel Henrique (1933–) Brazilian painter and sculptor, born in São Paulo. Some of his most important paintings and sculptures are on permanent show at the Museum of Modern Art in Rio de Janeiro.

as it might be for someone carving from wood. And the material he creates is religious: it has the solidity of convent beams. It is compact, and as dense as a closed door. But crevices have been sculpted there, as if scratched open by fingernails. And it is through those crevices that we can penetrate the synthesis. Coagulated colour, violence and martyrdom, are the beams which sustain the silence of his religious symmetry.

THE MIRRORS OF VERA MINDLIN[1]

What is a mirror? The word mirror does not exist — only mirrors, for any one mirror is an infinitude of mirrors. — Somewhere in the world there must be a mine of mirrors. Few mirrors are needed to create a scintillating and somnambulistic mine: two suffice for the one to throw up the reflection in the other, with a vibration which travels like a tense, insistent message *ad infinitum*, a liquid into which you can plunge your fascinated hand and retrieve it dripping with reflections, the reflections of that hard water. — What is a mirror? Like the crystal ball of the fortune-teller, it draws me towards that void which becomes the clairvoyant's field of meditation, and for me the field of endless silence. — That crystallized void which encompasses enough space to allow us to advance at will without ever stopping: for the mirror is the deepest space which exists. — And it is a magic thing: anyone in possession of a broken fragment may carry it with him when he goes into the desert to meditate. Whence he will also return empty-handed, enlightened and translucent, and with the same vibrant silence as that of the mirror. — Its form is of no importance: no form is capable of circumscribing or altering it; no quadrangular or circular mirror exists: the tiniest fragment is always the entire mirror: remove its frame and it spreads like

[1] Vera Mindlin (1920–) Brazilian engraver and painter. She was born in Rio de Janeiro, and studied art in Brazil and Paris. Her work has been exhibited extensively throughout Europe and the Americas, and several of her pictures are included in the permanent collection at the Museum of Modern Art in Rio de Janeiro. In 1969, Vera Mindlin published an album of engravings alongside poems contributed by major contemporary Brazilian poets.

spilling water. — What is a mirror? It is the only invented material which is natural.

Anyone who, like Vera, can observe a mirror while remaining detached; anyone who succeeds in seeing the mirror while not seeing it, anyone who grasps that its depth is due to its emptiness, anyone who penetrates its transparent space without leaving any vestige of his own image — will have perceived its mystery. To achieve this, you must take it by surprise and on your own when it is hanging in an empty room, without forgetting that the finest needle dangled before the mirror can transform it into the simple image of a needle.

Vera must have relied on her own delicacy in order not to pass through the mirror with her own image, for the mirror in which I see myself is I, but the empty mirror is the living mirror. Only an extremely delicate person may enter an empty room with an empty mirror, and this must be achieved with subtlety and detachment, so that their image will leave no trace. In recompense, that delicate person will have succeeded in penetrating one of the inviolable secrets of objects: Vera has seen what is strictly speaking the mirror.

And she has discovered the immense congealed spaces within, interrupted only by the rare tall glacier. At other moments, and these are extremely rare — it is necessary to be vigilant night and day and to practise self-denial in order to capture those moments — at such moments Vera succeeded in capturing the sequence of shadows which exist inside the mirror. Then, working only in black and white, she has recaptured the mirror's quivering, rainbow-coloured luminosity. With the same black and white, she has also recaptured at a chilling stroke, one of its most difficult truths: its frozen silence devoid of any colour. It is essential to grasp the violent absence of colour in a mirror in order to be able to recreate it, as if you were recreating the violent absence of taste in water.

BECAUSE THEY WERE NOT DISTRACTED

There was the gentlest ecstasy in walking out together, that happiness you experience upon feeling your throat rather dry and upon realizing that you are so astonished that your mouth is wide open: they were breathing in anticipation of the air ahead of them, and to have this thirst was their very own water. They walked through street after street, conversing and laughing; they conversed and laughed to give substance and weight to the most gentle of ecstasies which was the happiness of their thirst. Because of the traffic and crowds, they sometimes touched, and as they touched — thirst is the grace, but the waters are the beauty of darkness — as they touched there shone the brilliance of their waters, their throats becoming even more dry in their astonishment. How they marvelled at finding themselves together!

Until everything transformed itself into denial. Everything transformed itself into denial when they craved their own happiness. Then began the great dance of errors. The ceremonial of inopportune words. He searched and failed to see; she did not see that he had not seen, she who was there in the meanwhile. He who was there in the meanwhile. Everything went wrong, and there was the great dust of the streets, and the more they erred, the more they craved with severity, unsmiling. All this simply because they had been attentive, simply because they were not sufficiently distracted. Simply because suddenly becoming demanding and stubborn, they wanted to possess what they already possessed. All this because they wanted to name something; because they wanted to be; they who were. They were about to learn that unless one is distracted the telephone does not ring; that it is necessary to go out for the letter to arrive, and that when the telephone finally does ring, the wasteland of waiting has already disconnected the wires. All this, all this, because they were not distracted.

A NIGHT IN FEBRUARY

I swear, believe me — the drawing-room was in darkness — but the music summoned me to the centre, to the centre of the room — the entire room became dark within the darkness — I was in darkness — I felt that however dark, the room was bright — I took refuge in fear — just as I had already taken refuge from you within you yourself — what did I find? — nothing except that the dark room filled itself with the brightness one senses in the greatest darkness — and that I was trembling in the midst of this awkward light — believe me, even though I cannot explain — there was something perfect and delicate — as if I had never seen a flower — or as if I were a flower — and there was a honey-bee — a honey-bee paralysed with fear — before the unbreathable grace of this light of darkness which is a flower — and the flower was paralysed with fear before the honey-bee which was very sweet — believe me, for even I cannot believe it — even I do not know what a honey-bee alive with terror could want in the dark life of a flower — but believe me — the room was filled with a penetrating smile — a fatal rite was being fulfilled — and what is known as fear is not fear — it is whiteness emerging from the shadows — no proof remained — I can assure you of nothing — I am my only proof.

THE SCEPTRE

But if we, who are the avowed monarchs of nature, must not show fear, then who will?

BODY AND SOUL

In Italy, *il miracolo* is night fishing. Mortally wounded by the harpoon, the fish releases its crimson blood into the sea. The fisherman unloading his catch before sunrise, his face livid with guilt, knows that the great burden of miraculous fishing he is dragging over the sands — is love. *Milagre* is the tear of the leaf which trembles, escapes and falls: behold thousands of miraculous tears glistening on the ground. The *miracle* has the sharp points of stars and much splintered silver. To pass from the word to its meaning is to reduce it to splinters just as the firework remains a dull object until it becomes a brilliant flare in the sky and achieves its own death. (In its passage from the body to the senses, anger reveals the same supreme achievement — by dying.) *Le miracle* is a glass octagon which can be turned slowly in the palm of the hand. It remains in the hand but only for gazing at. It can be viewed from all angles . . . very slowly . . . and on each side there is revealed a glass octagon. Until suddenly — threatened and turning quite pale with emotion — the person understands: in the palm of his hand he no longer holds an octagon but a miracle. From this moment onwards, he no longer sees anything. He possesses it.

THE FUTURE OF SOMETHING DELICATE

— Mummy, I have seen a tiny hurricane but still so tiny, that all it could do was to rustle three tiny leaves on the street–corner . . .

PORTRAIT OF A LADY

She lived in a boarding-house on São Clemente Street. She was voluminous and smelled like a chicken when it is brought half-cooked to the table. She had five teeth and a parched mouth. Her reputation had not been invented: she still spoke in French whenever she found an opportunity, even if the other person spoke Portuguese and would have preferred to be spared the embarrassment of listening to their own accent. The absence of saliva rid her voice of any trace of glibness, and gave her an air of restraint. There was majesty in that huge body supported on tiny feet, in the strength of those five teeth, in those sparse hairs which trembled with the slightest breeze (as in a snapshot of someone in exile).

But there came a Monday morning when instead of leaving her room, she came in from the street. Her skin looked smooth, her neck washed, and there was no longer any smell of half-cooked chicken. She explained that she had spent

Sunday at her son's house where she had remained overnight. She was wearing a dowdy black satin dress; instead of going up to her room to change and reverting to being an ordinary guest at the boarding-house, she sat in the lounge and commented that the family is the pillar of society. She referred in passing to the leisurely bath which she had enjoyed in her daughter-in-law's comfortable bathroom. She sat for hours by the tall vase of flowers in the lounge — her eyes moist, her mouth parched, conducting a conversation meant for an invisible audience — and making the other guests, who were still wearing their dressing-gowns, feel awkward. As the afternoon wore on, it became clear that her boots were hurting her feet, but she continued to sit there, all dressed up, holding her large head erect like an oracle. When she enthused about the sumptuous meals served at her son's house, her eyes closed with nausea. She retired to her room, vomited, and refused any assistance when they knocked on her door. When it was time for dinner she came down to fetch a cup of tea; brown circles showing around her eyes, and wearing an ankle-length floral-patterned dress, and once again *sans soutien*. What did seem strange was the clearness of her skin. The other guests avoided looking at her. She spoke to no one: King Lear. She was silent, huge, dishevelled, and clean. She was happy to no purpose.

PAUL KLEE

Were I to spend too much time looking at *Paysage aux oiseaux jaunes*[1] by Klee, I should never be able to turn back. Courage and cowardice are in constant play. I am terrified by this vision which could be irremediable and perhaps even a vision of freedom. The habit of looking through prison bars, the comfort of holding on to the bars with both hands, while looking.

[1] *Paysage aux oiseux jaunes* [*Landscape with yellow birds*]: large watercolour on paper with a black background. Painted in 1923 by Klee (1879–1940), the work is now in a private collection in Basle.

The prison offers protection, the bars support for my hands. Then I recognize the freedom which is only for the chosen few. Once more, courage and cowardice form an endless game: my courage, altogether possible, terrifies me. For I know that my courage is possible. I then begin to think that among the insane there are some who are not insane. The fact is that any possibility which is truly realized, is not meant to be understood. And the more you try to explain, the more your courage fails you, the more you find yourself asking; *Paysage aux oiseaux jaunes* asks for nothing. At least I am calculating what freedom might be. And it is this which makes the protection of the bars intolerable; the comfort of this prison strikes me in the face. All that I have endured — simply in order not to be free . . .

AN UGLY DUCKLING

When in flight, its awkward arm became apparent: it was a wing. Its eye a trifle stupid, but that stupid expression functioned in open space. It waddled clumsily, but it flew. It flew so well that it even put its life at risk, which was a luxury. It waddled, looking ridiculous and cautious. On the ground it became an invalid.

THE SECRET

There is a word belonging to a kingdom which leaves me dumbfounded with horror. Do not startle our world. Do not cast our ship upon the seas forever more with an incautious word. I fear that once the word has been touched we become too pure by far. What shall we make of our pure lives? Leave the sky to hope alone. With trembling fingers I seal your lips. Do not utter that word. In dread, I have suppressed it for so long now that I have forgotten the word beyond recall, and made of it my mortal secret.

MUCH MORE SIMPLE

If in life he is a silent man, why did he write as if he was speaking? Silent men only speak when it is necessary. Does this prevent the others from listening? We are dealing with a silent person; which explains his air of mystery.

SINCE ONE FEELS OBLIGED TO WRITE . . .

Since one feels obliged to write, let it be without obscuring the space between the lines with words.

THE DIVINE SUPPER

An orange on the table. Blessed be the tree that gave you birth.

'SHE HAS JUST GONE OUT'

Her immense, understanding intelligence; that heart of hers which is void of me and demands that I should be admirable in order to be able to admire me. My enormous pride: I prefer to be found in the street. Rather than in this imaginary palace where no one will find me because — because I have given instructions that I am not at home: 'She has just gone out'.

THE HOUR OF THE MISSIONARY

When the ghost of this living person possesses me, I know that for several days I shall be a missionary's wife. Her thinness and delicacy have already taken possession of me. With a certain fascination and a persistent weariness, I succumb to the experience I am about to live. And with some apprehension from a practical point of view: for the moment I am much too occupied carrying out my duties to be able to cope with the burden of this strange, new existence, whose evangelical pressures I am already beginning to experience. I notice that even in the plane I have already started adopting the gait of a lay missionary. Upon landing, I shall probably find myself with an expression of physical suffering and moral hope. Yet when I boarded the plane, I was so strong. I was? No, I am. All my strength is being consumed so that I may succeed in becoming weak. I am a missionary in the wind. I understand, I understand, I understand. I do not understand means nothing: except that 'I do not understand' with the same purged fanaticism of this pale woman. I already know that within the next few days I shall succeed in recommencing my own life, which was never my own, except when my ghost possessed me.

SUNDAY AFTERNOON

The garden is drenched with rain; the raindrops are so thick, and the air glistens. The corolla keeps its opaque appearance. The pebbles scatter, the window-panes in the room trickle, the leaves hang heavy in the air; a towering rosebush shakes its thorns over the mud. The rain becomes heavier. Whereupon I ask myself most solemnly: Will this have ruined the pleasure of the Horse Trials?

TO ERR

To err is a much more serious matter among intelligent people: for they have all the arguments to prove their point.

ROMANCE

It would be more attractive if I were to make it more attractive. Exploiting, for example, some of the things which have framed a life, a thing, a romance, or a person. It is perfectly lawful to become attractive, except that there is the danger of a picture becoming a picture because the frame made it a picture. When it comes to reading, I clearly prefer the attractive. It tires me less and entices me more, confining and encircling me. In order to write, however, I must distance myself. The experience is worth the effort, even though it may only benefit the person who is writing.

HOW DOES ONE DESCRIBE IT?

If I receive a present given with affection by someone I do not like — how can I describe my feelings? A person whom I no longer care for and who no longer cares for me — how can I describe the mortification and resentment? To be occupied, and then suddenly to stop overcome by some idle moment — blessed, miraculous, radiant and idiotic — how can I describe the feeling? So far, I have only succeeded in naming it with my own question. What is the name? and this is the name.

ONCE UPON A TIME

I replied that what I wanted most of all was to write a story one day which would begin as follows: 'Once upon a time . . .'. A story for children? they enquired. No, for adults, I replied, my thoughts already elsewhere, struggling to recall my first stories at the age of seven, which all began with 'Once upon a time'. I submitted them to the editors of the children's page which appeared every Thursday in the *Recife Journal*, and not one, not a single one of them was ever published. And it was easy to understand why. None of them actually told a story with the necessary elements for a plot. I read the stories the *Journal* published and all of them related some occurrence. But if the editors were stubborn, so was I.

But since then I had changed so greatly that it seemed just possible that I was ready at last for the real 'Once upon a time'. So I asked myself at once: What is stopping me from making a start? Right now? I felt it would be so easy.

And so I made a start. No sooner had I written the opening sentence, when I realized that I still found it impossible. I had written:

'Once upon a time there was a bird, my God.'

AFRICA

A trip to the settlements of Tallah, Kebbe and Sasstown, within Liberia, accompanied by the journalist Anna Kipper, Captain Crockett and Captain Bill Young. No missionary had ever set foot here. Some of the inhabitants worked at the air-base and talked a smattering of English as if it were a local dialect (in Monrovia alone there are twenty-four or twenty-five dialects). In the midst of conversation they pause to say with infinite care and pleasure: *hello* — they listen to the resonance of what they have just said, laugh among themselves, and then go on conversing. They love to wave goodbye. Their skin is of a uniform matt black which seems to repel water like the feathers of the swan which never gets wet. Some of the children have a navel the size of an orange. One of the women in our party is examined attentively by a black youth and, lost for words, the woman ends up by waving goodbye. The youth is delighted and, with the utmost care as if delicately presenting her with some gift, he makes an obscene gesture. The black women paint their faces with streaks of ochre, and tinge their lower lip with a colour reminiscent of gangrene and verdigris. One woman, whose baby I admire, says: *baby nice, baby cry money* — her voice is so mellifluous that it sounds like water filling a pitcher. Captain Young gives her a nickel. *Baby cry big money*, she protests, upsetting the pitcher with a voice which explodes into laughter. The natives laugh a good deal, even those with sad faces; there is no trace of mockery or ambition in their laughter; their laughter is a mixture of fascination, humility, inquisitiveness and merriment. One of the girls stares at me closely. And startling everyone, she blurts out a lengthy speech, a harangue without malice in which I cannot make out a single *r* or *s*, only variations on the scale of *l*, the undulating rhythms of a rigmarole. I have recourse to the interpreter. He gives me the briefest summary possible: *she likes you*. The girl then breaks into another rigmarole which this time fills several pitchers with singing rain. The interpreter points to my headscarf. I take it off and show the girl how it is worn. When I look up, I am surrounded by little groups of young black girls, half-naked, all very serious and quiet. None of them pays any attention to what I am showing them and I start to feel awkward, surrounded as it were by black does. The painted stripes on their opaque faces are watching me. The gentleness is contagious. I also calm down. One of them then glides forward, and as if carrying out some ritual — they are much given to observing formalities — she takes my head in her hands, runs her fingers through my hair and examines it with the utmost concentration. All the other girls look on. I dare not move lest I should startle them. When she has finished, there is still a moment of silence. And then suddenly there comes an outburst of laughter mingled with a jovial outcry, as if silence were being dispersed.

HUMAN LABOUR

Perhaps this has been my greatest struggle in life: in order to understand my non-intelligence, I have been obliged to become intelligent. (Intelligence is used in order to understand non-intelligence. Except that the instrument goes on being used — and we are unable to gather things with clean hands.)

THE GREATEST EXPERIENCE

I should first have liked to be other people in order to know what I was not. Then I understood that I had already been the others and this was easy. My greatest experience would be to be the other of the others: and the other of the others was I.

TO LIE, TO THINK

The worst of lying is that it creates a false truth. (No, this is not as obvious as it seems nor is it a truism; I know that I have something to say without quite knowing how to phrase it. Besides, what really annoys me is that everything has to be phrased *in a certain way* — an imposition with considerable limitations). What am I, in fact, trying to think? Perhaps this: if a lie were merely the negation of truth, then that would be one of the ways (negative) of telling the truth. But the worst lie of all is the *creative* lie. (There is no doubt: to have to think irritates me, for before I started trying to think I knew perfectly well what I had in mind.)

MIRACULOUS FISHING

To write, therefore, is the way of someone who uses the word as bait: the word fishes for something that is not a word. When that non-word takes the bait, something has been written. Once the space between the lines has been fished, the word can be discarded with relief. But here the analogy ends: the non-word upon taking the bait, has assimilated it. Salvation, then, is to read 'absent-mindedly'.

REMEMBERING

To write often means remembering what has never existed. How shall I succeed in knowing what I do not even know? Like so: as if I were to remember. By an effort of 'memory' as if I had never been born. I have never been born. I have never lived. But I remember, and that memory is in living flesh.

WRITING, HUMILITY, TECHNIQUE

This inability to perceive, to understand, makes me instinctively . . . instinctively what? makes me seek a way of expressing myself which might lead me to a quicker understanding. This way, this 'style' (!) has been called a variety of things, but never what it really and exclusively is: a humble search. I have never had to cope with only one problem of expression because my problem is much more serious: that of conception. When I speak of 'humility', I am referring to humility in its Christian meaning (as an ideal within or beyond attainment); I am referring to that humility which stems from total awareness of being utterly incapable. And I am referring to humility as technique. Holy Mother of God, even I have been appalled at my lack of modesty; but here there is some misunderstanding. Humility as a technique is as follows: things should be approached with humility, otherwise they will become entirely elusive. I have discovered this type of humility, which ironically is a subtle form of pride. Pride is not a sin, at least not a grave sin: pride is a childish failing which we succumb to like greed. Except that pride has the enormous disadvantage of being a grave error, with all the consequences which error brings into our lives, for it causes us to waste a great deal of time.

WITHOUT HEROISM

Even in Camus — this fondness for heroism. Is there perhaps no other way? No, even to understand already implies heroism. Is a man unable then simply to open his door and watch?

WITHOUT ANY WARNING

There were so many things which I did not know at that time. No one had told me, for example, about this sun at three o'clock in the afternoon. Nor had anyone told me about this rhythm which is so monotonous, this relentless dust. That it would be painful, I had been warned. But that the little bird which comes bringing me hope from afar should spread the wings of an eagle over me, this no one had told me. I had no idea what it meant to be protected by great outspread wings, the beak of an eagle lowered towards me and smiling. When, as a young girl, I triumphantly wrote in my diary that I did not believe in love, that was precisely when I loved most of all. Nor did I know the consequences of telling lies. I began to lie as a precaution, and because no one warned me about the danger of being cautious, I was no longer able to rid myself of the habit of lying. And I told so many lies that I began to lie even to my very lies. And this — I sensed to my astonishment — was to tell the truth. Until I became so degenerate that the lies I told were crude, naked and laconic: I was telling the brutal truth.

ADVENTURE

My intuitions become much clearer as I make the effort to transpose them into words. It is in this sense that writing for me is a necessity. On the one hand, because to write is a way of not falsifying sentiment (the involuntary transfiguration of imagination is only one way of arriving); on the other hand, I write because of my inability to understand except through the process of writing. If I assume a note of hermeticism this is not only because the important thing is not to falsify sentiment but also because I am incapable of transposing sentiment in any clear way without falsifying it — to falsify thought would be to rob writing of its only satisfaction. So I often find myself assuming an air of mystery — a trait which I find extremely irksome in others.

After something has been written, should I not then try to render it more clearly? Here I choose to be obstinate. Besides, I respect a certain clarity peculiar to the mystery of nature which cannot be substituted by any other kind of clarity. I also believe that things can only be clarified with time: just as with a glass of water, whenever something is deposited at the bottom of the glass and the water turns clear.

. . . If ever that water should turn clear, so much the worse for me. I am prepared to take the risk. I have taken greater risks like every other creature who chooses to live. And if I take risks it is not because of some arbitrary freedom or insensibility or arrogance on my part. Each day when I awaken, as if by habit, I take new risks. I have always relished a deep sense of adventure and here I use the word deep to imply inherent. This sense of adventure is what gives me a dimension of security and reality in relation to living, and in some strange way, in relation to writing.

BERNE CATHEDRAL ON A SUNDAY EVENING

Every Sunday evening (I believe every Saturday evening as well) they lit what seemed like thousands of lamps tracing the outlines of the Cathedral: gothic, solid, and pure. This gave the impression from a distance that the masonry had been transformed into a simple design created from light. The light dematerialized the Cathedral's solid structure. And however much I tried to go on visualizing the substance of those walls, I felt myself to be passing through them. Not to find myself touching the other side of transparency, but my own transparency.

IN THE MANGER

In the manger all was calm and peaceful. It was late evening and no star had yet appeared. For the moment, the birth of

Jesus was an intimate affair. As darkness fell, lying on straw the colour of gold and tender as a lamb, the child Jesus looked radiant; as tender as our own little son. Nearby, an ox and an ass kept watch, and warmed the air with the breath of their great bodies. The birth had taken place and the moisture was settling; the moisture and warmth were breathing. Mary rested her weary body, her task in this world was to fulfil her destiny, and now she was resting and watching. Joseph, with flowing beard, turned to meditation; his mission, which was that of understanding, had been accomplished. The destiny of the child Jesus was to be born. And that of the animals continued to renew itself there in the manger: the destiny of loving without knowing that they loved. The innocence of children was something those gentle animals understood. And, before the arrival of the three wise kings, they offered to the newborn child everything they possessed: their large watchful eyes and their gentle warmth like that of the womb.

Humanity is the offspring of Christ made man, but children, beasts, and lovers are the offspring of that moment in the manger. Because they are the offspring of the child Jesus, their weaknesses are illumined: the symbol of the lamb marks their destiny. They recognize each other by a certain pallor on their foreheads, like that of the evening star, the odour of straw and earth, the patience of an infant. Because children, the poor in spirit, and lovers, are also turned away from the inn. Their shepherd, however, is the child Jesus, and they will want for nothing. For centuries they have hidden themselves away in mysteries and stables, where for centuries they have continued to commemorate the moment of the infant's birth: the happiness of mankind.

SKETCH OF A WARDROBE

It looks penetrable because it has a door. Upon opening it, you realize that its penetration has been deferred: because inside there is another wooden surface, like another closed door. Its function: to keep transvestites in the dark. Its nature: the inviolability of things. Its relationship with people: people always see themselves reflected in its mirror in an awkward light because the wardrobe is never in the right place: it stands wherever it can be accommodated; it is invariably colossal, humped and self-conscious, without quite knowing how to be more discreet. A wardrobe is invariably clumsy, obtrusive, sad and kind. Should its mirrored door close, however — then, as it moves, glass filter upon filter comes into the new composition of the room plunged into shadow. (A sudden dexterity, a contribution to the room, an indication of its dual existence, influential in the world, a dark eminence, the real power waiting in the wings.)

LITERATURE AND JUSTICE

Today, quite unexpectedly, as in any real discovery, I found that some of my tolerance towards others was reserved for me as well (but for how long?). I took advantage of this crest of the wave to bring myself up to date with forgiveness. For example, my tolerance in relation to myself, as someone who writes, is to forgive my inability to deal with the 'social problem' in a 'literary' vein (that is to say, by transforming it into the vehemence of art). Ever since I have come to know myself, the social problem has been more important to me than any other issue: in Recife the black shanty towns were the first truth I encountered. Long before I ever felt 'art', I felt the profound beauty of human conflict. I tend to be straightforward in my approach to any social problem: I wanted 'to do' something, as if writing were not doing anything. What I cannot do is to exploit writing to this end, however much my incapacity pains and distresses me. The problem of justice for me is such an obvious and basic feeling that I am unable to surprise myself on its account — and unless I can surprise myself, I am unable to write. Also because for me, to write is a quest. I have never considered any feeling of justice as a quest or as a discovery, and what worries me is that this feeling of justice should not be so obvious to everyone else. I am aware of simplifying the essence of the problem. But nowadays out of tolerance towards myself, I am not entirely ashamed of contributing nothing human or social through my writing. It is not a matter of not wanting to, it is a question of not being able to. What I am ashamed of is of 'not doing', of not contributing in an active way. (I know all too well that the struggle for justice inevitably leads to politics, and I should get hopelessly lost in a maze of political intrigue.) Of this, I shall always be ashamed. But I have no intention of doing penance. I have no desire, through oblique and dubious means, to achieve my own absolution. Of this, I wish to go on feeling ashamed. But, of writing what I write, I am not ashamed. I feel that if I were to be ashamed, I should be committing the sin of pride.

WHO SHE WAS

— (I love you)
— (Is that what I am then?)
— (You are the love which I have for you)
— (I feel that I am about to recognize myself . . . I can almost see myself. I am almost there)
— (I love you)
— (Ah, that's better. I can see myself. So this is me. Which I portray full-length)

THE SAILOR'S FAREWELL

— You do understand, don't you, Mummy, that I cannot love you for the rest of my life.

SPRING WITHOUT SENTIMENTALITY

I know that I ate the pear and threw away half of it — I never feel compassion in the spring. Afterwards we drank water at the fountain and I did not dry my mouth. We walked together, silent and overbearing. As for the pool, I know that I remained in the pool for hours. Look at the pool — that was how I saw the pool, pointing it out with tranquil eyes. For I was tranquil, and void of compassion.

FLYING THE FLAG

— Today I wrote an essay about Flag Day which was so beautiful, but so beautiful — for I even used words without being entirely certain of their meaning.

ABSTRACT AND SYMBOLIC

In painting as in music and literature, what is often termed abstract strikes me as being merely symbolic of a more delicate and elusive reality which is scarcely visible to the naked eye.

THAT'S NATURE, MY DARLING

— It's so funny, Mummy. I've found out that nature isn't dirty. Take a look at this tree. It's full of husks and cobwebs but nobody would call it a dirty tree. Yet just because that car is covered in dust, it is really dirty.

ONE STEP HIGHER

Until today, I did not realize that you can live without writing.
Little by little the thought dawned upon me: Who knows?
Perhaps I, too, might be able to live without writing. How
infinitely more ambitious that is. And almost unattainable.

GLORY BE TO GOD ON HIGH AND . . .

— I was about to make a noise in the room, almost on
purpose, to see if Father would wake up, but he was sleeping
so peacefully that I didn't have the courage.

AN ANGEL'S DISQUIET

Upon leaving the building, I was taken by surprise. What had
been simply rain on the window-panes and been shut out by
the curtains and cosy warmth indoors, was tempest and darkness outside on the street. Had this change taken place while I
was going down in the lift? A Rio downpour without any
shelter in sight. Copacabana with water seeping under the
doorways of shops at street-level, thick muddy currents
reaching half-way up my legs, as I probed with one foot to try
and make contact with the invisible pavement. It was like an
incoming tide which brought enough water in its wake to
activate the moon's secret influence: there was already a tidal
ebb and flow. Worst of all was that age-long fear engraved on
the flesh: I am without shelter and the world has banished me
to my own world. I, who can only be accommodated in a
house, will never again possess a house. I am these soaking
clothes. My drenched hair will never dry again, and I know
that I shall not be among those destined to enter the Ark, for
the best couple of my species has already been chosen.
On street-corners, cars have been abandoned, their engines

paralysed, and there is not a taxi in sight. The ferocious happiness of several men who find it impossible to return to their homes is unmistakable. The diabolical happiness of men on the loose presented an even greater threat to a woman whose only desire was to return home as quickly as possible. I walked at random along street after street, dragging myself rather than walking: to stop, even for a second, would have meant danger. I barely managed to hide my overwhelming sense of desolation. Some fortunate soul under an improvised tent, called out: By jove, you're a courageous lady! It was not courage, it was definitely fear. Because everything was paralysed, I who am terrified of that moment in which everything comes to a standstill, felt I had to go on.

When suddenly, through the downpour, a taxi appeared. It advanced cautiously, moving centimetre by centimetre, as if testing the ground with its wheels. How was I to secure that taxi? I approached it. I could not afford the luxury of asking; I remembered all the times when, however sweetly I pleaded, my plea was refused. Suppressing my panic, which gave a false impression of strength, I said to the taxi-driver: 'I must get home! it's late! I have small children who must be wondering where I am, it's already dark, do you hear me?' To my great surprise, the man simply answered: yes. Still puzzled, I got in. The taxi could scarcely move through the muddy currents, but it was moving — and it would eventually arrive. I was only thinking: this is more than I deserve. Soon I was thinking: it never occurred to me that I should be so deserving. And very soon, I was the mistress of my very own taxi. I had taken possession as if by right of something which had been given to me gratuitously, and I briskly set about tidying myself up: I wrung the water from my hair and clothes, pulled off my squelching shoes, and dried my face which looked tear-stained. I confess without shame that I had been weeping. Not much and for different reasons, but I had been weeping. After settling into my new domain, I leaned back comfortably in what was mine, and from my Ark, I watched the world come to an end.

Just then, a woman approached the car. As the taxi slowly advanced, she succeeded in accompanying it, holding on to the door-handle in a state of distress. And she literally implored me to allow her to share my taxi. I was already very late, and her route would have meant making a lengthy detour. I remembered, however, my own desperation five minutes earlier, and decided that she should not suffer a similar crisis. When I said yes, her note of pleading immediately ceased, and was replaced with an extremely practical tone of voice: 'Good, but wait a minute while I go across the road to collect a parcel which I left with the dressmaker so that it wouldn't get soaked.' 'Is she taking advantage of me?' I asked myself in my customary doubt as to whether I should or should not let people take advantage of me. I ended up by giving in. The woman took her time. And she came back carrying an enormous parcel which she held on outstretched arms, as if contact with her own body might stain the dress. She made herself comfortable on the back seat beside me, making me feel inhibited in my own home.

And my Calvary for being an angel began at once — for the woman, with that authoritarian voice of hers, had already started to call me an angel. Her situation could scarcely have been less endearing: there was to be a *première* that night and, were it not for my generosity, her dress would have been soaked in the rain or she would have been late and missed the *première*. I had already experienced my own *premières*, and had not been enthusiastic about any of them. 'You have no idea what a miracle this has been,' she told me firmly. 'I started to pray in the street, to pray that God would send an angel to my rescue; I made a vow that I would fast all day tomorrow. — And God sent you.' Feeling ill at ease, I fidgeted in my seat. Was I an angel destined to salvage *premières*? The divine irony left me disconcerted. But the woman, with all the force of her practical faith, and she was a forceful woman, vehemently insisted upon acknowledging me as an angel, something which very few people have ever acknowledged in the past, and even then with the greatest discretion. I tried to shrug it off with some mild sarcasm. 'Don't over-estimate me, I am merely a means of transport.' While she made no attempt to grasp my meaning, I unwillingly conceded that the argument did not really excuse me: angels are also a means of transport. Intimidated, I remained silent. I am always greatly impressed by anyone who shouts at me: the woman was not shouting, but she was clearly towering over me. Incapable of facing up to her, I took refuge in sweet cynicism: that woman who handled her own ecstasy with such vigour, must be a woman who was accustomed to paying with money, and almost certainly she would end up by rewarding her angel with a cheque, also bearing in mind that the rain must have washed away all my distinction. With a little more consoling cynicism, I silently informed her that money would be as legitimate a way as any other of thanking me, since her money was really money. Or — I thought in amusement — she could easily give her dress for the *première* as a token of her gratitude, because what she really ought to be grateful for was not that she had protected her dress from the rain, but that she had attained a state of grace through me as it were. With ever mounting cynicism, I thought to myself: 'Everyone gets the angel they deserve, and just look at the angel she got: here I am, out of pure curiosity, coveting a dress which I have never seen. Now let's see how her soul is going to conform to the idea of an angel who is interested in dresses.' It struck me in my arrogance, that I had no desire to be assigned as an angel to the fervid stupidity of that woman.

To be frank, being an angel was beginning to weigh upon me. I am all too familiar with the ways of the world: they call me good-hearted, and at least for some time I am disturbed by my own malice. I also began to understand why angels get upset: they are at everybody's beck and call. This had never occurred to me before. Unless I happened to be an angel rather low down in the hierarchy of angels. Who knows, perhaps I was just a novice angel. The complacent happiness of that woman began to depress me: she had exploited me to the full. She had converted my indecisive nature into a definite profession, she had transformed my spontaneity into an obligation, she had enslaved me, I who was an angel. Who knows, however, if I had not been sent into the world just for that moment of usefulness. This then, was my true worth. In the taxi I was not a fallen angel: I was an angel who came to her senses. I came to my senses and showed my displeasure. Any more nonsense and I would tell that woman in open revolt whose guardian angel I was: do me the favour of getting out of this taxi at once! But I curbed my tongue and supported the weight of my wings which felt ever more contrite because of the woman's enormous parcel. As my protegée, she continued to say nice things about me, or rather, about my function. I fumed inwardly. The woman sensed this and fell silent as if confused. By the time we reached Viveiros de Castro there was mute hostility between us.

— Listen, I said to her abruptly, because my spontaneity is a double-edged knife even for others, the taxi will drop me first then take you on.

— But, she said in surprise, a note of indignation creeping into her voice, then I shall have to make an enormous detour and end up by being late! You, on the other hand, would only have the slightest detour if you were to drop me off first.

— Of course, I replied dryly. But I will not allow any detours.

—I'll pay the whole fare! she insulted me with the same money with which she would have remembered to reward me.

— I shall pay the whole fare, I insulted her in return.

Upon alighting from the taxi, like someone who asks for nothing, I took great care to leave my wings folded on the taxi seat. I alighted with that profound lack of finesse which has saved me from angelical abysses. Free of wings, with a great swish of my invisible tail and with the hauteur which I reserve for taxi-drivers, I swept through the imposing entrance of the Visconde de Pelotas apartment block as regal as a queen.

AN IMAGE OF PLEASURE

I have a very nice picture in my mind, which I can conjure up at will, and it invariably comes back to me in its entirety. It is the image of a forest, and in that forest I can see a green clearing, plunged into semi-darkness and surrounded by elevations, and in the midst of this pleasing darkness there are innumerable butterflies, and a tawny lion is reclining, while I sit knitting on the ground nearby. The hours pass like countless years, and the years pass in reality; the butterflies are replete with great wings and the tawny lion is speckled but the speckles are only there to make me see that he is tawny, and from the speckles I can see what the lion would look like if he were not tawny. The nice thing about this image is the darkness, which demands nothing beyond my powers of vision.

And there I sit with butterfly and lion. My clearing has a number of mineral ores which are colours. There is only one threat: to know with dread that outside the clearing I am lost. Because it will no longer be the forest (the forest I know beforehand, out of love) but only an empty field (which I know beforehand, out of fear) — so empty that I might just as easily go in one direction as in the other, a wilderness so void of protection and ground-colour that I should never be able to find an animal there that would be mine. I put my fears aside, take a deep breath to regain my composure and settle down to enjoy my intimacy with the lion and the butterflies; we do not think, we simply enjoy. I, too, am not in black and white; without being able to see myself, I know that for these creatures I am coloured; without exceeding their powers of vision (for I give no cause for disquiet). I am speckled with blue and green which only shows that I am neither blue nor green — behold what I am not. The shadows are of a moist, dark green. I know that I have mentioned this already, but I am repeating it out of my zest for happiness: I want the same thing over and over again. So that, as I have been perceiving and saying, there we are. And we are extremely contented. Frankly, I have never felt so contented. Why? I do not wish to know why. Each one of us is in his right place, and I submit quite happily to being in my right place. I am even about to start repeating myself again, for things are getting better all the time: the tawny lion and the silent butterflies, while I sit on the ground knitting, and we are thoroughly enjoying our clearing in the forest. We are happy.

SILENT NIGHT, HOLY NIGHT

In Natal, Rio Grande do Norte, I woke up in the middle of the night, as peaceful as if I were awakening from a peaceful bout of insomnia. And I heard ethereal music which I had heard once before. It was extremely sweet and without any melody, yet it consisted of sounds which could be orchestrated into melody. It was undulating and uninterrupted. The sounds emerged like fifteen thousand stars. I felt certain that I was capturing the most primitive vibrations of air, as if silence were speaking. Silence was speaking. It had a low and constant pitch without any edginess, and it was criss-crossed with horizontal, oblique sounds. Thousands of resonances which had the same pitch and the same intensity, the same relaxed pace, a night of bliss.

It resembled a trailing veil of sound, with variations largely of shadow and light, sometimes of density (such as when the veil fluttered and folded over). The music was incredibly beautiful, and impossible to describe because there are no words to denote silence. The composer's presence was not felt; only angels in countless groups, impersonal as angels, anonymous as angels. When silence manifests itself, there is no warning; silence simply manifests itself in silence. As if you were to ask: what is the number 1357217? And this number were to come forward and reveal itself as 1357217. Silence can achieve the maximum: by becoming evident. And so my hotel room was inundated with the choral song of silence which became evident. And I was blessed in this manner. But I have no desire to renew the experience.

THE RESTORATION OF A LADY

She was born in the Castle of Possonnière in the Loire Valley. Her dress pleated from a high waistband, her long tresses scarcely ever washed. She was spinning flax. The castle set amongst woodlands. The green moon like an ambuscade. Nightingales and a well. Her voice humming ever so softly. The vast territory was divided into military regions. Ruddy-complexioned servants were grooming the horses. Great iron keys. The wind was blowing, and in the shadows the lady's pristine couch. Dogs in the courtyard: some fifteen were barking. The blacksmith at his forge, the bellows and the anvil, the hammering of metal. Galloping horsemen approached in a cloud of dust; they alighted. Forming a garland around the well, the daisies tremble in the breeze. Copper and silver. The avuncular bishop. The golden chalice. A visit from her spiritual mentor: his hands crossed on his lap. Her epoch was her life. Deceased in the year 1513, buried in the chapel in the forest: one hundred years later her bones were transferred, and subsequently transferred anew. Until all that remained of her was the castle in which she lived and the beautiful valley of the Loire. And in the museum, signed *By an anonymous artist sec. XVI*, a vase the lady had painted one day: now a relic of the decorative arts of her epoch.

ITALIAN VILLAGE

The men have crimson lips and produce offspring. The women become deformed from breast-feeding. As for the elderly, the elderly do not betray any emotion. The work is strenuous. The night, silent. There are no cinemas. On the threshold, the beauty of a young woman is to remain there standing in the dark. Life is sad and abundant as one would expect life to be in the mountains.

CONVERSATION WITH MY SON

— You know, Mummy, sometimes I feel I'd like to experience what it's like being mad.

— Whatever for? (I know, I know what you are going to say, for through me my great grandfather must have said the same; I know that it takes fifteen generations to form a single person, and that this future person has used me like a bridge and is now using my son, and will use the son of my son, like a bird perched on an arrow which is slowly advancing.)

— In order to free myself, then I could be free . . .

(But can there be freedom without first having experienced madness? We cannot experience it just yet: we are only the progressive stages of madness, of this person who is coming.)

SUMMER IN THE DRAWING ROOM

With her fan she ponders something. She ponders the fan and with the fan she fans herself. And with her fan she suddenly arrests her thoughts with a sharp click, vacant, smiling, taut, distracted. The fan, distracted and open over her bosom. 'Life is really very amusing' she agrees like a visitor being received in the drawing-room. But suppressing her excitement, she suddenly starts fanning herself with a thousand sparrow wings.

A DISCREET MAN

God has bestowed innumerable small gifts upon him which he has neither used nor developed for fear of becoming perfect and ostentatious.

STYLE

— What's that?

— It's a petition.

— Did you write it? Let me see. 'The undersigned requests of your Excellency . . .' Good heavens, Mummy, you've never written with such elegance.

FIVE DAYS IN BRASILIA

Brasilia is built on the line of the horizon. — Brasilia is artificial. As artificial as the world must have been when it was
created. When the world was created, it was necessary to
create a human being especially for that world. We are all
deformed through adapting to God's freedom. We cannot say
how we might have turned out if we had been created first, and
the world had been deformed afterwards to meet our needs.
Brasilia has no inhabitants as yet who are typical of Brasilia. If I
were to say that Brasilia is pleasant, you would realize immediately that I like the city. But if I were to say that Brasilia is
the image of my insomnia, you would see this as a criticism:
but my insomnia is neither pleasant nor awful: my insomnia is
I, it is lived, it is my terror. The two architects[1] who planned
Brasilia were not interested in creating something beautiful.
That would be too simple; they created their own terror, and
left that terror unexplained. Creation is not an understanding,
it is a new mystery. — When I died, I opened my eyes one day
and there was Brasilia. I found myself alone in the world.
There was a stationary taxi. Without any driver — Lúcio
Costa and Oscar Niemeyer are two solitary men. — I look at
Brasilia the way I look at Rome: Brasilia began with a final
simplification of ruins. The ivy had not yet grown. — Besides
the wind there is another thing which blows. — It can only be
recognized in the supernatural rippling of the lake. — Wherever you stand, you have the impression of being on the
margin of a dangerous precipice. Brasilia stands on the
margin. — Were I to live here, I should let my hair grow down
to my feet. — Brasilia belongs to a glorious past which no
longer exists. That type of civilization disappeared thousands
of years ago. In the 4th century B.C., Brasilia was inhabited by
men and women who were fair and very tall, who were
neither American nor Scandinavian, and who shone brightly
in the sun. They were all blind. That explains why there is

---

[1] Lúcio Costa (1902–   ) and Oscar Niemeyer (1907–   ), the two Brazilian
architects who prepared and supervised the pilot-plan for the creation of
Brasilia in 1957.

nothing to collide with in Brasilia. The inhabitants of Brasilia dressed in white gold. The race became extinct because few children were born. The more beautiful the natives of Brasilia, the more blind, pure, and radiant they became, and the fewer children they produced. The natives of Brasilia lived for nearly three hundred years. There was no one in whose name they could die. Thousands of years later the location was discovered by a band of fugitives who would not be accepted in any other place; they had nothing to lose. There they lit a bonfire, set up their tents, and gradually began excavating the sands which buried the city. Those men and women were short and dark-skinned, with shifty, restless eyes, and because they were fugitives and desperate, there was someone in whose name they could both live and die. They occupied the houses which were in ruins and multiplied themselves, thus forming a human race which was much given to contemplation — I awaited the night, like someone awaiting the shadows in order to steal away unobserved. When the night came, I perceived with horror that it was hopeless: wherever I might go, I should be seen. The thought terrified me: seen by whom? — The city was built without any escape route for rats. A whole part of myself, the worst part, and precisely that part of me which has a horror of rats, has not been provided for in Brasilia. Its founders tried to ignore the importance of human beings. The dimensions of the city's buildings were calculated for the heavens. Hell has a better understanding of me. But the rats, all of them enormous, are invading the city. That is an invisible headline in the newspapers. — Here I am afraid. — The construction of Brasilia: that of a totalitarian state. — This great visual silence which I love. Even my insomnia might have created this peace of never-never-land. Like those two monks, I would also meditate in the desert where there are no opportunities for temptation. But I see black vultures flying high overhead. What is perishing, dear God? — I did not shed a single tear in Brasilia. There was no place for tears. — It is a shore without any sea. — In Brasilia there is no place where one may enter, no place where one may leave.

Mummy, it's nice to see you standing there with your white cape waving in the breeze. (The truth is that I have perished, my son.) — A prison in the open air. Besides, there is nowhere to escape to. For anyone escaping would probably find himself heading for Brasilia. They ensnared me in freedom. But freedom is simply what is conquered. When they strike me, they are ordering me to be free. — The human indifference which lurks in my nature is something I discover here in Brasilia, and it flowers cold and patient, the cold strength of Nature. Here is the place where my crimes (not the worst of them, but those which I should fail to recognize in myself) — where my cold crimes find sufficient scope. I am leaving. Here my crimes would not be crimes of love. I am leaving for my other crimes, those which God and I understand. But I know that I shall return. I am drawn here by all that is terrifying in my nature. — I have never seen anything like it in the world. But I recognize this city at the very core of my dream. The core of my dream is lucidity. — For as I was saying, Flash Gordon . . . — If they were to photograph me standing in Brasilia, upon developing the film only the landscape would emerge. — Where are the giraffes of Brasilia? — A certain twitching on my part, certain moments of silence, provoke my son into commenting: Gosh, grown-ups are the limit. — It is urgent. Were Brasilia not populated, or rather, not over-populated, it would be inhabited in some other way. And should that happen, it would be much too late: there would be no place for people. They would feel themselves tacitly expelled. — Here the soul casts no shadow on the ground. During the first two days I had no appetite. Everything had the appearance of the food they serve on board aeroplanes. — At night, I turned my face towards silence. I know that there is a secret hour when manna falls and moistens the lands of Brasilia. — However close one is, everything here is seen from afar. I have found no means of touching it. But at least there is one thing in my favour: before arriving here, I already knew how to touch things from afar. I never became too desperate: from afar, I was able to touch things. I possessed a great deal, and not even that which I have touched, suspects this. A rich woman is like that. It is pure Brasilia. — The city of Brasilia lies outside the city. — 'Boys, boys come here, will you. Look who's coming on the street, all dressed up in modernistic style. It ain't nobody but . . .' (*Aunt Hagar's Blues*, played by Ted Lewis and his Band, with Jimmy Dorsey on the clarinet.) —

That astonishing beauty, this city traced out in the air. — Meantime, no samba is likely to emerge in Brasilia. — Brasilia does not permit me to feel weary. It persecutes me to some extent. I feel fine. I feel fine. I feel fine. I feel just fine. Besides, I have always cultivated my weariness, as my most precious manifestation of inertia. — Everything just for today. God alone knows what will happen to Brasilia. Here the fortuitous takes one by surprise — Brasilia is haunted. It is the motionless profile of something. — Unable to sleep. I look out of my hotel window at three o'clock in the morning. Brasilia is a landscape of insomnia. It never sleeps. — Here the organic being does not disintegrate. It becomes petrified. — I should like to see five hundred eagles of the blackest onyx scattered throughout Brasilia. — Brasilia is asexual. — The first time you set eyes on the city you feel inebriated: your feet do not touch the ground. — How deeply the people breathe in Brasilia. Anyone who breathes here starts to experience desire. And that is to be avoided. Desire does not exist here. Will it ever exist? I cannot see how. — It would not surprise me to encounter Arabs on the street. Arabs of another age and long since dead. — Here my passion dies. And I gain lucidity which makes me feel grandiose for no good reason. I am immense and futile, I am of the purest gold. And almost endowed with a medium's powers. — If there is still some crime which humanity has not committed, that new crime will be initiated here. It is so very open, so well adjusted to the plateau, that no one will ever know. This is the place where space most closely resembles time. — I am certain that this is the right place for me. But I have become much too corrupted on earth. I have acquired all of life's bad habits. — Erosion will strip Brasilia to the bone. — The religious atmosphere which I sensed from the outset, and denied. This city was achieved through prayer. Two men beatified by solitude created me here, on foot, restless, exposed to the wind. — One greatly longs to see white horses unleashed in Brasilia. At night, they would change to green under the light of the moon — I know what those two men wanted: that peace and silence which also conform to my idea of eternity. Those two men created the image of an eternal city. — There is something here which frightens me. When I shall discover what it is, I shall also discover what I like about this place. Fear has always guided me to the things I love; and because I love, I am afraid. It was often fear which took me by the hand and led me. Fear leads me to danger. And everything I love has an element of risk. —

In Brasilia you find the craters of the Moon. — The beauty of Brasilia is to be found in those invisible statues.

SUNDAY, BEFORE FALLING ASLEEP

On Sunday evenings, the entire family would go to the pier to watch the ships. They would lean over the buttresses and, if Father were alive today, perhaps he would still be watching those oily waters which he used to examine so intently. His daughters became vaguely restless, they would summon him to come and look at something more interesting: look at the ships, Daddy! they would point out to him impatiently. As darkness fell, the illumined city turned into a great metropolis with high revolving stools in every café. The youngest daughter insisted upon sitting on one of those high stools and Father found this amusing. This was great fun. Then the child would demand more attention and it was no longer quite so amusing. She chose something to drink which was not expensive, although the revolving stool increased the price of everything. The rest of the family stood around, waiting. A child's timid and voracious reaching out for happiness. This was when she discovered the Ovaltine they served in cafés. Never before had she experienced such luxury in a tall glass, made all the taller because of the froth on top, the stool high and wobbly, as she sat *on top of the world*. Everyone was waiting. The first few sips almost made her sick, but she forced herself to empty the glass. The disturbing reponsibility of an unfortunate choice; forcing herself to enjoy what must be enjoyed, and thus adding the indecisiveness of a rabbit to her other character defects. There was also the startling suspicion that *Ovaltine* is good: it is I who am no good. She fibbed, insisting that her drink was delicious because the others were standing there watching her enjoy the luxury of happiness which cost money: was it dependent on her that they should believe or not in a better world? But she was extricated from this problem by her father, and she felt safe inside this small territory where to stroll holding hands constituted her family. On the way home, her father quipped: without actually having done anything, we have spent so much money.

Before falling asleep, in bed, in the dark. Through the window, on the white wall: the huge, swaying shadows of the branches, as if they belonged to some enormous tree, which in reality did not exist in the patio. All that grew there was a straggly shrub: or perhaps it was the moon's shadow. Sunday was always that immense night which generated all the other Sundays and generated cargo ships and generated oily water and generated a milky drink with froth and generated the moon and the gigantic shadow of a tiny shrub.

BECAUSE I AM IN LOVE

The spring is really dry, the radio crackles absorbing its static, clothing bristles as it sheds the body's electricity, and the comb lifts magnetized hairs; it is a cruel spring. And completely empty. From every point, you have the impression of going far away: never has a road seemed so long. There is little conversation: the body is weighed down with sleep; eyes in general are large and inexpressive. On the terrace, the goldfish gyrates in its tank; we sip our drinks looking at the countryside. The wind transports the dreams of goats from the fields. On the other table on the terrace, there is a solitary fawn. We dream in ecstasy, looking into the glasses in our hands. 'What?' 'I didn't say anything.' The days go by. But one moment of harmony is enough to capture anew the barbed static of spring: the insolent dreams of goats, the hollow fish, a sudden desire to steal something, the fawn acclaimed in solitary leaps. 'What?' 'I didn't say anything.'

But I can hear a murmur, like a heart beating below the

earth. Quickly, I put my ear to the ground and can hear the summer break through inside, and my heart beats below the earth — nothing, I said nothing — and I can sense the patient brutality with which the sealed earth is opening up inside, and I know with what burden of sweetness the summer will ripen a hundred thousand oranges, and I know that those oranges are mine, because I am in love.

THE ART OF NOT BEING GREEDY

— Moi, madame, j'aime manger juste avant le faim. Ça fait plus distingué.

PATIO IN GRAJAÚ

In the Northern Zone a warm wind blows. In the patio five girls with pale skin have already taken their afternoon bathe, and are drying their hair in the sirocco wind. They have black eyes, shapely arms and colourless lips. They are the daughters of the household. Why speak? Sit down and play your guitars. There is nothing to say to them. In that household there is nothing to salvage. Nor does everything mean something (that is as important as the opposite). They are five girls with colourless lips whom I leave in the patio itself, and let them remain there. And, if they do not wish to remain, then let them depart. Five girls with pale skin symbolize five girls without colour. I observe this harem of colourless lips, and without cruelty or love, I submit them to the laws of survival. Indulging neither in politics nor poetry, I find it neither right nor wrong: it is so.

But the sirocco will surely bring horses and sandstorms.

THE HAPPY COOK AND THE MIGHT OF SINCERITY

'Sweet Teresa, I love you. You are always in my heart. From the moment I first set eyes on you, my heart was captivated by your charms. On seeing you so tender and beautiful, my soul was troubled, for until that moment my life had been empty and sad. Suddenly my soul filled with light and hope, and the flame of love burned in my heart. You aroused such feelings of love. Teresa, my beloved, my heart is illumined by your purity and there you will discover the might of my sincerity. We shall find such happiness together one day, our hearts beating together, united by the joys and sorrows of life. Your warm heart to comfort me, your pure soul to adore me. I raise to heaven a sweet ballad of love dedicated to my beloved Teresa, who is always in my dreams. From your ever adoring Edgar. I beseech a reply from my beloved Teresa. My address is: Estrada São Luiz, 30-C, Santa Cruz.'

SOCIAL COLUMN

. . . The lunch is perfect, perfect, perfect. It could be transported in its entirety — table, guests, food, waiters — to another household, perhaps even to another country (it knows no frontiers, as one might say in discussing a work of art). And the awareness that the avoidance of any *faux pas* is up to each and every one of us. Does a reunion mean a reunion around a *faux pas* which is not committed? The tension of perfection growing, the drum-skin stretching. An exciting risk. For each and every one of us, the *faux pas* which is not committed. What *faux pas* in the end? I. Everyone is his or her own silent *faux pas*. Which beneath that dreamy smile sadistically attracts, attracts, attracts. I am drawing nearer and nearer, in the smiling torture of a nightmare. One more minute, one more second — and — I emerge. Amidst the brandy and the smoke, tightly stretched perfection becomes ever more tenuous. Truly, a dangerous sport.

LIVING JELLY

I dreamt about a sad apparition. There was a jelly which was alive. What were the jelly's feelings? — silence. Alive and silent, the jelly dragged itself with difficulty to the table, descending and rising, slowly, without toppling over. Who grabbed it? No one had the courage. When I looked at it, I saw my own face mirrored there, slowly merging with the jelly's existence. My essential deformation. Deformed without toppling over. I, too, barely alive. Plunged into horror, I wanted to escape the jelly; I went on to the terrace, prepared to throw myself from my top-floor apartment on to the Rua Marquês de Abrantes. From the terrace I looked into the pitch-black night, and I felt gripped by fear at the thought of my approaching end: everything which is much too strong appears to be approaching some end. But before jumping, I decided to put on some lipstick. It struck me that my lipstick was curiously soft. I then realized that my lipstick, too, was living jelly. And there I stood on the dark terrace, my lips moistened by this living substance. My legs were already over the edge and I was just about to let go, when suddenly I saw a pair of eyes in the darkness. The darkness was watching me with two enormous eyes set wide apart. So the darkness, too, was alive. Where could I find death? Death was living jelly. Everything was alive. Everything is alive, primary, slow, involved; everything is fundamentally immortal.

With almost insuperable difficulty, I succeeded in rousing myself, as if I were pulling myself by the hair in order to escape from this living quagmire. I opened my eyes. The room was in darkness, but it was a familiar darkness, not the profound darkness from which I had dragged myself. I felt more peaceful. It had all been a dream. But I noticed that one of my arms was exposed. With a start, I pulled it under the sheet: no part of me should be exposed, if I still hoped to save myself. Did I want to save myself? I think I did: so I switched on the light. And I saw the room with its solid outlines. I had hardened the living jelly into a wall, I had hardened the living jelly into a ceiling; I had murdered everything that could be murdered, in my efforts to restore the peace of death around me; fleeing from what was worse than death: pure life, the living jelly. I switched off the light. Suddenly a cockerel crowed. A cockerel in an apartment block? A hoarse cockerel. In that white-washed building, a living cockerel? Outside, a freshly-painted house, and inside that cry? thus spoke the Book. Outside death accomplished, clean, definitive — but inside the living jelly. This was what I learned at dead of night.

SOME USELESS EXPLANATIONS[1]

It is not always easy to recall how and why I came to write a particular story or novel. Once they leave my pen, I too find them surprising and even strange. It is not a question of having been in a 'trance', but the degree of concentration required in writing is such that it seems to take away all consciousness of everything extraneous to the actual writing. Some details, however, I can try to reconstruct, in the hope that they might be relevant and of some interest to my readers.

What I remember of the story entitled 'Happy Birthday', for example, is the impression of a birthday party that was not so very different from any other birthday party. I recall that it was held on a hot summer's day although I make no mention of summer in the story itself. I received an 'impression' and this resulted in a few vague lines being jotted down in haste in the hope that one day I might be able to probe further into the feelings I experienced. Years later, upon rediscovering those lines, the entire story was suddenly born and written with the speed of someone faithfully transcribing a scene in every detail — although nothing of what I wrote had actually occurred at that or any other birthday party. Some considerable time afterwards, a friend asked me to identify the old lady in the story. I explained that she was someone else's grandmother.

---

[1] Clarice Lispector refers here to her collection of short stories *Laços de Família* (1960), translated into English as *Family Ties* (University of Texas Press 1984; Carcanet Press 1985).

But two days later to my utter astonishment the real answer to the question came to me: I discovered that the old lady was my very own grandmother whom I had never seen or known apart from a portrait seen as a child.

'Mystery in São Cristóvão' remains a mystery. I began writing the story as tranquilly as someone unwinding a bobbin of thread. I did not experience the slightest difficulty and I believe that the absence of any technical problems may have resulted from the conception itself of the narrative. The very atmosphere in this story dictated a mood of detachment even to the point of non-participation. The remarkable ease with which I developed the theme might well have stemmed from the *internal technique* and my individual treatment of the central episode with its emphasis upon delicacy and feigned distraction.

As for 'The Daydreams of a Drunk Woman', I can confidently say that I have rarely enjoyed anything so much. While writing this story, I was in a most happy frame of mind and, although others failed to notice, I even found myself speaking like the Portuguese woman in the narrative. 'The Daydreams of a Drunk Woman' involved me in a novel linguistic experience and I enjoyed myself enormously.

Of the circumstances surrounding 'Family Ties', the title story of the collection, I remember nothing.

About the writing of 'Love', two things come to mind. One is the intensity with which I suddenly identified with the woman in the sinister Botanical Garden, where we almost found ourselves trapped — ambushed and semi-hypnotized as we were — so that I had to force my woman character to summon the park attendant in a state of hysteria; otherwise we might still be locked up together in that park even now. The second thing I can clearly remember is a friend reading the manuscript of the story aloud in a familiar voice in order to allow me to assess its merits. Suddenly I felt that only at that moment was my story being born, perfectly formed as the child is born. This was the greatest moment of all: the story was given to me there and then and I received it, or I gave it and it was received, or both things happened, since they are one and the same thing. I have nothing to reveal about 'The Dinner'.

'The Chicken' was written in about thirty minutes. I had been asked to write a chronicle. I tried half-heartedly to comply and finished up submitting nothing. Then one day I observed that what I had written constituted a complete narrative and that it had been written with enormous love and care. 'The Chicken' betrays the affection which I have always felt towards animals, whom I find more congenial than human beings.

'The Beginnings of a Fortune' was written as an experiment. I was curious to see what would emerge if I attempted a technique of such extreme simplicity that it would barely intermingle with the plot. The story was elaborated almost with indifference and my pen was guided by curiosity alone.

One more exercise on the scales.

I find 'Preciousness' somewhat irritating and I finished up by disliking intensely the young girl in the narrative. At one point I felt like asking her forgiveness for my dislike only to back out at the eleventh hour. In the end, I tried to sort out her life, more in order to ease my conscience and discharge my responsibility than out of love. But to write in this manner is simply not worth the effort. It involves one in quite the wrong way and exhausts one's patience. I now feel that even if I could make something worthwhile out of this story, intrinsically it would still be unsatisfactory.

'The Imitation of the Rose' made use of several fathers and mothers in order to be born. There was the initial shock upon hearing the news about someone who had fallen seriously ill and I failed to understand why. On that same day, I received a bunch of roses which I shared with a friend. And there were other details which I no longer remember and which form the sap of any narrative. 'The Imitation of the Rose' gave me an opportunity to use a monochromatic tone which I find most pleasing: repetition always gratifies me, for the deliberate use of repetition denotes a gradual process of penetration, an insistent cantilena which has something to express.

'The Crime of the Mathematics Professor' was first published with the title of 'The Crime'. Years later, I realized that the story seemed unfinished. So I decided to write it again. Somehow the impression lingers that the story is still unfinished. To this day I do not understand the Mathematics

Professor, although I am convinced that he is exactly as I have described him.

'The Smallest Woman in the World' reminds me of Sunday, of spring in Washington, of a child asleep in my arms while taking a stroll, the first warm days in May — while 'The Smallest Woman in the World' (an article read in a newspaper) intensified all these impressions in a location which I consider to be the world's birthplace — Africa.

I am convinced that this narrative, too, stems from my affection for animals: I tend to regard them as the species closest to God, matter which did not invent itself, something still warm from its own birth — yet something already on its feet and totally alive, living each moment to the full rather than taking life in easy stages, never sparing itself and virtually inexhaustible.

'The Buffalo' vaguely reminds me of the expression I once saw on a woman's face, perhaps several women or even men; the story also reminds me of one of the countless visits I used to make to the zoological gardens. On this occasion, a tiger stared at me and I stared back. He sustained his gaze while I was obliged to turn my eyes away, and I can see him staring at me even now. The story itself bears no relation to this episode. It was written and put to one side. One day, I read it again and suddenly felt quite uneasy and horrified.

EAT UP, MY BOY

— The world appears to be flat but I know that it is otherwise.

— . . .

— Do you know why it appears to be flat? Because, wherever you look, the sky is always above, never below, or to one side. I know that the world is round because I have been told that it is so, but it would only appear to be round if you were to look and find that sometimes the sky is down there below. I know that it is round, but for me it is flat, but Ronaldo only knows that the world is round, for him it does not appear to be flat.

— . . .

— For I have been to many countries, and I have observed that even in the United States the sky is up above. Therefore, the world has always struck me as being on a straight line. But Ronaldo has never been abroad and he probably thinks that it is only here in Brazil that the sky is above and that in other countries it is either below or to one side. He probably thinks that the world is only flat in Brazil, and that in other countries which he has never visited it becomes round. When people tell him something, it is simply a question of believing them, for him nothing has to appear either one thing or another. Do you prefer a soup plate or a dinner plate?

— Dinn . . . — I mean a soup plate.

— So do I. A soup plate gives the impression of holding more, but that is only because of its depth; with a dinner plate the food rests on the sides and one can see at a glance how much it will hold. Don't you find cucumber somewhat unreal?

— Unreal.

— Why should you think that?

— That's what people say.

— No. Why should you think that cucumber looks unreal? I once thought so, too. One looks and sees something of the other side, the overall appearance is uniform, it feels cold in your mouth, it sounds a little like glass being crushed when you chew it. Don't you think that cucumber looks invented?

— Yes, it does.

— Where were black beans and rice invented?[1]

— Here in Brazil.

— Or in Arabia, as Pedrinho said about something else?

— Here in Brazil.

— In the Café Gatão the ice cream is delicious because it has a taste to match its colour. Do you find that meat tastes like meat?

---

[1] *Feijoada*. Brazil's national dish of black beans stewed with various kinds of meats, sausages and tripe, served with rice, kale, manioc meal and onions. (There are regional variations to the ingredients and accompanying dishes.)

— Sometimes.

— I don't believe you! Prove it! . . . Does it taste of the meat hanging up in the butcher's shop?

— No.

— Not even of the meat we were talking about. It doesn't have that taste you talk about when you say that meat has vitamins.

— Don't chatter so much, eat up.

— But when you keep looking at me, it's not to make me eat up; it's because you love me dearly. Am I right or wrong?

— You're right. Eat up, Paulinho.

— All you think about is food. I've been chatting all the time to keep your mind off food but that's all you ever think about.

SUBMISSION TO THE PROCESS

The process of writing consists of errors — most of them necessary — of courage and indolence, despair and hope, of growing awareness, of sustained feeling (not thought) which leads nowhere, leads nowhere, and suddenly what you thought was 'nothingness' turns out to be your own terrifying contact with the fabric of life. That moment of recognition, that nameless submersion in a nameless fabric, that moment of recognition (akin to revelation) must be received with the greatest innocence, with the same innocence with which we are born. The process of writing is difficult? That is like defining as difficult the extremely capricious and natural manner in which a flower is formed. (As my little boy pointed out to me: the sea is beautiful, green and with blue, and with waves! It's all *naturalised*! Nobody manufactured it!) The monstrous impatience as you work at something (standing beside a plant to watch it grow yet without seeing anything) is not in relation to the thing itself, but to the monstrous patience you must exercise (for the plant grows at night). As if I were to say to myself: 'I cannot bear to be patient for another moment', 'the patience of the watchmaker puts my nerves on edge', etc.

What makes me most impatient of all is that tedious, germinating patience: the ox pulling the plough.

THE WOMAN BURNED AT THE STAKE AND THE HARMONIOUS ANGELS

Invisible angels: Behold we are almost there, travelling the long road which existed before your time. But we are not weary, for our route requires no effort, and were it to demand vigour, not even that of your plea would sustain us. It is vertigo alone which makes us swirl and wail like leaves before the advent of some birth. How can we know if vertigo suffices? If men mistrust men and angels ignore angels; the world is immense and blessed be all that it embraces. We are not weary, our feet have not been washed. Chuckling at the thought of pleasures to come, we watch suffer what must be suffered, we who have not yet been touched, we who are not yet children. We are enmeshed in a real tragedy, from which we shall extract our primary form. When we open our eyes after birth, we shall remember nothing: we shall be babbling infants and we shall wield your own weapons. Blind on the route which precedes our footsteps, blind we shall advance where we are born with seeing eyes. Nor can we explain why we have come. All we need know is that what must be done, will be done: an angel's downfall orientates us . . . Our true origin precedes our visible origin, and our true demise will come after our visible demise. Harmony, some harmony, is our only previous destiny.

Priest: I have not lost myself in loving the Lord. I am ever secure in Your day as in Your night. This simple woman lost herself for so little and lost her own nature. Behold how she is dispossessed of everything and, now pure, they will burn all that remains to her. Strange paths exist. She consumed her destiny by surrendering her entire being to one sin: now behold her on the threshold of salvation. Every way, however humble, is a way: vile sin is a way, ignorance of the commandments is a way, lust is a way. The only thing which was not a way was my premature happiness as I followed the sacred way with such ease. The only thing which was not a way was that I should think myself safe half-way along the road. Lord, grant me the grace to sin. The freedom from temptation which you bestowed on me is too onerous a burden. Where is the water and the fire through which I have never passed? Lord, grant me the grace to sin. This candle which I have embodied and lit in Your holy name, has always burned in the light, yet I have seen nothing. But let hope open the gates of Your violent heaven: I now perceive that, if you did not destine me to be a burning torch, at least you have destined me to set the torch alight. Ah hope, wherein I still see pride at being elected: confessing my guilt, I strike my breast and with a happiness which I would wish mortified I say: The Lord has ordained me to sin more than this woman, and at last I shall consume my tragedy. For You exploited my angry tirade so that I might not only commit sin, but the sin of punishing sin. So that I might descend so low from this dangerous peace of mine, let total darkness — where no candelabra, nor papal purple, nor even the symbol of the Cross are to be found — let total darkness be You. For as is written in the Psalms: 'Thou shalt not be afraid for the terror by night . . .' '. . . the eyes of the blind shall see out of obscurity, and out of darkness.'

People: For days now we have suffered hunger and have come in search of food.

The sinner enters between two guards.

Priest: 'She took her pleasure as the slave of her senses', by the sign of the Holy Cross.

People: Behold her! Behold her! Behold her!

Drowsy child: Behold her!

Woman in the crowd: Behold her! She is the woman who sinned, the woman who, in order to sin, needed two men, a priest, and the people.

First Guard: We are the guardians of the fatherland. We are suffocating from this oppressive peace, and we have even forgotten the bugle calls of the last campaign we fought. Our beloved king assigns us to positions of the utmost trust, but with all this useless waiting, we have almost lost our manliness. Destined to die with glory, we live here in shame.

Second Guard: We are the guardians of a Lord whose domain is somewhat confusing: one minute it extends to the frontiers marked by custom and usage, and then we raise our lances to a flourish of bugles. The next minute, the same domain penetrates into lands where an older law prevails. So here we are guarding what, in its own right, will always be guarded by the people and by destiny. Under this sky of stifling calm, there may be a dearth of bread, but the mystery of achievement will never be wanting. So what do we imagine ourselves to be guarding here unless it be the destiny of a heart?

First Guard: How those closing words of yours remind me of the cannon's echoes. Such longing to guard a smaller world at last where our lances might wound unto death all that is destined to die. But here we are guarding a woman who, in a manner of speaking, has already been burned by her own hand.

Invisible angels: Burned by harmony, by that sweet, gory harmony which is our previous destiny.

The Husband enters.

People: Here is the husband, the man who was betrayed.

Husband: Behold her, the woman who is about to be burned to appease my anger. Who has spoken through me to have given me such deadly power? It was I who incited the priest's words, who assembled the troops of this people, who raised the lances of the guards, and gave such an air of glory to this courtyard that it has brought down the walls. Ah, wife whom I still adore, how I should like to be rid of this invasion. I dreamed of being alone with you and of recalling the happiness we once shared. Leave her alone with me, for since yesterday I live but do not live; leave her alone with me. In your presence — strangers to my former joy and to my present misfortune — I no longer recognize in this woman she who was mine yet was not mine; nor in our former rejoicing, she who was ours yet was not ours; nor can I feel the bitterness that this woman is mine and only mine. What is happening to this heart of mine, which no longer recognizes the fruits of its Revenge? Ah remorse: I should have brandished the dagger with my own hand, and then I should know that, if I were the man betrayed, I would also be the man revenged. But this scene is no longer part of my world, and this woman, whom I received in chastity, I now lose to a fanfare of trumpets. Leave me alone with the sinner. I wish to regain my former love, then become sated with loathing, then assassinate her myself, then adore her once more, and then nevermore forget her. Leave me alone with the sinner. I want to enjoy my misfortune and my revenge and my loss, and all of you are preventing me from being master of this holocaust. Leave me alone with the sinner.

Priest: Many years have passed since a saint was born. Many years have passed since a child prophesied from the cradle. For many years the blind man has not seen and the leper has not been healed. Ah, such barren times! We are under the cloud of a great mystery, which will be revealed in a flash to whomever it may be directed. For Your awaited miracle must come to pass.

First Guard: Each man speaks and no one listens.

Second Guard: Each man is alone with the guilty woman.

The Lover enters.

First Guard: The farce is complete: Behold the lover, I am overjoyed.

People: Behold the lover! Behold the lover! Behold the lover!

Drowsy child: Behold the lover!

Lover: This irony which brings no mirth: to call lover, he who burned of love, to call lover, he who lost that love. No, no, he is not the lover. But the betrayed lover.

People: We do not understand. We do not understand. We do not understand.

Lover: This woman who deceived her husband in my embrace; in her husband's embrace deceived the lover who deceived her husband.

People: Because she then concealed her lover from her husband, and concealed her husband from her lover? Behold the sin of sins.

Lover: But I am not laughing and momentarily I do not even suffer. I open my eyes hitherto blinkered by conceit and I ask of you: who? Who is this strange woman, who is this solitary woman for whom one heart was not enough?

Husband: She is the woman for whom I brought silks and precious stones from my travels, and for whom all my commerce of worth became the commerce of love.

Lover: Radiant with happiness, she came to me with such perfection that I should never have suspected her to have come from any household.

Husband: There was no jewel which she did not covet, and which she did not enhance with her comeliness. There was nothing which I would have refused her because for the humble and weary traveller peace resides with his wife.

Priest: 'And a man's foes shall be they of his own household.'

Husband: In a diamond's transparency she was already scanning the arrival of a lover. He who told you is the man who tasted the poison: beware of a woman who dreams.

Lover: Ah, wretched woman, who was given to dreaming even when she lay at my side. What more was she craving then? Who is this strange woman?

Priest: She to whom on Holy Days I vainly addressed words of Virtue which might cover her nakedness with a thousand mantles.

Woman of the people: All these words have strange meanings.

Who is this woman who has sinned and appears to warrant praise rather than blame?

Lover: She is the mysterious woman who has unveiled nothing but sorrow to my eyes. For the first time, I am in love. I am in love with you.

Husband: She is the woman to whom sin tardily announced me. For the first time I love you while destroying my peace.

People: She is the woman who gave herself to no one, and now she is completely ours.

Invisible angels: The harmony is awesome.

People: We do not understand. We do not understand. We do not understand.

Invisible angels: Even from this remote place on the edge of the universe, we can barely understand, so what hope is there for you who are hungry, or you who are sated? Let the generative decree suffice: what must be done, will be done. This is the one perfect principle of law.

People: We do not understand. We are hungry. We are hungry.

First Guard: This troublesome populace. Perhaps if they were summoned to a feast or burial, they would sing . . .

People: . . . we are hungry.

Second Guard: It is always the same commotion and the same monotonous refrain . . .

People: . . . we are hungry.

Priest: No more complaints about hunger. Be silent now, for yours is the Kingdom of Heaven.

People: Where we shall eat, and eat and eat and become so overfed that eventually we shall be unable to pass through the eye of a needle.

Priest: What has brought the people here? What has brought the husband, the lover and the guards? For were she to be left alone with me, this woman would be burned at the stake.

Lover: What has brought the people here? For were she to be left alone with me, she would love me anew, she would sin anew, she would repent anew — and so in one brief moment Love would be fulfilled anew, that Love which carries both dagger and death. I shall remind you of these words at nightfall. The restless horse waited, a lantern shone in the courtyard . . . And then . . . ah earth, your fields began to dawn, a certain window lit up in the darkness. And then the wine which I drank with joy, even with tears in my inebriation. (So it is true that even in a state of joy, I tried to recapture in tears the former taste of misfortune.)

Invisible angels: The former taste of awesome harmony.

Drowsy child: The woman is smiling.

People: She is smiling. She is smiling. She is smiling.

Husband: And her bright eyes glisten as if she were enraptured . . .

Women of the people: Who can explain why this woman who is to be burned at the stake is being transformed into her own history?

People: Why is this woman smiling?

Priest: Perhaps she is thinking that, if she were left alone with me, she would already have been burned.

People: Why is this woman smiling?

First and Second Guards: She is smiling at sin.

Invisible angels: She is smiling at harmony, harmony, harmony, which is now at hand.

Lover: You smile beyond my reach, and rage wells up inside me. Remember that in the chamber where I knew you, that smile was different, and the embers in your eyes were the only

tears you shed. By what strange grace has abject sin trans-
figured you into this woman who smiles in total silence?
Husband: Impotent rage! Behold her smiling! even less mindful
of me than when she belonged to another. Why has this people
caused me to reveal more than I would have them know? Ah
cruel mechanism which I myself unleashed with my lamen-
tations as a wounded man. For see how I have made her
unattainable even before she meets her death. The incitement
to have her burned was mine, but for me there will be no
victory: that has been usurped by the people, the priest, and
the guards. For wretched creatures that you are, you cannot
deny that you thrive on my misfortune.
Lover: You smile at having used me so that you might be
burned by fire, even while still alive.
Husband: Hear me once more, wife. (How strange, perhaps
she hears me, but it is I who can no longer find the words of
old. Doubt which knows no more frontiers: when was it I and
when was it not I? It was I who loved her, but who is about to
be revenged? He who previously spoke through me fell silent
the moment he had achieved his design. Why can I no longer
recognize the face of my beloved as in bygone times? Perhaps
she can hear me, but I have nothing more to say.)
Invisible angels: Remove your hands from your face, husband.
You are no longer the same man. The curtain has opened to
reveal that this is the lowermost, lowermost, lowermost circle
of awesome, awesome harmony.
Lover: I believed myself to be alive, but it was she who was
living me. I was lived.
Husband: How can I recognize you, if you smile like someone
sanctified? These chaste arms are not the arms which deceit-
fully embraced me. Can these be the same tresses which I once
untied? Stay! who testified that this is the same body which
incited you? Here I detect some error, I detect some crime, and
a monstrous confusion: for she sinned with one body and they
are burning another.
Priest: 'But, thou art the same'.
First Guard: Everyone grieves when the time for grief is already
over, and everyone disagrees for the sake of disagreeing, when
they know full well that they come here with revenge in their
hearts.

Second Guard: The moment has come at last when we shall enjoy the taste of battle.

Priest: The moment has come when, by the grace of God, I shall sin with the sinner, I shall burn with the sinner, and after descending to the depths of hell with the sinner, I shall be saved in Your name.

Invisible angels: Behold the moment has come. We can already feel the strenuous dawn. We are on the threshold of our primary form. It must be good to be born.

People: Let the sinner who is about to die speak.

Priest: Let her be. I fear even a single word from this woman who is ours.

People: Let the sinner who is about to die, speak.

Lover: Let her be. Do you not see how she is abandoned?

People: Let her speak. Let her speak. Let her speak.

Invisible angels: Let her be silent . . . let her be silent . . . we have no further use for her . . .

People: Let her speak. Let her speak. Let her speak.

Priest: Accept her death as her word.

People: We do not understand. We do not understand. We do not understand.

First and Second Guards: Draw back, for the fire might spread and set your clothes alight and burn down the entire city.

People: This fire was already ours, and the entire city is ablaze.

First and Second Guards: Behold the first flare. Long live the King.

People: The city is branded by the Salamander.

First and Second Guards: Branded by the Salamander.

Invisible angels: Branded by the Salamander.

First and Second Guards: Look at the brilliant sky. Long live the King.

People: Hurrah! Hurrah! Hurrah!

Invisible angels: Ah . . .

Priest: Ave Maria, to what depths have I fallen? (for though I am beyond reproach, that in itself is not enough to exonerate me), Lord, remove this burden from me. Pray, pray . . .

Invisible angels: . . . tremble, tremble; a plague of angels already darkens the horizon . . .

Lover: Alas, I have not been sent to the stake. I share the same sign and destiny, yet my tragedy will never be consumed by fire.

Newly-born angels: How good to be born. To see this pleasant land, to hear its gentle and perfect harmony . . . From what is being accomplished, we are born. In the spheres where we hovered, it was easy not to live and to be the free shadow of a child. But in this land where there is sea and spray, and fire and smoke, there exists a law which precedes the law and even the preceding law, and which gives form to the form, and to its form. How easy it was to be an angel. But on the night of fire there was such desire, furious, restless and shameful, to be boy and girl.

Husband: She sinned with one body and they have burned another. I was wounded in one soul, yet I am revenged in another.

People: Burnt flesh is the colour of burnished wheat.

Priest: Not even the colour is any longer hers. It is the colour of the flame. Ah, how purification burns. At last, I am suffering.

People: We do not understand, we do not understand, and we hunger for roasted meat.

Husband: With my cloak I could still smother the flames of your garments!

Lover: He does not even fathom her death, he who shared with me this woman who belonged to no one.

Priest: How I suffer. But 'ye have not yet resisted unto blood'.

Husband: If with my cloak I were to smother the flames of your garments . . .

Lover: Certainly you could. But try to understand: would she have the strength to prolong the pure fire of this instant forever more?

Priest: Behold her, she who will turn to dust and ashes. Ah, 'verily thou art a God that hidest thyself.'

First Guard: I tell you, she burns more quickly than a heathen.

Priest: The world passes and her concupiscence with it.

Second Guard: I tell you, there is so much smoke that I can scarcely see the body.

Husband: I can scarcely see the body with which I was once united.

Priest: Praised be the name of the Lord, 'Your grace suffices'. 'I counsel thee to buy of me gold tried in the fire, that thou mayest be rich', for thus it is written in the Book of Revelation. Praised be the name of the Lord.

People: Amen. Amen. Amen.

Priest: 'She took her pleasure as the slave of her senses.'

Husband: She was nothing but a degenerate woman, a degenerate woman, a degenerate woman.

Lover: Ah, she was so sweet and degenerate. You were so completely mine and degenerate.

Priest: I am suffering.

Lover: For me and for her there began what will endure forever.

Newly-born angels: Good day!

Priest: 'Waiting for eternal light to dawn and the shadows of the symbols to disperse.'

First and Second Guards: Everyone speaks and no one listens.

Priest: It is a melodious confusion: I can already hear the angels of those who are dying.

Newly-born angels: Good day. Good day. Good day. Already we do not understand. We do not understand. We do not understand.

Husband: Be accursed, if you think you have freed yourself of me and that I have freed myself of you. Under the spell of fatal attraction, you will not escape my orbit and I shall not leave yours, and *ad nauseam* we shall revolve until you pass beyond my orbit and I pass beyond yours; and in superhuman hatred we shall become one and the same person.

Priest: The beauty of a night without passion. Such abundance, such consolation. 'Great things doeth he, which we cannot comprehend.'

First and Second Guards: Just as in war, burning all that is evil does not guarantee that the good will remain . . .

Newly-born angels: . . . we are born.

People: We do not understand. We do not understand.

Husband: I shall now return to the house of the deceased. For there my former wife awaits me, bedecked in her hollow jewels.

Priest: The silence of a night without sin . . . Such light, such harmony.

Drowsy child: Mother, what has happened?

Newly-born angels: Mother, what has happened?
Woman of the people: My children, it happened like this . . .
A voice from the people: Forgive them, they believe in fate, and
therefore they are fatal.

GENTLE CRITICISM

— In the book of Pelé[1] things start to happen and go on and
on happening. It is quite different from your book, because
you merely invent. Yours is the more difficult book to write,
but his gives more pleasure.

HARSH CRITICISM

— I am about to write a story in imitation of you. And I am
going to type it as well: little beggar girl.
  She was something. Quiet, pretty, abandoned. Restricted
to the one street-corner and nothing else. She begged for
money in a timid way. Her remaining possessions: half a
biscuit and a photograph of her mother who had died three
days before.

WRATH

— 'This' — the man said to himself, as he knelt like a warrior
about to engage in battle — 'is the prayer of a man who is
possessed. I am experiencing the hell of passion. I cannot put a

---

[1] Pelé (Edson Arantes Nascimento, b. 1940): the internationally-acclaimed
   Brazilian footballer.

name to what possesses me, nor to what I find myself voraciously possessing, save that of passion. What is this overwhelming violence which causes me to beseech clemency even from myself? It is the will to destroy, as if I had been born for this moment of destruction. This moment may strike or pass: but my choice depends on my being able or unable to hear myself. God hears, but shall I be able to hear myself? The force of destruction is momentarily still under my control. I cannot destroy anyone or anything, for pity is as strong in me as rage; therefore I wish to destroy myself, I who am the source of this passion. I have no intention of asking God to pacify me. My love for God is so great that I fear to touch Him with my plea; my plea inflames, my very plea is dangerous, such is its ardour, and it could destroy the image of God within me, which I still want to cherish. Meantime, I can only ask God to lay His hand upon me, even while facing the risk of burning God's hand. Ignore my plea, for it is so violent that it terrifies me. But to whom shall I turn in this brief moment of respite, if I have already dismissed mankind? I have dismissed mankind, I have gradually sealed every trace of sweetness in my nature with every blow I have received, and those suppressed reserves of sweetness have blackened like simple clouds which gradually intensify their darkness. I lower my head before the approaching storm. What will divine wrath be like, if my own is so overwhelming that it blinds me? A wrath capable of destroying others with me. But I must protect the others — the others have sustained my hope. What can I do to resist this omnipotence which possesses me? What can I say? Except speak the truth; except speak the truth. I have only experienced one other thing as overwhelming, blind, and powerful as this craving within me to wallow in violence: the sweetness of compassion. This alone will serve to balance the scales — for on the other side there is blood and the hatred of blood and the laughter of blood which is painful. What am I asking? I am asking that every one of my sorrows should correspond here and now to an act of wrath.

'But I know what my sorrows have been. Wrath is easy to demonstrate. But sorrow made me somewhat ashamed. For my sorrow stems from the unhappy consequences of my other mortal sins. My violence — which is flesh and blood and will only be nourished on flesh and blood — this violence is the result of other essential forms of violence in my nature having been suppressed. Those other forms of wicked violence, which seemed so righfully mine . . . At the outset, they so closely resembled all that was sweetest in my nature. I had simply been born and I simply wished to take possession of the things I craved. And each time I failed, each time I was restrained, each time I was denied. I smiled and believed my smile to be one of docile resignation. But it was sorrow masquerading as goodness. I knew that my sorrow was offensive in the eyes of God and, worse still, in my own eyes, whoever I might be. Each time my sins failed to triumph, I suffered, but without my feeling that I had the right to suffer, and I was forced to hide not only my sorrow but, above all, the reasons for my sorrow. What was being trampled inside me? My mortal sins.

'Mortal sins clamoured within me for freedom to live, and they clamoured with shame: my mortal sins demanded the right to live. How I hungered for the world: I wanted to consume the world; and I wanted to spread throughout the world this hunger for milk with which I was born. But the world had no desire to be edible. Or rather it wanted to be edible, but demanded that I should consume it with the same humility with which it offered itself. But violent hunger is demanding and proud and, when you are proud and demanding, the world becomes hard on the teeth and on the soul. The world only gives itself to the simple man, and I was about to consume it with my strength and this wrath which has now become part of me. And when the bread turned to stone and gold between my teeth, I proudly insisted that I felt no pain. I believed that to feign strength was the noble path of mankind and the path of my own strength. I believed strength to be the substance from which the world is made, and that I would meet the world with strength. It was only later that love for the world possessed me: and this was no mean hunger: it was voracious hunger. It was the great happiness of living — and I believed this, to be truly free. But how did I come to transform, completely unaware, the joy of living into the rich abundance of existing? Meantime, in the beginning it was simply good and it was not a sin. It was love for the world when heaven and earth were dawning, and my eyes still knew how to be tender. But suddenly my nature was destroying me, and it was no longer the sweetness of love for the world; it was an avid hunger for the world's abundance. And the world retracted once more, and I called that betrayal. This lust for life terrified me in my insomnia, for I failed to understand that the night of the world and the night of existence are so sweet that one even sleeps, that one even sleeps, dear God. And the water, in my lust for life, the water trickled through my fingers before reaching my lips. And I loved the other being with the abundance of someone who wants to save and to be saved by happiness. I did not know that mortal sin could only be avoided by taking a middle-course; I felt ashamed of any such compromise. My sins are mortal, not because God kills, but because I perish for my sins. It was I who could not cope with mortal sins. What I could not achieve with mortal sins is that very same thing which now does me violence, and to which I respond with violence. My clumsy and pitiful efforts have gained me neither heaven nor earth, and I am possessed by rage. Ah, if only for one moment I might understand that this rage is directed at my own crimes and not at those of others, then this rage would be transformed into flowers in my hands; into flowers, into flowers, into delicate things, into love. I have not learned as yet how to control my hatred, but I now realize that my hatred is a frustrated love, my hatred is a life still waiting to be lived. For I have lived everything — except life. This is what I cannot forgive in myself, and since I cannot bear not to forgive myself, I cannot forgive others. This is the point I have reached: having failed to achieve life, I want to destroy it. My rage — what is it except revindication? — my rage, I know, I must know at this rare moment of choosing, my rage is the reverse of my love; were I to choose at last humbly to yield to the world's sweetness, then I should call my rage love. I was so afraid of pledging myself forever with that first word which I can scarcely bring myself to utter (love), that I took refuge in violence and in the bloodshot eyes of passion. All, all for fear of prostrating myself at Your feet and at the anonymous feet of the "other" who always represented You. What monarch am I who refuses to pay homage? I must choose between losing my pride and the love-current of ignorance and sweetness. Will my ancient truth continue to serve me? God forbade the seven sins not because He demanded perfection, but simply out of His compassion for mankind. And for me, who, like the others, tries to evade Him, just as I try to evade the others, even while recognizing that the others are God. Now I must choose between loving or hating. I know that to love is slower, and urgency devours me. Cover my fury with Your love, for I also know that my wrath is simply not to love, my wrath is to cope with the unbearable responsibility of not being a plant. I am a plant which senses its own omnipotence and yields to panic. Rid me of this false destructive omnipotence, do not allow the wound they have inflicted on me to be inflicted on You; ordain that, at the moment of choosing, I might understand that he who wounds is as guilty of sinning as me: he is possessed by that pride which leads to wrath, and therefore he wounds just as I should wound, simply because he has no faith, simply because he has no confidence, simply because he sees himself as an unthroned king. Assist those who are suffering from wrath for it suffices that they should submit to Your grace. But since Your greatness is beyond my understanding, present Yourself to me in a guise which I might recognize: in the guise of a father, a mother, a friend, a brother, a lover, a son. Wrath, transform yourself into forgiveness within me, for you are the sorrow of not loving.'

DO NOT UNLEASH THE HORSES

As in everything, so in writing I am almost afraid of going too far. What can this be? Why? I restrain myself, as if I were tugging at the reins of a horse which might suddenly bolt and drag me who knows where. I protect myself. Why? For what? For what purpose am I saving myself? I was already aware of this when I once wrote: 'It is important not to be afraid of being creative'. Why fear? Fear of knowing the limits of my ability? Or the fear of the sorcerer's apprentice who did not know how to stop? Who knows, perhaps like a woman who

keeps herself inviolate so as to offer herself to love one day,
perhaps I, too, wish to die inviolate so that God may possess all
of me.

AVARICE

Just to have been born has ruined my health.

SHADY DEALINGS

After I discovered in my own mind how people think, I was no
longer able to believe in the thoughts of others.

REMEMBRANCE OF A DIFFICULT SUMMER

Insomnia pervaded the poorly-lighted city. There was not a
single closed door, and every window had a warm glow.
Around the street-lamps the spectres hovered. On the river
bank there were tables, several weary conversations, children
asleep on laps. The buoyant night air made sleep impossible:
like vagrants, we strolled at leisure. We were part of the amber
death-watch created by the street-lamps, of the winged
spectres, of the billowing clouds, suspended in the heavens, of
the vigil of the entire celestial dome. We were part of the
eternal waiting which, by itself and in itself, is what engages
the entire universe. Since the time of those other enormous
spectres, who in bygone ages drank slowly from the waters of
that river.

But within the totality of that eternal waiting, which was a
way of being, I pleaded for a truce. That summer's night in
August was of the finest weave, forever impenetrable, and full

of expectancy. I wished for the night to start trembling at last in a gentle spasm, thus initiating its agony; so that I, too, might sleep. But I knew that a summer's night neither fades nor dawns, it merely perspires in the lukewarm fever of dawn. And it is always I who has gone to sleep: it is always I who has entered into agony, while the night remains like a naked eye. It is beneath the world's great, watching eye that I have planned my sleep, shrouding my grain of insomnia in a thousand burial cloths, for insomnia is the diamond which befell me. I was on the corner and I knew that nothing would ever enter into agony. It is an eternal world. And I know that it is I who must die.

But I did not want to go alone, I wanted a place which might correspond to my needs, I wanted them to receive my necessary agony. My deaths are not caused by sadness — they are one of the ways in which the world inhales and exhales, the succession of lives is the respiration of an eternal waiting, and I myself, who am also the world, need the rhythm of my agonies. But if as the world, I harmonize with my death, I, like that other thing which I so completely am, need merciful hands to receive my corpse. I, who am also the hope of waiting's redemption, need love's pity to save me and the spirit of my blood. That blood which was so black in the black dust of my sandals, while my forehead was surrounded by mosquitoes like a fruit. Where could I take refuge, and free myself from the vibrant summer's night which enchained me to its splendour? My tiny diamond had become so much greater than I. I noticed that the stars are also hard and brilliant and I needed to be the fruit which rots and rolls to the ground. I needed the abyss.

Then I saw the cathedral of Berne towering before me. But the Cathedral, too, was warm and alert. Encircled by wasps.

CONQUERED LOVE

I met Ivan Lessa[1] at the local bus stop, and we were conversing when Ivan, sounding a little startled, said to me: look at that odd sight. I looked behind me and saw a man coming round the corner, with his placid little dog on the lead. Except that it was not a dog. The animal behaved like a dog, and the man behaved like a man walking his dog. But this was no dog. It had the elongated snout of an animal capable of drinking from a tall glass, and a long, hard tail — it could have been, admittedly, simply an unusual crossbreed. Ivan suggested that it might be a raccoon, but I thought the animal was much too like a dog to be a raccoon, unless it was the most docile and deceptive raccoon I had ever seen. Meanwhile, the man was calmly approaching. No, not calmly: there was a certain tenseness about him, it was the calm of someone who has accepted a challenge: he had the look of a born fighter. There was nothing eccentric about his behaviour; it was an act of courage that he should appear in public walking his pet. Ivan suggested some other species, the name of which he had momentarily forgotten. But I was not convinced. Only later did I understand my embarrassment; it was not exactly mine, but stemmed from the fact that the animal no longer knew what it was, and was unable, therefore, to project any clear image of itself.

Until the man passed us. Unsmiling, his shoulders drawn back, proudly appearing in public — no, it has never been easy to walk past a queue of people. The man pretended to have no need of our admiration or pity; but each of us recognizes the martyrdom of someone who is cherishing a dream.

— What animal is that? I asked the man, and intuitively I adopted a gentle tone so as not to offend him with my curiosity. I asked him what animal it was, but the tone of my question also implied: 'Why are you doing this? What has driven you to invent a dog? Why not a real dog? for dogs do exist! Or had you no other means of capturing the grace of this creature except with a collar? Don't you realize that you destroy a rose

---

[1] Ivan Lessa, Brazilian journalist and humorist who regularly wrote a column for the satirical newspaper *O Pasquim*.

if you crush it in your hand?' I know that tone is a unity which cannot be divided by words, I know that I am crushing a rose, but to shatter silence into words is one of my awkward ways of loving silence, and it is in this way that I have so often killed what I understand. (Although, thank God, I am more familiar with silence than with words.)

The man, without stopping, replied briefly but without any discourtesy. It *was* a raccoon. We stood there staring. Neither Ivan nor I smiled, no one in the bus queue laughed — that was the key, that was the intuition. We just stood there staring.

It was a raccoon which believed itself to be a dog. At times, with dog-like gestures, it would pause to sniff at things, which caused the lead to tighten and delayed its master with that common synchronization between man and dog. I stood there watching the raccoon which did not know what it was. I thought to myself: if the man is taking it to play in the park, there will come a moment when the raccoon will start to feel uneasy: 'But, dear God, why do dogs always stare at me?' I also thought to myself that, after spending a perfect day as a dog, the raccoon might sadly think to itself as it looked up at the stars: 'What have I achieved in the end? What is missing in my life? I am as contented as any dog, therefore, why this emptiness, this longing? What is this anxiety, as if I were only destined to love what I do not know?' And the man, the only person capable of freeing the raccoon from its uncertainty, that man is never likely to answer those questions, for fear of losing the raccoon forever.

I also thought about the imminence of hatred which existed in the raccoon. It felt love and gratitude for the man. But within, there was no way of the truth ceasing to exist; only the raccoon did not perceive that it hated the man because it was essentially confused.

Suppose the mystery of its true nature had suddenly been revealed to the raccoon? I tremble to think of the fatal chance which might have brought that raccoon to an unexpected confrontation with another raccoon, and therefore to self-recognition. I tremble to think of that moment when the raccoon would have experienced the most blissful shame which is given to us: to me . . . to us . . . I know full well that the raccoon would have every right, on discovering the truth, to massacre the man with all the hatred which one creature can inflict upon another — to defile the other's essence in order to exploit him. I sympathize with the animal, I side with the victims of evil love. But I beseech the raccoon to pardon the man and to pardon him with infinite love. Before abandoning him, of course.

THE TEA-PARTY

The imaginings which frighten me. I imagined a party — without drink or food — a party simply to be observed. Even the chairs had been hired and transported to an empty third-floor apartment on the Rua da Alfândega, an ideal setting for a party. I would invite all my former friends of both sexes, with whom I have now lost touch. Only former friends, excluding any of the mutual friends of friends. Individuals who shared my life and whose life I shared. But how could I climb those dark stairs to a rented room on my own? And how does one get back from the Rua da Alfândega at night? I know for certain that the pavements would be dry and hard.

I preferred another imagining. It began by mingling affection with gratitude and rage: only afterwards did the two wings of a bat unfold, like someone coming from afar and drawing quite close; but those wings were also shining. It would be a tea-party — on a Sunday at the Rua do Lavradio — to which I would invite all the housemaids I had ever employed. Those whom I had forgotten would mark their absence with an empty chair, just as they exist inside me. The others would be seated, their hands folded on their laps. Silent — until that moment when they would open their mouths and, restored to life, resuscitated corpses, each would recite in turn what I can recall of their conversations. Almost like a tea-party for society ladies, except that at this tea-party there would be no talk about housemaids.

— Well, I wish you much happiness — one of them gets to her feet — May you be blessed with what no one can give you.

— When I ask for something — another rises from her chair — I can never control my laughter, so people never take my requests seriously.

— I like films with a gun fight. (And that was all I could remember about an entire person.)

— Plain, everyday home-cooking, madam. I only know how to cook for the poor.

— When I die, one or two people will miss me. But that's all.

— My eyes fill with tears when I speak to a lady, it must be because of the spirits.

— He was such a pretty child that I really felt like giving him a good thrashing.

— Early this morning — the Italian maid told me — when I was coming to work, the leaves started to fall, along with the first snow. A man on the street said to me: 'It's raining gold and silver.' I pretended I hadn't heard him because, if I'm not careful, men always get their way with me.

— Here comes Her Ladyship — the oldest of all of my former housemaids gets up, the one who only managed to show soured affection and who taught me so early in life how to forgive love's cruelty. — Did Your Ladyship sleep well? Being a lady means enjoying every luxury. She's full of whims: she wants this, she doesn't want that. To be a lady means being white.

— I want three days off during the Carnival, madam, for I'm tired of playing Cinderella.

— Food is a question of salt. Food is a question of salt. Food is a question of salt. Here comes Her Ladyship: may you be blessed with what no one can give you, that's all I ask when I die. That was when the man said that the rain was gold and silver, what no one can give you. Unless you're not afraid to stand all alone in the dark, bathed in gold, but only in the dark. The upper classes have seen better days: leaves or the first snow. To taste the salt in what you are eating, not to give a pretty child a good thrashing, to avoid laughter when you are asking for something, never to pretend that you haven't heard when someone says: It is raining, my good woman, it is raining gold and silver. It really is!

THE RECRUITMENT

The footsteps are growing louder. A little closer. Now they sound almost at hand. Nearer still. Now as close as possible. Meantime they continue to approach. Now they are no longer close, they are inside me. Will they outstrip me and travel on? I hope so. I can no longer tell with which sense I measure distance. For those footsteps are no longer simply close and pounding. They are no longer simply inside me. I am marching with them.

FAIR TIDINGS FOR A CHILD

In everything, in everything your body will be an asset. Our body is ever at our side. It is the one thing which stays with us to the end.

FIRST IN THE CLASS

His secret is a snail. His hair is cropped, his eyes delicate and attentive. His soft skin at nine years is still transparent. He is refined by nature and handles things without breaking them. He lends books to his school-mates, helps them with their lessons and does not lose his patience with the square and the rule like so many indolent children. His secret is a snail. Which he does not forget for a single moment. His secret is a snail which sustains him. He tends it lovingly in a shoe-box. With daily solicitude he pierces it with a needle and thread. With care and attention, he postpones its death. His secret is a snail, nurtured with insomnia and precision.

SKETCHING A LITTLE BOY

How can one ever come to know a little boy?

In order to know him, I must wait for him to deteriorate, and only then will he be within my grasp. There he is, a point in the infinite. No one will know his today. Not even the little boy himself. As for me, I look, and it is useless: I cannot understand anything which is simply real, completely real. What I know about him is his situation. He is the little boy whose first teeth have just started to appear, and he is the same little boy who one day will become a doctor or a joiner. In the meantime — there he is sitting on the floor, with a reality which I define as vegetative in order to be able to understand. There are thirty thousand such little boys sitting on the floor; will they have the chance to build another world, one that will take into account that absolute reality to which we once belonged? In union there will be strength. There he sits, initiating everything anew, but for his own future protection, and without any real opportunity of truly initiating anything.

I do not know how to sketch the little boy. I know that it is impossible to sketch him in charcoal, for even pen and ink stains the paper beyond that subtle line of extreme actuality within which he lives. One day we shall domesticate him into a human being and then I shall be able to sketch him. For this is what we have done with ourselves and with God. The little boy will assist his own domestication; he is diligent and co-operative. He co-operates without knowing that the assistance we expect of him is for his own self-sacrifice. Recently, he has had much practice. And so he will go on progressing until little by little — because of the essential goodness with which we achieve our salvation — he will pass from actual time to daily time, from meditation to expression, from existence to life. Making the great sacrifice of not being mad. I am not mad out of solidarity with the thousands of people who, in order to construct the possible, have also sacrificed the truth which would constitute madness.

But meanwhile, there he sits on the floor, sunk in a void.

From the kitchen his mother reassures herself: are you behaving in there? Roused into action, the little boy gets up with difficulty. He totters on his tiny legs, all his attention concentrated within: his entire equilibrium is something internal. And once that has been achieved, all his attention is directed outwards: he observes what the act of getting to his feet has provoked. For getting up has had consequence after consequence: the floor moves unsteadily, the chair is taller than he is, the wall confines him. And on the wall there is a portrait of THE LITTLE BOY. It is difficult to look up at the portrait without leaning against a piece of furniture, and that is something which he still has not practised. But his own awkwardness ironically supports him: what keeps him on his feet is precisely focusing his attention on the portrait above; to look up serves him as a hoist. But he makes one mistake: he blinks. To have blinked detaches him for a fraction of a second from the portrait which was supporting him. He loses his balance — and, in one total gesture, he falls on his bottom. His mouth gaping from so much human effort, the clear spittle runs and drips on to the floor. He examines the spittle at close quarters, as if it were an ant. He raises his arm and brings it forward in slow mechanical stages. Then suddenly, as if he were capturing something ineffable, with unexpected violence he squashes the spittle with the palm of his hand. He blinks and waits. Finally, having allowed sufficient time to elapse, he carefully removes his hand and looks at the floor, examining the fruit of this experience. The floor is empty. With another brusque movement, he examines the palm of his hand: the spittle is stuck there. He has learned something else. Then, with his eyes wide open, he licks the spittle which belongs to the little boy. He thinks loud and clear: little boy.

— Who are you calling? his mother enquires from the kitchen.

With effort and decorum he looks round the room and searches for the person whom his mother says he is calling; he turns his head and falls backwards. As he sobs, he sees the room distorted and refracted by his tears, the white volume grows until he cries out — Mother! — he is gathered into strong arms, and suddenly the little boy finds himself in mid-air, cradled in an embrace which is warm and comforting. The ceiling is closer now: the table down below. Overcome with exhaustion, the pupils of his eyes revolve before disappearing beneath the horizontal line of his eyelids. He closes his eyes before the final image, the wooden bars of his cot. The little boy falls asleep, worn out and pacified.

The saliva has dried in his mouth. The fly beats on the window-pane. The little boy's sleep is streaked with light and warmth, his sleep vibrates in the atmosphere. Until in a sudden nightmare, one of the words he has learned comes to mind; he shivers violently, and opens his eyes. And to his alarm, he sees nothing but the warm, clear emptiness of air — and no mother. His thoughts explode into sobbing which pervades the entire house. As he sobs, he begins to recognize himself, transforming himself into the child whom his mother will recognize. He almost grows faint from so much sobbing: he must transform himself immediately into something which can be seen and heard, otherwise he will remain alone, he must transform himself into something comprehensible, otherwise no one will comprehend him, no one will respond to his silence, no one will know him if he does not speak and confide. I shall do everything necessary so that I might belong to the others and the others belong to me; I shall leap over my real happiness which will only bring me abandonment; and I will be popular, for I barter in exchange for love. It is altogether magical to weep in order to receive in exchange: a mother.

Until a familiar noise comes through the door and the little boy, silent as he ponders what the power of a little boy can provoke, stops sobbing: mother. He will exchange all the possibilities of a world for: mother. Mother is: not to die. And his reassurance is to know that he has a world to betray and to sell, and that he will sell it.

Yes, it is mother, mother holding a clean nappy. The minute he sees the nappy, he begins to sob once more.

— But if you're soaking wet!

— The news alarms him, his curiosity is reawakened, but now it is a curiosity which is comfortable and guaranteed. He looks blindly at his own wetness and, in a new phase, looks at his mother. But suddenly, he recoils and listens with his whole body, his heart beating heavily in his tummy: honk-honk! he recognizes the noise with a sudden cry of victory and terror — the little boy has just recognized something!

— That's right! his mother says proudly, that's right, my

darling, honk-honk has just passed along the street, I shall tell daddy what you've learned today, that's just what it sounds like: honk-honk, my darling! his mother repeats, bouncing him up and down on her lap, lifting him by his legs, throwing him backwards, and then bouncing him up and down again. In all these postures, the little boy keeps his eyes wide open. As dry as a fresh nappy.

AN ITALIAN WOMAN IN SWITZERLAND

Rosa lost her parents when she was small. Her brothers and sisters dispersed throughout the world and she was sent to an orphanage attached to a convent. There she led an austere and deprived existence with the other inmates. During the winter the great mansion was permanently cold, and the work never ceased. Rosa did the washing, she swept out the rooms, and mended clothes. Meantime, the seasons passed. With her head shaved and wearing a long tunic made of coarse material, she often interrupted her sweeping to gaze out of the windows. Autumn was the season she liked best for she could savour it without going outdoors: through the window-panes she would watch the yellowing leaves fall into the courtyard, and that was autumn.

In this particular Swiss convent, whenever a man crossed the doorway, the floor had to be scrubbed and alcohol burned over the spot where he had been standing. Then winter would return once more and Rosa's hands became inflamed and covered with chilblains. Her bed was so cold that it was impossible to sleep. In that darkened dormitory, with her open eyes peering over the sheet, she would espy those tiny glancing thoughts. In some strange way those thoughts were paradise.

How and why at the age of twenty Rosa suddenly decided to leave the convent, I cannot say, nor could she herself explain. But she had made up her mind although everyone opposed the idea. Her resolve was firm, her resistance passive. The nuns were horrified and warned her that she would go to Hell. But because Rosa made no attempt to justify her decision, she got her way. She left the convent and found employment as a housemaid.

She left carrying her small bundle of possessions, her head shaved, her skirt down to her ankles. 'The world struck me as being . . .' but she could not explain.

With her Southern Italian features, her oval eyes, and curves which were slow in asserting themselves, Rosa went to live with a family which had been recommended. There she remained day and night, month after month, never going out. She explained to me that at that time she did not know how 'to go out'. She contemplated the wonders of winter from the windows without venturing out into that Paradise: she observed everything through those windows and no one could say for certain whether she was happy or sad. Her face was still incapable of expressing emotion. She looked through those windows with the wrapt attention of someone at prayer, her arms folded, her hands tucked into her sleeves.

One afternoon when everything struck her as being much too vast — a free afternoon without any household chores was almost sinful — she felt that she should apply herself to something, adopt a much more disciplined, even pious attitude. She went downstairs, went into the drawing-room and selected a book from the bookcase. She went back upstairs and sat in a chair without leaning back, for she was still unaccustomed to seeking comfort or pleasure. She began to read with concentration. But her spherical head where tufts of vigorous hair began to sprout — her head became muddled. She closed the book, lay down, and shut her eyes.

The family waited for her to serve dinner, but Rosa did not appear. They went to look for her. Here eyes were swollen, inflamed, expressionless: she was burning with fever. The mistress of the house spent that night looking after her, but there was nothing to do: Rosa complained of nothing and asked for nothing as the fever gripped her. Next morning, she looked thinner, her eyes more subdued. And she passed another day and night in the same condition. The family sent for the doctor.

He enquired what had happened, for there were clear symptoms of a nervous disorder. Rosa made no reply, nor did it occur to her to answer the doctor's questions, for she was not accustomed to speaking for herself. At this point, the doctor chanced to look at the bedside table and his eye caught sight of the book. He examined it, and looked at her with some alarm. The book was entitled *Le corset rouge*. He warned Rosa that she should not read such a book under any circumstances. She had barely left the convent, and her innocence constituted a threat. Rosa said nothing. The doctor continued:

— You must not read such books because they are false. Rosa opened her eyes a little more widely for the first time. The doctor swore to her that the book was full of lies. He had sworn . . .

Rosa sighed and shyly gave a wistful smile:

— I thought that everything which is written and published in a book is the truth, she said, looking modestly at the first honest man she had ever known.

The doctor said — and you can imagine in what tone of voice:

— That is not the case.

Rosa slept, thin and pallid. Her fever abated and she was soon back on her feet. With time, people began to notice: what lovely black hair you have. Rosa, touching her hair, would reply: really!

How Rosa could be so happy at the age of forty continues to puzzle me. How she laughed. I also know that on one occasion, she tried to commit suicide. Not because she had left the convent. But because of a love affair. She explained that when she fell in love she had no idea that 'things were really like that'. Like what? She made no attempt to answer my question. Ten years older than her lover, she laughs under that great mane of black hair and insists: I really cannot explain why I prefer autumn to the other seasons. I think it's because in the autumn things wither so quickly.

She also insists: I am not very bright. I have the impression that Madam is much more intelligent than I am. She also asks me: 'Has Madam ever cried like a fool without knowing why? for I have!' — and she bursts out laughing.

BROTHERS

— Let's play at something else now. Let's see if you're clever. Is this painting concrete or abstract?

— Abstract.

— No, you idiot. It's concrete. I painted it myself and put my own feelings into it and those feelings are concrete.

— Fair enough, but not all your feelings are concrete.

— Yes, they are.

— No, they're not. They're not all concrete, because fear is not concrete. Only a small part of you is concrete.

— I am a genius and I find that everything is concrete.

— Oh, I had no idea that you were a famous painter.

— Well, I am. My name is Bergman, Maurice Bergman. I am Swedish, and I'm a genius. You can tell by my face. Take a good look: I am suffering! Now let me see if you understand anything about painting. Is that painting concrete?

— Of course, because you can see at a glance that it's a map, simply by following the lines.

— Ah, is that so? and what about that one?

— Abstract.

— Wrong! That picture, too, would have to be concrete because it also has lines.

— I shall explain to you what concrete means, it means . . .

— . . . you're quite wrong.

— Why?

— Because I don't understand. When I don't understand what you're talking about, you must be wrong. And now I want to know: what is *comprete*?

— You mean concrete.

— No, I mean *comprete*. Because I'm a genius and every genius has to come up with at least one invention. I have invented the word *comprete*. Is music *comprete*?

— I believe it is, because one listens, and feels the music simply by listening.

— Ah, but you cannot draw!

— Do you think the ceiling is concrete?

— Certainly!

— But if I were to change over that wall and put it in the

position of the ceiling, it would become a wall-ceiling. Would that wall-ceiling then become concrete?

— I think perhaps it might. Is a ghost concrete?

— What do you mean by a ghost? Someone with a sheet over his head?

— No, a genuine ghost.

— Well . . . Well, it would presumably be concrete.

— Is mother concrete or abstract?

— Concrete, of course, you idiot.

In the adjoining room, their mother interrupted her sewing, her hands resting on her lap, her head bowed, over a concrete heart which could be heard beating.

A PUBLIC MAN

To what extent will he have understood his own act? I can barely imagine his solitary confusion. When an irrational act provokes a monstrous echo, the man probably feels himself to be almost acquitted before whatever provoked his cry: from vibration to vibration, the toppling of the avalanche. He himself does not know the truth, and perhaps may never know it, for the truth has already been buried under various pretexts. He was 'private', which is considered to be a crime in a public man. The sacrifice of a leader or of a saint or artist — who has come to be precisely what he is through having been private — is that of not being private any longer. A man's cross is to forget his own sorrow. It is in this forgetting of self that the most fundamental human truth comes into being, that which constitutes his humanity. His own sorrow attains a vastness which accommodates all his fellow-men, wherein they take refuge, and are understood. Those who are close to death are revived by means of the love which exists in the renunciation of a private man's sorrow. The true meaning of Christ is the imitation of Christ. Christ Himself was the imitation of Christ.

The whole of Brazil could be elevated through that man's

suffering, through what he himself knew about fear, ambition, and his own tendency towards madness. Just as the transcendence of the will to kill consists in preventing others from killing, for that abyss is all too familiar. But that public man restrained himself. From the magnitude of human imperfections, he derived tiny imperfections. Criminal because petty. He was more in need of help than able to offer help to others.

ANNIVERSARY

— Tomorrow, I shall be ten years old. I intend to make good use of this last day of my ninth year.

— The child paused, then said with some sadness:

— Mummy, my soul is not ten years old.

— How old then?

— Only eight years old.

— Don't worry, that's how it should be.

— But I think we should count our years according to the age of our souls. Then people would say: that chap died at twenty. And the chap had died, but with a seventy-year-old body.

ANNIVERSARY

We began to sing, then stopped and said:

— I am singing to celebrate my own birthday. But, Mummy, I haven't taken full advantage of my ten years of existence.

— Yes, you have.

— No, no, I don't mean taking full advantage in the sense of doing things, of doing this and doing that. What I mean is that I have not really been happy. What's wrong? Why are you looking so sad?

— I'm not sad. Come here and let me give you a kiss.

— You see? Didn't I say that you were sad? Haven't you noticed how many times you've kissed me? When a person kisses another person that many times, it's because she is sad.

NOTES ON INDIAN DANCING

The male dancer makes solemn, priest-like gestures, then comes to a halt. To stand still for several moments forms part of the dance. It is the dance of being motionless: the dancer's movements arrest things. The dancer passes from one motionless pose to another, allowing me time for wonder. His sudden stillness is often the resonance of the previous leap: the still air retains the whole vibration of a gesture. The dancer now stands quite motionless. To exist becomes sacred as if we were merely the protagonists of life.

This is the dance of the male, who has the knowledge of numbers and altitudes, and to whom greater strength of feeling is permitted.

As for the female Indian dancer, she is neither alarmed nor alarming. Her movements are as fluent and enveloping as the motionless current of a river. She has the elongated curves of women of ancient times. The hips of this particular dancer are unusually broad, thus limiting her latent powers of thought. These are women void of malice. And in silent dance they renew the primitive meaning of grace. Even sensuality becomes part of that grace, except that it is a little more intense.

The audience is restless because this dance, which has existed for centuries, is extremely monotonous. Besides, it is inevitable that we should feel uneasy when confronted by Eastern culture: theirs is another way of knowing life — their way. There is yet another reason for our disquiet: we sense that they do not believe in us. For there are certain movements executed by the dancers which leave us dismayed in the West. They believe in masks, they believe in a greater love: they are ancient things, and much too serene.

The interminable programme I am leafing through announces that the next item for three female dancers will 'display every aspect of feminine allure'. What a disappointment. The three women who come on stage barely move. I look in vain for the promised 'feminine allure', and what I see are three women who move with utter tranquillity, as if that in itself were enough. And . . . worst of all, suddenly it is enough. As if they were saying to the audience: behold the rarest of fruits, while showing us nothing more remarkable than a simple orange. To my surprise, I can see that the orange is rare among the rarest of fruits.

My fondness for satiety is amazed at how little they offer. Fat and pale, we are settled in our seats, awaiting the offerings of the Three Wise Kings. But they consign us to our poverty, as people whose greed has been satiated, tacitly accepting that hunger is simple. They start to dance without malice, turning their backs on our darts. By now, we are ashamed at having let them see that we possess so much more — not what they possess, it is true, but so much more. Smiling with embarrassment, we try to do justice to this poor man's banquet, pretending, with gratitude, that we are eating pheasant. Feeling awkward, we allow them to remove our shoes and anoint our feet with oils. Which they proceed to do, smiling and transparent, without humility. Will ancient custom ordain that we in return should anoint their swarthy feet? I feel that it should be so. But what I find offensive is that they do not even expect it of us.

The dance is so placid that little by little it extends the hours. Will the programme never come to an end?

Finding myself trapped in that auditorium, I realize that they can torture me at their leisure, revealing little by little how naked feet have the same expressive powers as hands, how dark skin is much more definite; revealing how people lived subsequent to a Bible which is so immense that it is even profane — bewitching me with the exhaustive repetition of the same truth. Until, by virtue of so much watching, I understand spices, galleons, and the odour of cinnamon. The significance of rivers unfolds; cities rise along river-banks. The cymbal makes a sound which I can only describe as being 'exotic'. The pure spirits can only be invoked with cymbals. The bells attached to the dancers' ankles and wrists convey with gentle tinkling the most subtle intentions of their bodies.

The printed programme carefully explains what is happening on stage. The dancers have no confidence in our visual judgement. The programme describes the next item and informs us, in parentheses, that two female dancers will appear on stage playing at ball. I look in vain for a single gesture which might represent the imaginary existence of a ball. Then they disarm me: they know how to play without any toy.

The names of the dancers are sweet and mellow, and fall easily on one's lips. Mrinalini, Usha, Anirudda, Arjuna. Sweetness with a hint of bitterness and strangely familiar: have I already tasted or not tasted these fruits? Unless it was when I, bored Eve, tasted the fruits in the Garden of Eden.

The musicians sit on the stage itself, their legs crossed as if they were practising yoga. The music is a plangent cantilena, which sounds like the wind when it puts your nerves on edge. It is a monotonous cantilena which has been transplanted from wider spaces to the dimensions of the theatre; like a beast of the jungle, quietly pacing its cage. Among the musicians, there is a desperately thin man who performs as the cantor. His song is gentle and gives the impression of having been intended for the throat. It sends me slowly to sleep in my seat; slowly hypnotizing me into a snake.

POSTERITY WILL JUDGE US

When a preventive cure is discovered for influenza, future generations will no longer be able to understand us. Influenza, while it lasts, is one of the most irretrievable of organic disorders. Having influenza is to know many things which, if not known, would never need to be known. Having influenza is to experience a useless catastrophe, a catastrophe without tragedy. It is a cowardly lament which only another person suffering from influenza can understand. How will future generations ever be able to understand that for us, having influenza was a human condition? We are flu-stricken creatures who will be subjected to censure or ridicule by future generations.

THE SECRET ROOM, YOUR ROOM

Poisoned flowers in the vase. Red, blue, pink, they carpet the air. Enough flowers to fill a hospital ward. I have never seen such lovely flowers. So this is your secret. Your secret resembles you so closely that it tells me nothing beyond what I know already. And I know so little, as if your enigma were I. Just as you are my enigma.

'AD ETERNITATEM'

— They tell me that we're in the twentieth century, is that right?
— Yes.
— Gosh, Mummy, we are behind the times!

GRADUAL APPROXIMATION

If I had to give a title to my life, it would be the following: in search of my own thing.

UNDERSTANDING

All the visitations I have received in life have been the same: they came, sat down, and said nothing.

PROLONGED, DISTENDED TRANQUILLITY

Such perfume! It is Sunday morning. The terrace has been swept. He then switches on the radio. A late lunch gives one ideas. He smiles, and gives those ideas some form. There is water on the table, but on Sunday no one is thirsty. And the craving to drink water starts up without the weariness of thirst. At four o'clock that same afternoon, they will hoist the flag on the pavilion. (But what he really fears are those tranquil Sunday evenings.)

PROFILE OF ELECTED BEINGS

He was a being who was electing. Among the thousand things which he might have been, he was choosing himself. Engaged in a task which obliged him to wear spectacles, distinguishing whatever he could and probing with moist hands the things he could not see: the being was choosing and, for this reason, he was indirectly choosing himself. Little by little, he gathered the essentials in order to be. He went on and on selecting the essentials. In relative freedom, if one discounted the furtive determinism which discreetly operated without giving itself a name. Having discovered this furtive determinism, the being was freely choosing himself. He was guided by the will to discover his own determinism, and to pursue it vigorously, for the true line is extremely blurred and other lines are much more visible. He went on and on selecting the essentials. The being separated the so-called wheat from the chaff, then ate only the best. Sometimes, he ate the worst. He separated perils from the great peril, and to his horror, it was with the great peril that he was left. Only to measure the weight of things in terror. He pushed aside the lesser truths which he ended up ignoring. He craved those truths which were difficult to bear.

Because he ignored the lesser truths, the being appeared to be enshrouded in mystery; because he was ignorant, he was a mysterious being. He had also become: a knowing ignoramus; an ingenuous sage; a forgetful creature who remembered very well; an honest villain; an absent-minded thinker; a creature full of nostalgia for things long since forgotten, a creature pining for things irretrievably lost; and a courageous human being for he was already much too late. Paradoxically, all this bestowed on the being the wholesome contentment of the peasant who only struggles with basic reality, and has no idea what film is currently being shown at the nearest cinema. All this bestowed on the being that unintentional austerity which every vital task confers. When it came to choosing and assembling the essentials for existence, there was no established hour for starting or finishing: it was the task of a lifetime.

Paradoxically, all this gradually bestowed on the being that deep happiness which must manifest, reveal and communicate itself to others. In order to communicate, the being was assisted by his innate gift for enjoyment. This was not something he had chosen or gathered: it was truly a gift. He enjoyed the deep happiness of others, and by means of an innate gift, he discovered the happiness of others. By means of the same gift, he was also able to discover the solitude which other human beings experienced in relation to his own deeper happiness. By means of the same gift, the man also knew how to amuse himself. An inborn instinct taught him that gestures, without causing offence or scandal, could convey the liking he felt for others. Completely unaware that he was using this gift, the being manifested himself; he gave to others, unaware that he was giving; he loved, unaware that this was what other people called love. The gift was truly like the missing shirt in the life of the contented man: since the being was very poor and did not have anything to give, he gave himself. He gave himself in silence, and gave what he had gathered of himself, just as one summons others to come and take a look as well. He did all this with discretion, for he was a timid creature. With the same discretion, the being saw in others what they had gathered of themselves: he knew just how difficult it was to distinguish the faint line of one's own destiny, how easy it was to lose sight of it, or to obscure it with pencil marks, making mistakes, erasing, putting the details right.

This was how the being came to be surrounded by misunderstanding. The others believed in an almost simplistic way that they were seeing an immovable and fixed reality, and they looked at the being the way one looks at a painting. An extremely valuable painting. They failed to understand that for the being, to have gathered the fragments of himself together, had been a task of denudation rather than embellishment. And, because of a misunderstanding, the being was elected. Because of a misunderstanding, the being found himself being loved. But to feel oneself being loved would have been to recognize oneself in love. And that being was loved as if he were another being: as if he were an elected being. The being shed the tears of the equestrian statue which weeps unseen at night in the square, without stirring astride the marble horse. Falsely loved, the being was aching in every limb. But those who had elected him did not offer a hand to help him dismount from that horse of solid silver, nor had the being any desire to mount the horse of heavy gold. The suffering endured by the being disintegrating alone in the public square was the suffering of stone. Meantime, those who had elected him were asleep. Out of fear perhaps? But they were asleep. The darkness in the square had never been so intense. Until dawn began to break. The earth's rhythm was so generous that dawn was breaking. But when night returned, darkness fell once more. The square loomed once more. And once more, those who had elected the being were asleep. Out of fear, perhaps, but they were asleep. Were they afraid because they thought they would have to live in the square? They did not realize that the square was only the being's place of work. That in order to walk, he did not need a square. Those who were asleep did not know that the square had been a battlefield for the elected being and that war was striving to conquer everything outside the square. Those who were asleep thought that the elected being, wherever he might go, would open up a square like someone unrolling a canvas in order to paint. They did not know that the canvas for the elected being was simply a means of mapping out the world where he wished to travel. The being had prepared his entire life in order to function outside the square. It is true that the elected being, on feeling himself prepared like someone who has been annointed with oils and perfumes, realized that there was no time left to learn how to smile. Yet this did not worry him, for this was also his great expectation: the being had relinquished an entire territory to be given to him by whosoever might wish to give it to him. The calculation in the being's dream was deliberately to leave himself incomplete.

But something had gone wrong. When the being saw himself in the photograph which the others had taken, he was horrified and embarrassed when confronted by the image the others had made of him. They had turned him, no more, no less, into an elected being; that is to say, they had imprisoned him. How could he rectify the misunderstanding? In order to make their task easy and save time, they had photographed the being. And now they no longer referred to him but to the photograph. Besides, they only had to open a drawer in order to take out the photograph. Besides, anyone could acquire a copy. Besides, it cost very little.

When they said to the being's image: I love you (but what about me? me? why not me as well? why only my portrait?), the being felt uncomfortable because he could not even express his gratitude: he had nothing to express gratitude for. And the being did not protest, for he knew that the others were not doing this out of malice. The others had pledged themselves to a photograph, and people do not jest: there is too much at stake. Nor could they take any risks: it must be the photograph or nothing. The being, as an act of kindness, sometimes tried to imitate the image in the photograph so as to give some value to what the others possessed, namely, the photograph. But he was unable to match up to the simplified image captured in the photograph. And at times he became quite confused: he found himself unable to copy the portrait, and forgot what he was like outside it, so that, like the laughing clown, the being often wept under the painted mask he wore as court jester.

Then the being tried secretly to destroy the photograph. He did or said things which were so loathsome to the photograph that the latter raged in its drawer. In the hope of becoming more real than his own image so that it would have to be replaced by something inferior: by the being himself. But what happened in the end? It turned out that everything the being did only served in effect to retouch the portrait. The being had become a mere contributor. And a fatal contributor: it no longer mattered what the contributor gave, it no longer mattered what the contributor did not give; everything, even were he to die, merely embellished the photograph.

And so it continued. Until, profoundly disillusioned in his most ingenuous aspirations, the elected being died as people do. He ended up trying to dismount unaided and with great difficulty from the stone horse; he tumbled a number of times, but finally learned to walk about on his own. And, as the saying goes, the land had never looked so beautiful. The being recognized that that was precisely the land for which he had prepared himself. So he had not been mistaken, after all, for the map locating the treasure had given the correct indications. As he walked about, the being touched everything in sight, and smiled. The being had learned, unaided, how to smile. One fine day . . .

WRITING AND PROLONGING TIME

I am unable to write when I am worried or awaiting solutions, for at such moments I do everything possible to make time pass; and to write is to prolong time, to break it down into particles of seconds while giving to each of them an irreplaceable life.

RECOGNIZING LOVE

— I only had this one, she said, pointing to her youngest son with an affectionate smile, because it was much too late when I discovered him and there was no way of getting rid of him.

The child lowered his eyes and gave a bashful smile.

TWO WAYS

In trying to ignore immediate life in favour of a deeper existence, I have two ways of being. In life, I observe a great deal and I am 'active' in my observations. I have an eye for the absurd, I am good-humoured and ironic and fully capable of participating. But when writing I have insights which are 'passive' and so intimate that they 'write themselves' the very instant I perceive them almost without the intervention of any so-called thought processes. For this reason, I make no choice when writing. I am incapable of multiplying myself a thousand-fold. And despite myself, I can sense my own destiny.

AN ABSTRACT DOOR

From a certain point of view, I consider making things abstract as the least literary approach. Certain pages, void of any events, give me the sensation of touching my own essence, and that is the greatest sincerity. It is as if I were sculpting — what is the most authentic sculpture of a human form? — the body, the outlines of the human form, the expression of the form itself of the human body — and not the expression 'given' to the body. A naked Venus, standing 'expressionless', is so much more than a literary concept of Venus. What I mean by 'a literary concept of Venus' is a Venus, for example, which has the smile of Venus on its face, the look of Venus as if it were a title. The Venus de Milo — is an abstract woman. (Were I to make the detailed drawing of a door, without adding any embellishments of my own, I would be making an objective drawing of an abstract door.)

BERNE

The foreign visitor, confronted with such perfection and beauty, may find it difficult to elucidate its mystery: the picturesque beauty of Switzerland is all too evident. After the initial impression of accessibility, there comes the feeling of something impenetrable. A picture postcard, certainly. But little by little, the repose and symmetry begin to provoke disquiet.

You observe the mountains in the distance, and see a vertiginous and tranquil expanse. But in the tiny city above, with its houses and churches confined by walls now reduced to ruins, there is an intimate and sober concentration of forms. In this city of towers, alleyways, arches and silence, the Devil has been expelled beyond the Alps. Once rid of the Devil, an uneasy peace has remained, the marks of a life which has been formed with harshness, the might of the Reformation, signs of slow conquest, of tenacious and wearing perfection.

Determination to keep the Devil at bay? A determination which is perfected in the Swiss obsession with cleanliness, their anxiety to reproduce the cleanliness of the atmosphere on land, an obedience to the law of purity dictated by the mountains on their implacable frontiers. This desire to sacrifice the human element, fatally contaminated and disordered, to the pure abstraction of nature. Order is no longer a means, but a moral necessity in its own right. Order is the only ambience where the native of Switzerland can breathe in Switzerland. Outside Switzerland, he loses his nerve, bewitched by that Devil which he himself expelled.

In the streets, ascetic faces, economy of expression. And in their peaceful but dour expressions, a mute strength reminiscent of fanaticism. As someone once pointed out, the native of Switzerland is not a soldier; he is a warrior. And if the Swiss male is a warrior, his female counterpart is the wife of a warrior. She is a severe, unyielding creature, who has been elected for some sacrifice. Watcher her listening to music in the Cathedral without a trace of make-up on her face, impassive, immersing herself with an enjoyment which is scarcely discernible, in the strains of the organ and the soprano voices of the choir; purifying music which harmonizes with the austere happiness of this race. The Swiss woman does not recline in her seat but sits upright looking rather solemn and enigmatic, lacking in any languorous appeal, but endowed with that puritan grace of uncertain origin, and dressed in a subdued manner without the slightest hint of vanity.

She overcomes this modesty in spring with a few bold touches. Colourful blouses are donned, tiny white collars enhance dresses in muted tones, a delicate feminine contribution to the spring sunshine. The elderly sit in the parks looking grave: this is the land of respectable old ladies and gentlemen. From their benches they contemplate the shimmering lakes, the snow-covered alps, the air of hasty pleasure on every bough. Later, summer will arrive, and in the tepid perfume the outlines of the landscape will become harsher, the flowers more urgent and violent, the wind will merrily bring dust in its wake. Sport, sport, sport — a form of blossoming without any demons. Autumn comes and darkens the waters: no sounds of hunting can be heard, yet there is game for sale everywhere; mountains, slopes, tiny forms, all assume the intimacy of the homeland beneath that icy wind and that light without sun. Finally, winter comes: sport, sport, sport.

But meanwhile, it is early spring once more and the days are passing all too quickly: beneath the bridges of Berne, the freezing river flows rapidly. Light, silence, mystery: that is what I can see from my window in Berne.

VENGEANCE AND PAINFUL RECONCILIATION

I found myself strolling along the Avenida Copacabana, looking distractedly at buildings, a strip of sea, people on the sidewalk, thinking of nothing in particular. I still had not realized that I was not really distracted but imbued with an effortless attention: I was being something that is all too rare — free. I was absorbing everything at my leisure. Little by little, I began to realize that I was, in fact, perceiving things. My freedom became more intense without ceasing to be freedom. It was not a *tour de propriétaire*, nothing of what I perceived was mine nor did I covet it. Yet it seems to me that I was deeply satisfied with what I saw.

Just then, I experienced a feeling which I had never heard anyone mention. Out of sheer affection, I felt myself to be the Mother of God — God who was the earth and the world. Out of sheer affection, truly, without any suggestion of arrogance or vanity, without the slightest trace of pride or equality; out of sheer affection. I found that I had become the Mother of all things. I also knew that if all this were *really so* and not some misunderstanding, then God would allow Himself to be loved without pride or pettiness and without any concessions on my behalf. He would find the intimacy with which I loved Him acceptable. This feeling was new to me but unequivocal and if it had not occurred to me before that was simply because it could not be. I know that one loves He whom we call God with grave and solemn love, with respect, fear and reverence. Yet no one ever told me about loving Him as a Mother. With this maternal love I bear Him, God is not diminished but enlarged and in becoming Mother of the World my love finds a new freedom.

It was just at this moment that I stepped on a dead rat. I bristled immediately with the terror of being alive; within a second I felt shattered by fear and panic, struggling to control the piercing scream inside me. Almost running, oblivious to everyone around me, I ended up leaning against a lamp-post, my eyes firmly closed and refusing to witness anything further. But the sight of that dead rat was glued to my eyelids: a reddish-brown rat with an enormous tail, its paws crushed . . . dead, silent, reddish-brown.

Trembling from head to foot, I managed to go on living. Wholly perplexed, I walked on, my expression almost infantile from sheer surprise. I tried to sever the connection between the two facts: what I had been feeling some moments previously and the sudden encounter with the rat. The two episodes were linked in time and, however illogically, revealed some connection. It terrified me to think that a rat should have acted as my counterpart. Repugnance suddenly overwhelmed me: was I unable to surrender to sudden love? What was God trying to tell me? I am not the sort of person who needs to be reminded that there is blood inside everything! Far from forgetting that blood, I welcome and desire it. There is too much blood in me to allow me to forget blood. For me, the word spiritual has no meaning and even the word earthly has no meaning.

There was no need to confront me with a rat, especially at that moment when I felt so exposed and vulnerable! You should have considered the terror that has hallucinated and haunted me since prehistoric times; those rats have already mocked me; in a distant age they have already devoured me with impatience and loathing! So, it was to be like this? Me walking through life asking for nothing, wanting for nothing, loving with a pure and innocent love, and all God could do was to confront me with His rat. God's vulgarity wounded and outraged me. God was behaving like a savage. Walking, my heart heavy with sorrow, my disappointment was as inconsolable as those disappointments I had suffered as a child. A child grown prematurely in order to escape the injustices of my childhood. I went on walking, trying to forget in vain. I could only think of revenge. But what revenge could I hope for against an Almighty God, against a God who only needed a rat crushed to death in order to crush me? Such was my vulnerability as a mere creature. In my thirst for revenge, I was unable even to confront Him. I did not even know where He might be found, in what object or thing He might be found, so that gazing upon it with hatred, I might finally see Him. Perhaps the rat? . . . the window? . . . the stones on the ground? For in me, He no longer existed! In me, He was no longer to be seen!

Then the revenge of the weak suddenly occurred to me: so that was what it was like? Very well, I shall break my silence and reveal everything. I know that it is ignoble to enter into someone's confidence and then reveal their secret, but I am going to speak. Say nothing, for love's sake, say nothing! Keep His shame to yourself! — but I am resolved to speak . . . to explain what has happened to me. This time I shall not be silenced, I shall reveal what He has done to me. I shall destroy His reputation.

. . . Who knows . . . perhaps because the world is also a rat and I had thought myself prepared . . . because I imagined myself to be stronger and converted love into an erroneous mathematical calculation. I foolishly believed that, by adding to my perceptions, I had fallen in love. I failed to recognize that it is only by adding up misunderstandings that one comes to love. Once having experienced affection, I believed love to be easy. I felt no desire for solemn love, failing to understand that solemnity makes a ritual of misunderstanding and transforms it into a sacrifice. Then I have always been quarrelsome by nature and have never learned to concede. At heart, I want to love what I would choose to love rather than what is there to love. For I am still not myself and my punishment is loving a world which is not itself. I am also quick to take offence, forgetting that my birth only came later. Perhaps I need to be told these things with brutality since I am extremely stubborn. I am also extremely possessive and began asking myself with some irony if I also wanted the rat for myself.

For I should only be the mother of a tree when I am able to pick up a dead rat in my hand. Yet I know that I should never be able to pick up that dead rat without dying my worst death. Let me then intone the *Magnificat* that exalts what it neither knows nor sees. Let me exploit the formality which isolates me because formality has not wounded my simplicity but rather my pride. For it is my pride at having been born that causes me to feel so intimate with the world — this world which still draws a cry from my heart. The rat exists just as I exist, but perhaps neither I nor the rat is capable of being seen by ourselves for distance makes us equal. Perhaps first of all, I must accept this nature of mine which seeks a rat's death. Perhaps I consider myself delicate simply because I have not committed my crimes. Simply because I have contained my crimes, I believe myself to be in possession of innocent love. Perhaps I cannot gaze upon the rat so long as I refuse to gaze with fury upon this soul of mine which I have barely managed to control. Perhaps I should call the 'world' this nature of mine, this tendency to be a little of everything. How can I love the world's grandeur if I fail to love the dimensions of my own nature? So long as I deem *God* to be good only because I am evil, I shall find myself loving nothing: it will simply be my way of accusing myself. Without even having taken the trouble to scrutinize myself, I have chosen to love my opposite and I want to call that opposite God. Without ever having become accustomed to myself, I have asked the world not to scandalize me. Having only succeeded in forcing myself to submit to myself (for I am so much more inexorable than myself), I hoped to compensate for myself with an Earth less violent than myself.

For so long as I love a God only because I do not love myself, I shall be a marked dice, and the game of my greater life will not be played. So long as I go on inventing God, He does not exist.

'APPEARANCES ARE DECEIVING'

My appearance deceives me.

'ALL THAT GLISTERS IS NOT GOLD'

So I did not pick up from the ground what lay there shining. It was gold, dear God. It was probably gold.

GRASSHOPPER

It took me some time to make out what I was seeing. I was seeing a green insect with long legs which was resting. It was a 'grasshopper' and people were always assuring me that it is an omen of good fortune. Then the grasshopper began to move very gently across the counterpane. It was bright green, with legs which supported its body on a higher and freer plane, a plane as fragile as the grasshopper's own legs which seemed to consist only of the colour of their outer shell. There was nothing inside those threadlike legs: the inside layer was so thin that it was indistinguishable from the outer layer. The grasshopper looked like a transparency which had come off the paper and was walking about in green. But however somnambulant, it moved with determination. Somnambulant: the tiniest leaf of a tree which had achieved the solitary independence of those who pursue the blurred traces of a destiny. The grasshopper walked with the determination of someone tracing out a line which I simply could not see. It walked without a tremor. Its inner mechanism was in no sense tremulous, but it had the regular oscillation of the most delicate clock. What was love like between two grasshoppers? Green and green, and then the same green, which, suddenly, because of a vibration of greens, turns green. Love predestined by its own aerial mechanism. But where were the glands of its destiny situated, and the adrenal glands of its parched, green entrails? For it was a hollow creature, a graft of splinters, a simple, elective attraction of green lines. Me? Me. Us? Us. In that slender grasshopper with its tall legs, which are capable of walking over a woman's bosom without arousing the rest of her body; in that grasshopper which cannot be hollow because a hollow line does not exist; in that grasshopper, atomic energy without any tragedy, walks in silence. Us? Us.

MUTE SINGING, MUTE DANCING

It could scarcely be called singing, in as much as singing implies exploiting the voice musically. It was scarcely vocal, in as much as the voice tends to speak words. It is something which precedes utterance, it is breathing. Sometimes, the odd word escaped, revealing what constituted that mute singing: it was a tale about living, loving and dying. Those three un-spoken words were interrupted by laments and modulations. Modulations of breath, that initial vocal phase which captures the opening outburst of sorrow, which captures the opening outburst of joy. And of exclamation. And then another exclamation, this time of happiness at the utterance of that exclamation. The participants sit huddled round the dancers, looking swarthy and unwashed. After a lengthy modulation which closes with a sigh, the flamenco group, sounding as exhausted as the cantor, murmur in response, *olé*, a dying ember.

But there is also that impetuous song which the voice alone cannot express: then the nervous, insistent tapping of feet intervenes, the 'olé' which continually interrupts the song is no longer a response; it is incitement, it is the black bull. The cantor, almost clenching his teeth, gives voice to the fanaticism of his race, but the participants demand more and more, until they achieve the climax of emotion: Spain.

I also heard them perform the non-existent song. It consists of silence interrupted by cries from the participants. Within that circle of silence, a short, emaciated, swarthy fellow, with inner fire, hands on hips and head thrown back, hammers out the incessant rhythm of the non–existent song with the heels of his shoes. This is not music. Not even dance. *Zapateado*[1] predates choreographed forms of dancing — it is the body manifesting itself and manifesting us, feet transmitting even wrath in a language which Spain understands.

The group intensifies its fury, absorbed in its own silence. From time to time, you hear the hoarse taunts of a gypsy, all charcoal and red tatters, in whom hunger has turned to passion and cruelty. It was not a spectacle, for there were no spectators: everyone present played as important a role as the dancer tapping his feet in silence. Becoming more and more exhausted, we communicated for hours through this language, which, if it ever possessed words, gradually lost them throughout the centuries — until the oral tradition came to be transmitted from father to son like the impetus of blood.

I also watched two flamenco dancers partner each other. I have never witnessed any other dance in which the rivalry between a man and a woman becomes so naked. The conflict between them is so open that their wiles are of no importance: at certain moments the woman becomes almost masculine, and the man looks at her in amazement. If the Moor on Spanish soil is the infidel, his female counterpart has lost any natural languor she possessed in the face of Basque severity. The Moorish woman in Spain is a cockerel until love transforms her into a *maja*.[2]

Conquest is an arduous business in flamenco dancing. While the male dancer speaks with insistent feet, his partner peruses the aura of her own body with her hands outspread like two fans: in this way she magnetizes herself, and prepares herself to become both tangible and intangible. But just when you least expect it, she puts forward one foot and marks three beats with her high heel. The male dancer shivers before this crude gesture, he recoils and freezes. There is the silence of dance. Little by little, the man raises his arms once more, and cautiously — with fear rather than modesty — attempts with splayed hands to shade his partner's defiant head. He circles her several times and at certain moments almost turns his back

[1] *zapateado*: the tap–dancing peculiar to Spanish flamenco.
[2] *maja*: low-class woman (especially in Madrid).

to her, thus exposing himself to the likely risk of being stabbed. And if he has avoided being stabbed, he owes his escape to his partner's unexpected recognition of his bravado: this then is her man. She stamps her feet, her head held high, with the first cry of love: at last she has found her companion and enemy. The two withdraw bristling with pride. They have acknowledged each other.

The dance itself now begins. The man is dark-skinned, lithe and stubborn. She is severe and dangerous. Her hair has been drawn back, proud of her severity. This dance is so vital that you can hardly believe that life will continue once the dance has come to an end: surely this man and woman must die. Other dances express the nostalgia of their courage. But this dance is courage. Other dances are joyful. But the joy of this dance is grave. Or joy is dismissed. What matters here is the human triumph of living.

The two dancers do not smile, nor do they forgive each other. But do they understand each other? They have never thought of understanding each other. They have brought themselves as their only banner. And whoever is vanquished — in this dance both of them will be vanquished — will not soften in submission; they will remain with those eyes parched by love and wrath: eyes which are triumphantly Spanish. Whoever is vanquished — and both of them will be vanquished — will serve wine to the other like a slave. Even though there may be death in this wine, when jealous passion finally explodes. The partner who survives will feel revenged. But forever alone. For this woman alone was his enemy, this man alone was her enemy, and they chose each other for the dance.

THE WOMAN WRITER

Ample bosom, broad hips, eyes chaste, brown, and dreamy. Now and then she would cry out suddenly. She exclaimed with a bright, afflicted air, uttering the words so quickly that they could scarcely be heard: I thought that I could never be a writer, I am so . . . so . . . !

One day, in a moment of distraction, she jotted down some sentences about the Sugar Loaf Mountain in her notebook. They consisted of only a few words, for she tended to be brief. Some considerable time afterwards, she was alone one evening, when she remembered that she had made a few notes about something or other — the Sugar Loaf Mountain? The sea? She went to look for her notebook. She searched the entire house. She systematically went through every piece of furniture. She even opened shoe-boxes in the hope of having been so secretive as to have hidden her notes in a shoe-box. That would have been an excellent idea. Gradually the sensation of choking grew worse. She put her hand to her forehead — now she was searching for something more than her notebook, no longer precisely for her notebook. Let's see, patience, let's have another look. What could she have written in the notebook? Hope — what could she have written? Let's have another look. It's a question of not giving up the search, of getting hold of it somehow. What a calamity — she said, standing motionless in the middle of the room, without any sense of direction, without knowing where to look. What a calamity. Her eyes became tender. What had been irretrievably lost weighed on her destiny and overwhelmed her: her eyes were tender, brown. The room, tranquil in the evening light. And somewhere there was something written. She unbuttoned the collar of her blouse. Don't be downhearted, she whispered to herself, look among your papers, among your letters, among the cuttings and reviews people keep sending you. Ah, if only they had written to her more often, then she would have more papers to search through. But her orderly existence was exposed, she had few places for hiding things, her rooms were tidy. In her home, the only hiding place was herself. But how happy she felt to have pieces of furniture and boxes where she might discover things by chance. She had places where she could go on searching indefinitely.

For a number of years that was precisely what she did from time to time. Periodically she would remember her notebook and be seized with fresh hope. Until one day, after several more years had passed, she said:

— When I was younger, I used to do a little writing.

A SPANISH GENTLEMAN

He was not simply Pepe, he was not simply a guide. In the heat
of summer, his face was bloated by alcohol as he downed one
glass of wine after another. The man paused unsteadily in the
middle of a shady little side-street with whitewashed houses in
Cordoba, looked at us and said very slowly in Spanish so that
the words might penetrate our slowness:
— I am not a guide. I am — Pepe The Guide!
We stopped in our tracks, impressed by what must have
been a singular coincidence. What coincidence? Pepe The
Guide stood there motionless, his eyes moist with emotion,
wine, heat, and despair. It must have been strange and
oppressive to be Pepe The Guide. Still standing there, the
perspiration running down his face, and smartly dressed in the
inevitable dark suit, he waited for us to grasp his meaning
through his own intense silence. We looked at him, our eyes
frowning in the sunlight. Until the faintest breeze passed
through us. The coincidence was his being Pepe The Guide,
his awareness of his own identity, of being Spanish among so
many other possibilities, of living under the naked sky of
Cordoba when at that very same hour it was raining in
London: these miraculous coincidences passed through us like
a faint breeze, as we wiped our foreheads with our hand-
kerchiefs.
All around us, the city extended sweet and warm. Un-
bearably sweet, full of hesitant blind men and of women who
appeared to be even more hesitant. There was, nevertheless, a
certain harshness. Where did it come from? We searched with
frowning eyes. It came from the intrepid dreams of those
youths who dozed in the doorways of bars and cafés. It came
from the desire to escape which could be sensed like an ambush
in the stillness all around us. Truly a dangerous city.
Amidst the overpowering heat, the source of so much
harshness, our man emerged, inebriated by his own stature: I
am Pepe The Guide, he repeated with open arms, and his
crucifixion filled him with joy. As if Pepe The Guide were a
pre-existent abstraction, and he, a simple Pepe, a simple guide,
were the embodiment of a symbol. Confronted with our

silence, not out of any respect but simply because we were lost
for suitable words of reply, he reassured us:

— In Pepe The Guide, you have found a friend.

Why did he say it with so much sadness? Sad, courageous
and drunk, sadly dominating what he alone could see in the
white, modest houses of Cordoba, and in us, too, for one
moment of disquieting grace. Intimidated, we thanked him.
Tyrannized, we repeated our thanks several times over. Yes,
he was a friend. Friendship pays, but with all the despair of
friendship: we were friends, but what could we give to each
other? Except acknowledge each other. In him, we acknowledged Pepe The Guide. In us, he recognized those who recognized him.

The friend we made that afternoon turned out to be touchy.
A careless word from any of us offended him, the merest hint
of indecisiveness wounded his feelings — he would come to a
sudden halt and draw back, as if preparing to brandish his
sword. Hastily, we explained that we did not mean to give
offence. Above all, we assured him that we had every confidence in his knowledge of the city which consisted of the
vaguest dates, and a muddled account of historical detail,
interspersed with anecdotes about English tourists, 'his friends
for life'. He listened to our apologies, and pondered awhile
before accepting them. During those lengthy pauses, he still
looked menacing. We waited anxiously, feeling more and
more frustrated. The afternoon was turning into a struggle for
human dignity. Then all of a sudden, Pepe The Guide decided
to make his peace with us and proceeded to make even more
vehement protestations of friendship, reinforced by misunderstanding.

To tell the truth, we learned precious little about Cordoba
which we did not know already. We had discovered for
ourselves that the nights were perfumed with spikenard and
jasmine. We knew about the things we could see and sense.
From Don Pepe, on the other hand, we learned that there was
not a living soul in Cordoba who did not admire him. We did
not dare to ask why, nor did he tell us. 'Only in Cordoba?' an
outraged Pepe asked us: 'No,' he himself rejoined with open
arms, 'throughout the length and breadth of Spain!' 'Only in
Spain?' he questioned us once more. He paused as if he were in

pain. We were confident that he himself would provide the answer. And suddenly, he conceded: 'In Morocco, Algiers, Egypt . . .'. That man engaged in the strangest commerce. He had bartered horses, no doubt belonging to others, for dates and olives; he had sold a caravan of camels to someone whose name 'unfortunately he could not disclose'. Commerce with a great tradition. More adventure than commerce, more travel than profit, more a question of making a living, than of amassing wealth, but ever glorified by his unfulfilled tragedy, that same tragedy which caused him to go on challenging with bared chest the enemy who never materialized, for he only attracted friendship and love. Not because he had shirked exposing himself to danger. You could tell that he had been prepared to face death at the age of twenty, but he had been robbed of his own tragic destiny, of that tragic destiny which had rightfully belonged to him. That unfulfilled tragedy had left Don Pepe scarred, a sixty-year-old monarch. For that villain was in every sense a king.

As for Don Pepe's family, it was not restricted to his gypsy wife and the innumerable children of his prodigality. He also supported the wife and children of a brother-in-law who had been killed in the Spanish Civil War, and two more women relatives who were widowed during the conflict — all of them assembled under the same roof, all of them taking a siesta in the same house, all of them fanning away the flies. Don Pepe insisted that we should meet his family, and he introduced them on the threshold with a broad gesture which could have been mistaken for either pride or accusation: that family was his open wound. And for family, you should visualize a bevy of women who were so sweet that they had been transformed into sugar, fanning themselves in the patio with lowered eyelids, the sly creatures. Visualize infants and youths with narrow hips, all of them turned somnolent by work, by their longing to become a bullfighter. Or by hope. And try to imagine what it cost Don Pepe to nourish all those dreams.

Yet this did not prevent Don Pepe from threatening to draw his sword when we offered to pay for 'the special sherry which only Pepe The Guide can provide'. Offended to the core, as only a Spaniard knows how, and shaking with the proverbial indignation of his race, he accused us:

'You are wounding me!'

Consoled by his own sense of outrage, he allowed us to pay for the sherry without any fuss. He gallantly accepted our gratitude for the privilege of being allowed to sample that unique sherry which is sold, in fact, by every Spanish wine-merchant. Never had we been so completely duped by anyone, but our contribution to his sense of tragedy was to allow ourselves to be duped. Nevertheless, it was a tense game, and we were worn out. Meanwhile, Don Pepe — still deeply moved by the drama of a friendship which had come close to being spoiled over the mere question of money — Don Pepe, as a magnanimous gesture, assured us, with his hand on his heart, that he would show his forgiveness by accepting several more glasses of wine. To our confusion and shame, we had forgotten to offer him a drink — another oversight which he was prepared to forgive — but only because we were not Spanish and we were not to blame. The fellow was very astute and dejected. Feeling somewhat drained by the story of Don Pepe's life, I went back to my hotel to take a siesta amidst the flies of Cordoba.

THE LEADER

The leader's sleep is troubled. His wife shakes him until he awakens from his nightmare. Half-asleep, he gets up and drinks a little water. In front of the mirror, he restores the expression of a middle-aged man, smooths the hair over his temples, and goes back to bed. He dozes off and the nightmare comes back. 'No, no!' he argues with himself, his throat becoming dry.

The leader experiences terror in his sleep. Are the people threatening their leader? No, for the leader takes care of the people. Are the people threatening their leader?

Yes, the people are threatening the leader of the people. The leader tosses and turns in his bed. At night, he experiences fear. But his nightmare is a nightmare without history. At night, his eyes firmly closed, he sees tranquil faces, one face after another. And those faces are expressionless. It is always the same nightmare. But each night, he scarcely sleeps, more tranquil faces assemble as if he were looking at the photograph of a silent multitude. For whom is this silence intended? For the leader. There is a succession of faces all looking alike, as if the same face were monotonously repeating itself. Those faces are utterly expressionless. Their lack of expression enlarged as in an enlarged photograph. A whole series of photographs, and each time with a greater number of faces all looking alike. And nothing more. Yet the leader perspires profusely when confronted with the innocuous sight of thousands of vacant, unblinking eyes. By day, the leader's speech gets longer on each occasion. With every speech, he keeps his audience waiting even longer for that resounding finale. He closes his speech by attacking, denouncing, denouncing, denouncing, ranting and, after reaching his moment of glory, he goes off to the lavatory, closes the door behind him and, alone at last, he leans against the locked door, and wipes the perspiration from his forehead with his handkerchief. But all in vain. At night, the silent multitude is ever greater. Each night, the faces draw a little closer. Until he can actually feel their hot breath. The expressionless faces can breathe — the leader awakens with a cry. He attempts to explain to his wife: I dreamed that . . . I dreamed that . . . But he has nothing to tell. He dreamed that he was the leader of living persons.

BE CAREFUL WITH SATURDAY

For me, Saturday is the rose of the week; on Saturday evening curtains blow in the breeze, and a bucket of water is thrown over the terrace. Saturday with a breeze is the rose of the week. On Saturday morning, the bee appears in the yard, and the breeze is blowing; a sting, a swollen face, blood and honey, a poisonous sting inflicted on me. Other bees will follow the scent and on the following Saturday morning I shall see if the yard is going to be full of bees. It was on a Saturday that the ants swarmed over the stone. It was on a Saturday that I saw a man sitting on the pavement and out of the sun as he ate stew and manioc meal out of a gourd. We had already bathed. In the afternoon, a bell announced in the breeze, the matinée performance at the local cinema: in the breeze, Saturday was the rose of the week. If it rained, I alone knew that it was Saturday; Saturday transformed into a dank rose? In Rio de Janeiro, just when you think that the week is about to come to an end, the week opens out vigorously into a rose: the car suddenly slams on its brakes, and suddenly, before the startled breeze can blow once more, I realize that it is Saturday afternoon. That was Saturday, but no one asks me any more. So I say nothing, feigning resignation. But I have already gathered my things and moved on to Sunday morning. Sunday morning is also the rose of the week. But rose is not exactly the word I am looking for.

BECAUSE IT IS TODAY

. . . for no good reason, without anticipating anything, one afternoon, this afternoon, I start applying myself to calligraphy which has occupied much of my time. Like one of those nuns who sits busy as a bee, embroidering in gold thread: Viva the 7 September.[1]

THE SENSITIVE WOMAN

At that point she went through a crisis which appeared to have nothing to do with her life: a crisis of deep compassion. That narrow, well-groomed head of hers could scarcely bear to

---

[1] Brazilian Independence Day.

forgive so much. She could not bear to look at the expression on a tenor's face while he was singing some joyful aria — she invariably averted her eyes in distress, unable to bear it, unable to bear the singer's glory. In the street, she would suddenly press gloved hands to her bosom — assailed by forgiveness. She suffered without recompense, without any sympathy even for herself.

That same woman who suffered from sensibility as if it were an illness, chose a Sunday when her husband was away to pay a visit to her seamstress. It was more of an outing than an errand. That was something she had always enjoyed: going on an outing. As if she were still a little girl strolling along the pavement. She tended to go on frequent outings whenever she 'sensed' that her husband was deceiving her. So she went to call on her seamstress one Sunday morning. She walked down a muddy, unpaved road which was swarming with chickens and naked children — where had she landed herself! Her seamstress lived in an overcrowded hovel, full of children with hunger written on their faces and a husband who was stricken with tuberculosis. The seamstress was reluctant to embroider the tablecloth the woman had brought with her, because she found cross-stitching awkward. So the woman left, feeling indignant and puzzled. She felt distinctly grubby as she walked home in the oppressive morning heat: it gave her pleasure to think that, ever since childhood, she had been fastidious about cleanliness. Back home, she lunched alone, then lay down in her semi-darkened room, full of mature sentiments and without bitterness. At least for once she did not 'feel' anything. Except perhaps bewilderment when confronted by the freedom of her poor seamstress. Except perhaps a sense of expectation. Freedom.

Until, several days later, when her sensibility was cured, just like a wound which has healed. One month later she also took her first lover, the first of a blissful succession.

INAUGURAL SPEECH

. . . the future we inaugurate today is like a metal line. It is something which has been deliberately left bare. Of our entire existence, only this line will remain. It is the result of the mathematical calculation of uncertainty: the more it is purified, the less risk it runs; the metal line does not run the same risk as the line of the flesh. The metal line will provide no food for the vultures. The metal line is in no danger of putrefying. It is a line which is guaranteed eternity. Those of us who are gathered here today, inaugurate this line with the intention that it should be eternal. We have chosen a metal line because from start to finish it consists of the same metal. We cannot say with any certainty if this line will be strong enough to save us, but it is certainly strong enough to last. To last in its own right, as our creation. It has not yet been verified whether the line will sag under the weight of the first soul to hang from it, as if hanging over the chasm of Hell.

What does this line look like? It is smooth and cylindrical. Like a thread of hair and, although extremely fine, it has sufficient volume to be hollow — so this line of ours remains empty. It is deserted within. But we who are gathered here today have an urge and longing for the desert as if we had already been disappointed by our lineage. We shall leave the line hollow so that the future may fill it. Vigorous as we are, we could fill the line with ourselves, but we abstain. So you will be our survival, but without us: our mission is one of suicide. This eternal metal line, the product of all of us who are gathered here today, this eternal metal line is our crime against the present; it is also our purest endeavour. We launch it into space, we launch it from our umbilical cord, and cast it towards eternity. Our secret intention is to cast our body with it by fastening the line to our umbilical cord. Then our bodies will also be pulled from the terrain of the present and be thrown into space. This is our hope, this is our resolve. This is our calculation of eternity. Our mission is one of suicide: we present ourselves as volunteers for the future. We are men of commerce who have no need of money, only of our own posterity. What we have taken for ourselves from the present has in no way abraded eternity. We have loved, but love does not abrade the future, for we have only loved after the fashion of today, which will end up as flesh for the vultures. We have also eaten bread and butter, which detracts nothing from the future because bread and butter is our only filial pleasure: and at Christmas we have been reunited with our family. But none of this prejudices the eternal line, which is our real commerce. We are the artists of commerce and make our sacrifice as if it were barter: our sacrifice is our most profitable investment. From time to time, also without any erosion of eternity, we give ourselves up to passion. But we can tranquilly take this from the present for ourselves, because in years to come, we shall simply be the ancient dead of others. We shall not behave like our own ancient dead who bequeathed us, as our legacy and burden, the flesh and the spirit, and both of them incomplete. Not we. Defeated by centuries of passion, defeated by a love which has been useless, defeated by a dishonesty which has borne no fruits — we are investing in honesty because it is more profitable and we are creating a line of the most legitimate metal. We shall bequeath a brittle and solid skeleton which is hollow. It will be as difficult for those who follow us to penetrate the metal line as to penetrate the narrow hollow in a strand of hair. We who are now gathered to inaugurate the metal line know that it will become a narrow door for those who follow us.

As for ourselves, just as our offspring find us strange, the eternal metal line will find us strange and feel ashamed of us even though we were responsible for its erection. We are aware, therefore, that this is a suicide mission on behalf of survival. We, the artists of important commerce, know that the work of art fails to understand us. And that to live is a suicide mission.

WRITING

I no longer remember how it started. It was, in a manner of speaking, all written at a single stroke. Everything was there

or ought to have been there as in the temporal space of an open
piano . . . on its simultaneous keys. I wrote, cautiously
pursuing the words which formed themselves within me, and
which only after the fifth copy had been patiently drafted, I
was able to absorb. My great fear was, that out of impatience
with the slowness with which I understand myself, I might
somehow be forcing things unduly.

I had the distinct impression that the more time I allowed
myself, the more readily the story would narrate what it had to
narrate without any crisis. More and more, I discover that
everything is largely a question of exercising patience, of love
begetting patience and patience begetting love. The entire text
came to life at once, with greater clarity emerging here and
there. I would interrupt a sentence in chapter ten, let us say, in
order to resume the writing of chapter two, interrupted in its
turn while I devoted myself to the writing of chapter eighteen.
I found that I had the necessary patience and it taught me a
great deal: for example, how to bear the frustrating discomfort
of disorder, without any guarantees.

Yet it is also true that order constrains me. As always, the
greatest difficulty was that of waiting. (I am feeling unwell —
the woman would explain to the doctor. You are about to
have a child — he would say. And to think that I imagined I
was dying — the woman would reply.

The deformed soul, growing, swelling, without even
realizing that this is waiting. Sometimes, faced with a still-
birth, one knows that it was expected.)

In addition to the trial of waiting, there is the laborious task
of reconstructing the vision that was instantaneous. And, as if
this were not enough, alas I am incapable of 'drafting' a
manuscript. I am incapable of 'relating' an idea or of 'dressing
up an idea' with words. What comes to the surface is already
expressed in words or simply fails to exist. Upon writing the
text, there is always the certainty (seemingly paradoxical) that
what confuses the writer is the necessity of using words. This
is the real trouble. If only I could write by carving on wood or
stroking a child's hair or strolling through the countryside, I
should never have embarked upon the path of words. I should
do what so many people who are not writers do, and precisely
with the same happiness and the same torment as those who

write, and with the same deep, inconsolable disappointments:
I should avoid using words. This might prove to be my
solution. And as such, it would be most welcome.

MINEIRINHO[1]

I suppose that I should search within myself as one of the
representatives of mankind, in order to ascertain why the
death of a criminal should cause so much sorrow. And why I
prefer to speak of the thirty shots which killed Mineirinho
rather than discuss his crimes. I asked my cook what she
thought about the matter. I detected the tiny spasm of conflict
on her face, the disquiet of not being able to rationalize her
feelings, of being forced to betray contradictory emotions
because she did not know how to conciliate them. Irreducible
facts, also an irreducible indignation, the violent compassion
of indignation. To feel ourselves puzzled and divided in the
face of our inability to forget that Mineirinho was dangerous
and had murdered far too often; yet we wanted him alive. The
cook was somewhat wary, perhaps because she was suspicious
of avenging justice. With an unmistakable tone of irritation
which came from the heart, she replied coldly: 'There is no
point in my telling you what I feel. Surely everybody knows
that Mineirinho was a criminal? But I'm convinced that his
soul was saved and that he's already in heaven.' I answered:
'Much more likely than in the case of lost of people who have
never killed anyone.'

Why? For the first commandment, which protects irreplaceable body and life, says that *thou shalt not kill*. That
commandment is my greatest guarantee: so do not kill me, for
I do not wish to die, and do not let me kill, because to have
killed would cast me into eternal darkness.

This is the commandment. But while I can listen to the first
and the second shot with a sense of relief, the third shot makes

---

[1] Mineirinho. A bandit killer of some notoriety, who operated in Rio de
Janeiro until he was finally tracked down and shot by the police.

me alert, the fourth leaves me restless, the fifth and sixth cover me with shame, the seventh and eighth cause my heart to beat with alarm, the ninth and tenth cause my mouth to tremble, the eleventh shot finds me invoking the name of God in terror, and at the twelfth shot I call for my brother. The thirteenth shot kills me — because I am the other. Because I want to be the other.

I repudiate this justice which watches over my sleep, and feel humiliated that I should need it. Meantime, I sleep, and falsely save myself. We, who are astute by nature.

So that my house may function, I make it my priority to be astute so as to give no outlet to the rebellion and love which rage inside me. Were I not astute, my house would shake. I must have forgotten that below the house there is the soil, the terrain where a new house might be erected. Meantime, we sleep and falsely save ourselves. Until thirteen shots awaken us, and with horror I say, but much too late — twenty-eight years after Mineirinho was born — that they should not kill the cornered bandit, that they should not kill this man. For I know that he is my weakness. And of an entire life, dear God, sometimes all that one salvages is weakness. I know that we shall not be saved as long as we do not value our weakness. My weakness is the mirror, wherein I behold what I silently made of a man. My weakness is the way I saw life open out in his flesh. I panicked, and I saw the matter of life, placenta and blood, the living quagmire. My way of life exploded in Mineirinho. How could I resist loving him, if he lived until the thirteenth shot when I was sleeping? His startled violence. His innocent violence— not in its consequences, but innocent in itself like the violence of a child neglected by its father. All that was violence in him is astuteness in us, and we avoid each other's gaze lest we should run the risk of misunderstanding each other. Lest the house should shake. Only if the hand of another man, the hand of hope, were to rest on his confused and fevered head, could the violence which exploded in Mineirinho be pacified and cause him to raise his startled eyes filled with tears at last. Only after a man has been found lying dead on the ground, without cap or shoes, am I aware that I forgot to say to him: I, too, feel desperate.

I do not want this house. I want a justice which will have

given a chance to something pure and helpless in Mineirinho — that thing which moves mountains; that same thing which made him 'fall madly in love' with a woman; that same thing which has led him to pass through a door so narrow that it has lacerated his nakedness. That intense, transparent thing inside us, like an ominous gram of radium, that grain of life which, once trampled, transforms itself into something menacing — into trampled love. That thing which in Mineirinho became a dagger, is the same thing which makes me offer water to another man, not because I have water to offer, but because I, too, have experienced thirst; and I, too, without losing myself, have experienced perdition. Being sentenced would cause me no shame. The time has come, with or without ridicule, for us to be more divine; if we have some perception of God's goodness, it is because we have some perception of goodness in ourselves, that which man perceives before he is contaminated by crime. I go on hoping, therefore, that God may be the father, in the knowledge that a man can be another man's father. And I go on living in my fragile house. That house, whose front door I bolt so carefully will not withstand the first gust of wind which will send a bolted door flying through the air. But the house is standing, and Mineirinho has lived wrath on my behalf, while I remained calm. He was shot in his wild frenzy, while a fabricated god at the eleventh hour hastily sanctions my wilful evil and my crude justice; what supports the walls of my house is the certainty that I shall always justify myself. My friends will not justify me, but my enemies who are accomplices will congratulate me: what sustains me is to know that I shall always fabricate a god to the image I require in order to sleep peacefully, and that others will quietly pretend that we are all justified, and that there is nothing to be done.

All this because we are astute by nature and the bastions of something. And above all, because we try not to understand.

Because anyone who understands is likely to cause disruption. There is something in us which is capable of disrupting everything — something which understands. That thing which remains silent before the man without cap or shoes. In order to possess a cap and shoes, Mineirinho plundered and killed. That thing which remains silent before the statue of Saint George, bedecked with gold and diamonds. That something which is very serious in my nature becomes even more serious in the presence of the man who is gunned down. Is that something the assassin in me? No, it is the despair in all of us. Driven mad, we know that dead man in whom the gram of radium ignited. And we have to be mad, rather than astute, in order to know him. It is as a madman that I enter this life which often has no door, and it is as a madman that I understand what can only be understood at one's peril. It is only as a madman that I feel deep love, that love which is confirmed when I perceive that the radium will somehow irradiate itself, if not through faith, through hope and love, then lamentably through the diseased courage of destruction. Were I not a madman, I should be eight hundred policemen with eight hundred machine-guns, and that would be my claim to honour.

Until the appearance of a justice which would be even madder. A justice which would take into account that we all have to speak through a man who became desperate because human speech failed him. A man who is now so mute that only a savage, disarticulated cry could serve him as an utterance. A sentence which might bear in mind that our great struggle is that of fear, and that if a man has killed compulsively, it is because he was extremely frightened. Above all, a justice which might examine itself, and recognize that all of us, a living quagmire, founder in darkness, and for this reason not even a man's evil should be consigned to another man's evil: so that the latter may not shoot to kill without restraint or censure. A justice which will not forget that we are all dangerous, and that at the hour when the executant of justice kills, he is no longer protecting us or seeking to eliminate a criminal; he is committing his own crime, which he has been harbouring for some considerable time. At the hour of killing a criminal — at that very moment, an innocent man is being put to death. No, no, I am not asking for the sublime, nor for the things which gradually became the words which help me to sleep peacefully. Those of us who take refuge in the abstract are a strange mixture of forgiveness and vague charity.

What I want is something much harsher and much more difficult: I want the terrestrial.

Acknowledgements

I should like to express my gratitude to Michael Schmidt, Robyn Marsack, and the staff of Carcanet Press; also to the following colleagues and friends who offered useful advice and criticism: Paul Berman, Eudinyr Fraga, Patricia Bins, Carlos Sachs, Teresa Nunes, Amelia Hutchinson and Arnold Hinchliffe; and finally to Stefanie Goodfellow for valuable material assistance, and to Nancy Stålhammer, who typed the manuscript with scrupulous care.

Giovanni Pontiero
Manchester, June 1985

Afterword

Clarice Lispector was born on 10 December 1925 in Tetchelnick in the Ukraine. She was barely two months old when her family emigrated to Brazil where they settled in Recife and subsequently in Rio de Janiero. She graduated in law before turning to journalism and creative writing. On 9 December 1977, Clarice Lispector died of cancer and three days later (her fifty-seventh birthday) she was buried in the Jewish Cemetery in the Caju district of Rio de Janeiro. With her death, Brazil lost one of its most gifted and influential writers.

The stories and chronicles of *The Foreign Legion* offer ample evidence of Clarice Lispector's unique sensibility and range as an exponent of experimental prose. The book was published in 1964 when her reputation had already been established with the publication of several prize-winning novels and a much-acclaimed collection of short stories entitled *Family Ties*.

The thirteen narratives which constitute the first part of *The Foreign Legion* illustrate the salient facets of Clarice Lispector's fiction. As a writer, she is less interested in conventional plot structure than a labyrinth of perceptions. The story, she always insisted, is not 'something a writer manufactures: the story exists like an animal or plant and should be allowed to grow naturally without interference'. As with most of her mature work, the stories of *The Foreign Legion* show her deep concern with the central problems of existence and individual identity. Conflicts abound between human ideals and actions, between imaginings and reality, between faith and logic.

Her narratives trace out the ages of man/woman from precocious childhood to oracular senility and each stage of intellectual and emotional development brings fresh insights.

In *The Foreign Legion* we encounter Clarice Lispector in a number of guises: woman, mother, artist and mystic. As a woman she confides her own vulnerability, her personal phobias and obsessions; she is the incurable insomniac whose days and nights merge, whose dreams and nightmares become almost interchangeable. Yet this fragile core to her fiction never entirely obscures her awareness of everyday existence. She studies her characters and their situations with shrewdness and compassion. Experience has taught her that private struggles with existence and the irreversible sentence of mortality go hand-in-hand with mute rebellion against the world's hypocrisy and indifference. Without resorting to documentation and propaganda, the author succeeds in exposing the psychological scars of living in a society without political stability or adequate social structures; and at a more personal level, in conveying her own preoccupations as a woman and writer striving to survive in such an environment.

The mystical dimension in Clarice Lispector's narratives stems from her concern with inner tranquillity, order and grace. The quotations from the Old Testament and the lessons of the Parables are a constant reminder of the belief she upheld in God and His laws. But if the surface of her mysticism is one of light and silence, the substance is compounded of guilt and remorse, of sacrifice and naked suffering.

As in most of her writing, children and animals play an important role in these stories. A close study of children (her own, as well as those of others) probes the beauty and perverseness of innocence, the refreshing yet disarming truths which emerge with awakening sensibility. Animals, on the other hand, reveal an ontological integrity and steadfast loyalty which appear to elude most human beings. The very presence of these animals provokes an uneasy confrontation with the inconsistencies of human motivation.

The Chronicles which constitute the second part of *The Foreign Legion* are a rich miscellany of arts criticism, character sketches, travel notes, conversations with her own children, aphorisms and personal reflections. There is even a drama about adultery which is reminiscent of the morality plays of the fifteenth century. The symbols and dialogue evoke the Middle Ages, but the moral implications are reappraised in conformity with contemporary thinking about sexual relationships.

Clarice Lispector's wholly personal responses to the visual arts, to music and dance, reveal a discerning critic with considerable flair and understanding. As a travel writer, her grasp of Brazilian and more remote cultures and traditions is invariably stimulating, and her account of a five-day visit to Brasilia must rank as one of the most penetrating accounts ever written about Brazil's new capital.

These chronicles also embody some of Clarice Lispector's most significant statements about her own approach to creative writing. The image which emerges is that of a compulsive and totally committed writer who lived in constant fear of betraying the things she felt and saw, once she came to transpose those insights into words.

At her most introspective, Clarice is wilfully capable of tying herself and her reader into metaphysical knots. Syntax and punctuation, for example, are often treated in arbitrary fashion in an attempt to capture fragmented patterns of inspiration. The conceptual intricacies, however, are offset by dazzling powers of insight and recognition. Her transcendental meditations unfailingly exude their own poetic lyricism. Here is clearly a talent to disturb. It is, moreover, a talent to amuse. She has an eye for all that is false and sham in human behaviour. She has a responsive ear for the knowing absurdities uttered by children and the preposterous clichés uttered by their elders. And, like most great humorists, she is also strong on self-parody.

Clarice Lispector has provided the key to any valid appreciation of *The Foreign Legion* when she writes: 'If I were to give a title to my life it would be: in search of my own thing'. The precious *thing* to which she alludes is her own persuasive truth, that artistic integrity which she valued above all things.